UEA CREATIVE WRITING ANTHOLOGY 2003

CONTAINS SMALL PARTS

UEA MA Creative Writing Anthology: *Contains Small Parts*

Published by Pen & Inc Press, School of English and American Studies at the University of East Anglia, Norwich, NR4 7TJ.

International © retained by individual authors, 2003

Pen & Inc Press is a member of Inpress Ltd. – Independent Presses Representation.

A CIP record for this book is available from the British Library

ISBN: 1-902913-14-0

Distributed by Central Books, 99 Wallace Rd, London, E9 5LN

Contains Small Parts is typeset in Hoefler Text & `Courier New`

Printed by Antony Rowe Ltd, Bumpers Farm, Chippenham, Wiltshire SN14 6LH

Contains Small Parts

Thanks to the following for making this anthology possible: Random House and the School of English and American Studies at the University of East Anglia.

We'd also like to thank the following people:

Sheryl Colk, Jon Cook, Patricia Duncker, Rachel Hore, Paul Magrs, Andrew Motion, Michèle Roberts, George Szirtes, Val Striker and Val Taylor.

Emma Forsberg, Sarah Gooderson, Julian Jackson and Katri Skala at Pen & Inc Press.

Naomi Alderman for the last minute subbing and Sam Byers for the title.

Editorial team:

Fiona Curran
W. David Hall
Margaret Johnson
Tom Lewis
Andrea Mason
Michael Miller
Sarah Raymont
Alyssa Russo
Chantal Schaul
Carol Thornton
Charlie Thurlow
Alex Watson

Contents

The Prosers

The Scripters

The Poets

The Prose

Introductions
Paul Magrs, Michèle Roberts
& Patricia Duncker

We sometimes get asked if Creative Writing courses are just like sausage factories turning out links of workshopped clones. Well, no.

The question always surprises me. You'd have to be crazy to think we spent time encouraging everyone to be the same, play it safe and to work within a certain paradigm. I've taught on the fiction MA for six years now and the variety of work produced is what keeps me doing it.

There used to be those LPs of songs – I'm thinking of the Seventies – they were called things like Chart Hits or Top of the Pops. They'd have some model in a bikini on the front and they would be cheaper than normal records because they were all cover versions. Faceless but proficient session musicians churning out fairly bland versions of recent hits. It was the more expensive compilation LPs that would boast of sporting 'original artists only', to differentiate themselves. And that's what our anthologies ideally have, too. Original artists presenting their three minute perfect pop songs. The kind of singles that make you want to buy their individual solo records.

The contents of this book are as broad and diverse as the writers we have here. These anthologies began as a showcase for just prose writers at UEA but, in recent years, we've included script and poetry as those courses have developed on campus. This is a school that is expanding all the time: the Lifewriting course is growing in size and renown; Critical and Creative hybrid writing is something UEA has been behind for years and, in the near future, we hope to start an MA focusing on Writing for Younger People.

Contains Small Parts

Writing at UEA is evolving. With this year, 2002/3, we have changed around the team that selects, teaches and mentors the writers here. Alongside myself, Denise Riley, George Szirtes and Val Taylor, we've been delighted to add two new professors on the prose strand: Patricia Duncker and Michèle Roberts. They're here to be part of the team and to help encourage the kind of idiosyncrasy and uniqueness that the writing programme at UEA has always championed.

– Paul Magrs

Writing fiction involves taking risks because it involves accessing the deep part of the self, the unconscious imagination, in which all the words we may be afraid of saying live and dance. If we just write out of the surface level of life then we may simply reproduce the commonsensical chitterchatter of the culture which formed us, all its clichés about life, love and death. Writing from deeper down we re-find the self which got away, gets away, from the authority figures in our heads. This process takes time. Safety and danger are connected to writing. We need to feel safe enough to embark on this dangerous adventure. It requires courage: who knows what we shall discover? It requires commitment: to endless re-writing. For the second risk involved in writing is finding, inventing, the form that adequately, beautifully, shapes our utterance. Form must express content, be integrated with it. So writing consists of struggle after struggle: to find language, find ways of embodying it. Teaching creative writing similarly involves taking risks: trying to work out when to support, when to suggest changes, when to try to inspire, when to wrestle, when to shout push. The MA writing workshop over the past year has nurtured all these activities, all these connections, all these relationships. I have witnessed everybody's work improve.

– Michèle Roberts

Prose Introductions

And where have I been for the last six months? Well, teaching on the MA has taken me to an orthodox Jewish synagogue in North London, Nigeria, the Far East, a run down housing estate in Liverpool, a night club in Lisbon, a bar stool in Spitalfields, Hong Kong, Dublin, Galway, Barcelona, a fish canning factory in an unspecified Northern town, Las Vegas, Scandinavia in the snow, a rural village just outside Shakespeare's London, Beauvais in Northern France, an upturned tank with my Horror Cousin, and a very strange holiday resort on the Suffolk coast.

Oh yes, and I have joined a coven in Bayswater.

I have been spending time in the 1940s, the 1590s, the 1980s and am still on the brink of the First Gulf War. You get the picture. Travelling with the writers whose work is showcased in the following pages has involved strange journeys in time and space. We have worked hard, been on research trips, read lots of other books, champed with impatience, written and re-written it all, again and again. And there are other journeys, here in this volume, which I have not yet taken but will now do – as their first readers. Writing is hard work. The process of making writing is one of endlessly stitching a provisional shape, and then watching it unravel, to be remade again. Many of the writers here are surprised, baffled, delighted by the changing directions their work has taken. Finding the way is part of the work. But writing is also a gift, from the writer to the reader. It's our turn now, as readers, to enjoy ourselves.

– Patricia Duncker

Two stories
Naomi Alderman

The final analysis

I had a call from my therapist last week. He was feeling low, just needed to talk to someone, just called to hear the sound of a human voice, he said.

I said: 'Dr Kingdom, I don't think this is a normal therapist-patient relationship.'

He said: 'I think I'm better qualified to make that judgment than you.'

And he was right.

I started seeing Dr Kingdom about six months ago. I'd been having terrible nightmares. I would be in a narrow room with bare floors or on a wide, empty desert plain. Always alone, but with a sense of menace. It's hard to explain.

Dr Kingdom said he knew what I meant. He'd been having bad dreams too. He dreamed of gathering together small pieces of string, which were then torn from his hand by the wind with personality and scattered across a devouring sea.

I wondered if it might be a castration anxiety dream. He told me to eat my copy of Freud page by page, to teach it a lesson. I swallowed the covers in small pieces, washed them down with a glass of water, but threw the rest away. I didn't tell Dr Kingdom.

A friend of mine, Bill, an actor, said: 'Do you think this guy's doing you any good, Bill?'

Bill calls everyone Bill. It's just his gimmick.

I said: 'He comes highly recommended. Anyway, the nightmares have stopped.'

And they had. But then I wasn't sleeping.

Dr Kingdom used to lie on a couch during analysis. He had me lie next to him. It was a big couch. Once, I leaned over and found that he had taken off all his clothes except for one sock, which he had placed over his penis.

I said: 'Dr Kingdom, why am I putting up with this?'

He said: 'Because you're paying $250 an hour.'

I felt that I was coming close to a breakthrough.

He asked me to tell him about his father. I said I didn't know about his father, so he told me. Then I told him. We agreed that the story sounded better the way I told it. We made a pact to write each other's autobiographies.

I began to wonder when I would be cured.

He placed his hand on my thigh and said: 'Darling, none of us is ever cured.'

During sex I heard a rustle of paper. I looked around and found that he was reading, rhythmically, a book with no covers. When I tried to see what it was, he threw it out of the window.

Once, I felt I was being watched. I ran to the curtain and found his mother standing behind it. I recognised her from his drawings.

He said: 'Don't worry, it's all part of her therapy. She needs to get out more.'

I said: 'Dr Kingdom I think this is an invasion of my privacy.'

He said: 'You have no privacy.'

I wondered what I'd been thinking.

I had lunch with a friend of mine, Grace. She's in finance.

She said: 'You look tired.'

I told her I felt alive with freshness.

She said: 'I'm beginning to worry about you, Bill.'

I told her she was spending too much time with Bill.

I told Dr Kingdom I thought I was falling in love with him.

He explained that it was a perfectly normal part of therapy and slapped me hard across the face. Then he sent me to bed without any dinner.

Later that night, I awoke to find him licking my face. He said he needed more salt in his diet. I suggested where he could find some.

Eventually, Dr Kingdom told me he thought I should leave.

'I feel,' he said, 'that I've moved past the point where these sessions are helpful.'

I sank to my knees and began to cry. I clung to his legs. I begged him not to leave me. I thought that was probably what he expected.

He stroked my hair and told me I'd always be a part of him. I wrote him my final cheque.

I wondered if my need for therapy was over. I slept without nightmares, but I had begun to feel oddly unhappy around other people. I had cocktails with a friend of mine, Nancy. She's in PR.

She said: 'I love your hair. What have you done with it?'

I said: 'Nancy, do you think I'm attractive?'

Later, during sex, she whispered: 'God, Bill, Grace said you were good, but I had no idea.'

I started to feel cheap. I threw her out when Dr Kingdom called.

I said: 'Dr Kingdom, do you think I'm ready to start seeing other therapists?'

He said: 'Hey, why not? I'm seeing other patients.'

So, now I'm seeing Bill's therapist, Dr Pink. He's been explaining to me that if I call everyone by my own name my inferiority complex will disappear completely.

I said: 'And then will I be well again?'

Dr Pink smiled.

Naomi Alderman

For they that hate me love death

As a young woman, I despised the old. I was disgusted by their slow movements, their collapsed forms, their smell. They seemed, to my young eyes, barely human.

Now age creeps upon me like a quiet hand, calming my limbs and bidding them be still. And I begin to see that I have more to fear from youth than age.

The young people came to me again today, their faces eager. They wanted to speak of my son.

I said: 'What would you have of me?'

They asked for tales of his glorious life.

I considered telling how he feared the dark. How he loved the roast lamb I cooked, its crisp flesh spiked with herbs and oozing fat. How he used to pull his younger sister's hair. They do not want such stories; these are not the deeds of a glorious hero.

I said: 'Why do you need my stories?'

'We will write them in our papers and tell the world. Your son will live forever.'

I spoke without emotion. 'He is dead, you fools. My son is dead.'

The old never come to me in this way. The men drink their brews in the shade of trees and doorways. The women scold and wheedle in the marketplace. And when they see me shuffling – for I walk now like a broken thing – they watch me quietly; we share an understanding.

Last week a bearded youth with rolling eyes preached in the square. There are many such. I paid him little mind, until I heard him call out my son's name.

'This man,' he declared, 'is a Holy Martyr! He died to free us from the oppressors! He gave his life willingly in our sacred struggle for the Holy Land.'

I pulled my scarf around my face and listened. The man's lips were cracked and bleeding. His words were confused; they bore no connection to the faith I have been taught. As he shouted his beard became flecked with creamy-white spittle.

'The mother of this man,' he declared, 'is filled with pride! She delights that her son died in a Holy War, as God has commanded.'

I scanned the crowd. I have known some of those faces for many years, but I did not know them then. They looked hungry. Fervent. Dangerous.

Nausea swept over me. I cast my eyes downward and walked away.

They tell me that at his last moment he shouted aloud the name of God.

I do not know. I was not there.

In my dreams he calls my name and I cannot answer him.

When he was a baby, I saved him from a scorpion. The thing had found its way into his cradle; it danced upon his chest, sting dripping black venom. I plucked it from him, threw it to the ground, trod it to yellow pulp.

Only when he was safe did I notice that my hand was stung. Two of my fingers withered, but I have not regretted it.

Now, though, I begin to wonder why I did not leave the scorpion to its work. Did I save him only for this? For the Holy Cause?

They tell me that he believed in the Cause, that he was glad to die. I cannot say what he believed.

Once, I went to hear him speak. I had not seen him for many months. His face was different, his eyes shining. He seemed to be inhabited and animated only by his words. Afterwards I tried to see him but they turned me away.

So it was not I who spoke with him the night before he died.

They tell me that he doubted that night. In my dreams he comes to me with his doubts. I tell him to turn back, for it is not too late. All at once, he is a trusting child again. He puts his small, smooth hand in mine and I lead him from that place.

But I was not there and the youths spoke fire to him. These same youths who come to me now to beg for tales of the martyr.

Naomi Alderman

I have thought about this a great deal. And I think that now I understand.

To the young, death is an affront. They scramble and scurry to deny it. He is not dead, they say. Or they say he has died but his death is glory. In their fear of death they run toward it crying out: 'Behold! We have no fear!'

The old know that death walks behind us like a shadow. That it waits with patience. That we must snatch a taste of sweetness from our lives, for not all our words nor all our prayers will check its slow and steady progress. Death is no glory. It is no triumph. We will all come to it by and by.

The old understand the words of King Solomon, who taught that only those who hate wisdom love death. Only a fool seeks death, for death finds they that seek and they that wait in equal measure.

In my dreams I see my son under the wedding canopy.

I see him dance with his bride, swooping her high in his arms, kissing her with kisses of the mouth.

I see him gaze wide-eyed at his first child.

And when I wake I understand that these things will never be.

For the Romans crucified him upon a hill.

And he is gone.

Three stories
Iain Ross

Carnivale

S he stalks the shifting alleys, where fog hangs and holds
hundreds of years of footfalls and stifled laughter. Black velvet
sky, black starless cape flicking at her heels. A shadow-pair,
fantastic-faced, confer gravely at the alley's end, but her arrival
reveals only two bone-white masks, blank-eyed on a pile of
butterfly silks. She ponders: grotesque, great-nosed Punchinello,
or the other, enigmatic? She selects the latter and, faceless now,
moves on.

Bridge over black water. A figure dandiacal atop it. Her prey!
She hastens, but he is gone at once, and she pauses at the spot on
which he stood, above the stinking waterway. Footfalls far away.
Distant laughter.

On she hunts, implacable. Her lover sometimes a corner away,
sometimes the length of the tear-shaped sinking city. At last he is
at bay: a silent square, teetering dark walls, the glitter of his coat
in the furthest gloom. Triumphant, she advances. Motionless, he
waits. Mask confronts half-mask. Only as she uncovers her face
and he presses his cold mouth to hers does she understand that
he is not the one she sought.

Iain Ross

The Cupboard

During half-term I found a man in the woods and killed him with a rock. I did not expect to find him; I did not expect to kill him. But the woods were silent, and the man was alone, and I knew these circumstances might not repeat themselves. I had a chance to kill, and I took it.

I hit his head many times with the rock before he lay still and silent. At the first blow he looked at me, surprised, through blood, and I immediately regretted what I had done and wanted to stop. But of course that was impossible. He shouted at the second and third blows, and I was afraid, and I redoubled my efforts to stop him from hurting me.

I left him where he lay and returned to my room, where I wondered what I had done. That night I dreamed I had taken him home with me and shut him in my cupboard. When I woke, at dawn, the thought of fingers behind that door disturbed me, and I opened the cupboard and checked that it was empty. It was empty. I have not dreamed of it since.

The Missing Link

Today is my hundred and twenty-third birthday. On my fifteenth birthday I was introduced to Oscar Wilde; today I was introduced to 'Tony' Blair. Wilde told me he liked my dress 'because it is green; and green is for Ireland'; Mr Blair asked me to repeat this story for the thousandth time since I turned one hundred. I felt inclined to respond with a string of profanities – what have I to lose? But even at my advanced age I am inhibited by propriety and convention.

A young man from a literary society was also present. 'What was Oscar Wilde like?' he asked me shyly.

'Large,' I responded. 'And gentlemanly. I met him only the once, you understand.'

'I am in love with him,' he said simply.

I nodded encouragingly and waved him away. The truth is I can't remember Wilde at all, not any more. All I remember is the story I have told so often for so many years that it has entirely effaced any genuine memory of our meeting. Was he really there that day? Sometimes I can smell the polish on my mother's silver, or hear the distant hansoms in the street, but these things mean nothing to anyone but myself. I am the last living link to Oscar Wilde, people value me for that alone; and the touch of so many hands has worn the relic away.

The Mustardseed Seduction
Laura Bridgeman

Three days after we stole from Cook, we took Miss Brown to the lake. You couldn't see the lake from the school but we knew it was there; deep in the wood beyond the west gate, where the footpath ran with primrose. We told Miss Brown we would rehearse well. Mandana, Edith, Spuddy and I. We promised to be good.

'Like hobgoblins,' said Mandana. 'Like blissful little sprites.'

The sun was below its zenith. We walked with our backs to Mapledene Close. All five of us clutching *A Midsummer Night's Dream*. I pushed my fingers between the pages, feeling the earmarks and the scribbles. Miss Brown walked beside me. Her shoulders grazed against mine: we were both five feet two. Miss Brown wore a calico dress with red buttons and cork-wedged sandals. We were in our summer uniforms with their dreary oval collars. As we approached the path I heard Miss Brown break twigs and her breath quicken. I heard her stomach grumble. Picking our way under the horse chestnuts, our shadows fell like stones. Mandana, Edith, Spuddy and I.

When we reached the wide oak, Miss Brown tucked her dress beneath her and dropped to the soil. 'Page 16 girls. Let's begin.' Mandana threw down her book and turned towards the water.

'I want to see the lake.'

'Sorry Mandana?'

'There's a lake Miss Brown, behind the bulrushes. I want to dip my toes in.'

'We are starting the rehearsal.'

Mandana winked as she walked backwards. I looked at Spuddy and then we both placed our books on the grass. It was the way we always worked: Edith and Mandana first, Spuddy and I at the rear. We all followed Mandana to the bulrushes. Spuddy tucked her hem into her knickers and ripped off her sandals and socks. She walked quickly to the water, pushing her feet in. 'Cold and dirty, but pleasant.' The sun was hot on my neck. I felt queasy. Rays bit into my skin. A dragonfly lifted across the water; its wings skeleton clear. Staying in my shoes and socks I came close to the edge. Squashing the mud and bits of bulrush.

Miss Brown stood up under the tree. Her voice was harder now.

'Girls, come back.'

'Just a minute Miss Brown.'

Turning right, I saw Mandana unhooking her buttons, teasing herself out of her uniform.

A flash of shoulder. Her collarbone raw against the day. She was the first of us to wear a bra. Against her dull Bengalese skin, the silk cups looked majestic.

'Now girls, this is enough.'

'It's so hot,' said Edith flapping her dress like a sail, 'we fairies need to dip.'

Soon all four of us were knee deep in the foul water. Squinting back I saw Miss Brown flick her head, as if the school was watching. Waiting for the strike. Mandana trickled water in droplets over her bra and the puckered run of her tummy. The light danced off the lake in endless shards; twinkling over the weeds. The light was waiting too.

'I only agreed to rehearse here if you all behaved.'

'But all fairies misbehave.' Edith's voice was sing-song. Then she looked at me. 'Don't we, Mustardseed?'

'Yes Mustardseed,' said Mandana.

'Yes, yes, yes Mustardseed,' echoed Spuddy, her dark hair brilliant, her face as a sweet as a boy's.

That was my cue. We agreed when all of them said my character name I was to draw Miss Brown nearer. Miss Brown had been such comfort to Cook ever since the money. Only that morning, she had told the whole class that since she came from the Congo, Cook didn't have a bank account and that was why she hid her wages in the tea urn. Miss Brown asked us all to consider Cook as if we were considering a friend. That if the money was returned, she was prepared to forget it was ever missing at all. Turning back I looked at Miss Brown. Her face was sombre as she bent down and collected up our copies of the play.

'Girls, if you can't behave, we are going back to school.'

Mandana was now taking off Edith's dress, undoing the long, checked tie. Edith was gamine; her chest covered by a wool vest with material roses. As Mandana yanked the uniform away, Edith giggled then they went deeper into the brackenish water. Only Spuddy remained on the edge; her dress a balloon of cotton, her hands clapped against her chest, nodding at me. Willing me on. Nodding, nodding, nodding.

I drew my legs from the water and walked over to Miss Brown.

'Thanks Jodie, I knew I could rely on you.'

I took our copies from her hand.

'If we start rehearsing, then the others will follow suit.'

I looked towards the lake. Edith and Mandana were swimming now, cutting the surface with slanted palms. Their hair stretching behind them.

'Miss Brown?'

'Yes Jodie?'

'I just want to say.'

'What?'

'You're very pretty in white.'

Mandana and Edith panted. Their mouths glistened in the light.

'Girls, out of the lake please.'

'So pretty.'

'Girls –'

'I'd like to always remember you in white.'

Miss Brown fixed her gaze beyond my shoulder, where Edith was pretending to be caught in the weeds. She was throwing her vest over the surface of the lake. Mandana was trying to assist her with phoney yanks and cries.

'Help! Emergency!'

Spuddy glared back at me and whispered, 'Mustardseed, they need you.'

Mandana pulled on Edith's ribs. Edith flipped about like a

delirious salmon. Then I heard the school bell over the field. It must have been teatime. Three hundred pupils would be making their way to the dining hall; towards the smell of bread and watery jam. Three hundred honest, obedient Mapledene girls.

I fixed on the bell, then turning to Miss Brown, I said –

'We need to rescue Edith. She's stuck.'

Just then I saw Miss Brown's hair shake. Her Alice band slid backwards. She looked anxious, lost. Her eyes dancing at mine.

'We must raise the alarm, Jodie.'

'We don't have time,' I said, 'let's form a line across the water.'

I took Miss Brown's hand and lead her to the lake. Edith was giving her best rendition of a drowning girl. Spluttering mud, flicking her arms at right angles with limp, desperate stabs. Mandana was pretending to help. I saw translucent reeds skid over her arms and pop about her midriff. Miss Brown wriggled her hand free from mine and told Mandana to lift Edith's chest.

'Turn her nose to the sky.'

Mandana attempted the instructions. Spuddy splashed at the edge, her feet bringing up mud and air bubbles. Miss Brown got nearer the lake. Her sandals touched the shore. Then I saw her hesitate. She turned her face to the school where the bell was still ringing.

'Miss Brown, I've got you.'

I took her hand again and it quivered at the edge of the lake. Then I fed myself into the water. My feet were sliding with mud. Spuddy took my hand and reached out towards Mandana who yelled, 'Pull.' Miss Brown pulled me and I, in turn, yanked Spuddy. Edith gave encouragement by lifting her head. 'Pull.' Spuddy got nearer Edith and put one arm around her. Mandana drew away. 'Keep going Miss Brown.' Mandana splashed towards the shore. Coming behind Miss Brown, Mandana lifted up her arms.

All I ever had was feeling, too much feeling. The others had more to lose: Mandana had already been expelled from Sherborne. Edith had brothers at Oxford. Spuddy was Captain of Games.

Mandana lifted her arms. I gripped Miss Brown's fingers but it was too late. Mandana pitched forward, knocking Miss Brown into me. My legs buckled. I went under the surface of the water. Through the dense particles I saw Spuddy's dress floating before me, twisting towards the light. Then Miss Brown's face came to mine, her blue eyes pulled open, her mouth goldfish taut. On the base of her crown I saw Mandana's fingers clamping. Spuddy pulled away leaving me to float upwards. On the surface Miss Brown's legs were thrashing but it was no use. Mandana had a grip. The other two had joined her. They were all pushing down.

I recoiled in the water. 'Let her go. Please. Let her –'

Mandana's face snarled with satisfaction, Edith bit her lip, Spuddy held her ankles as if holding a third former for the bumps.

I felt the bulrushes. 'She won't tell about Cook's money.'

My feet were sliding. 'I promise.'

Mandana shook her head. 'How can anyone promise that?'

They held on. All three of them. Six hands under the water. Miss Brown's white dress stuck to her; see-through now, like a second skin. Her pale arms snatching at liquid, air, sunlight. A jay flew up from the horse chestnut. Miss Brown sank lower. They held her under. They held her longer than the time it would take for a shock. The hold went on and on. Spuddy broke first, wheezing slightly, then Edith. Only Mandana stuck fast. Her fingers stretched out like frog feet, pushing down, onto the crown. We all stared. Miss Brown's arms sank lower. The calico rose. The surface rippled, then the surface stayed calm. A cork sandal bobbed free. Edith pulled back again, her wet face panting. Spuddy shivered. The jay called out over the wood.

Then someone said, with monotone precision.

'We're all suspended now.'

I looked through the chestnut leaves to the striped lawns of Mapledene Close. Sixth formers had smuggled out sandwiches. White bread and red jam triangles littered the grass.

When My Father Was Shot
Tash Aw

In 1957, on the day the country achieved independence after four hundred and fifty years of foreign rule, my father was shot by an unknown gunman. The assassin fired twice from close range but did not succeed in killing him. This was not the first attempt on Father's life – he had survived one previous assassination during the war, in 1944 – but it had a marked effect on his appearance. Whereas the first attack had merely left him with a scar (a pale puckered star on his left calf), this one shattered the bones and muscles in his right shoulder. Even the best doctors in the Valley were not able to prevent that shoulder from hanging awkwardly at a downward-sloping angle for the rest of his life.

The shooting happened as the nation gathered around television sets to watch the Independence Parade in Kuala Lumpur. Those scenes which have become fixed and stale in our memories were fresh and startling then, newborn images in our newborn world. The Padang – the stately cricket pitch in the middle of town – turned into a boiling sea of banners and bodies. We had only ever seen pictures of Englishmen on the Padang, a few dignified men on a vast expanse of lawn; behind them the black-and-white half-timbered Club House, huge and silent and brooding. Now there were *people*, thousands and thousands of them, filling that same space. It looked like a foreign country. We had never seen people dancing in public before. Not like this. Men with men, women with women, men with women even. They did the *joget*, swaying and step-stepping in little circles, lifting and dropping their shoulders to a strange, shared rhythm. They held their new flag above their heads, letting it catch the wind: thirteen stripes, a sickle-moon and a star. There, too, was the Tunku, the Father of the Nation, raising his hand and repeating the word 'Merdeka' three times; after each cry the people on the Padang echoed the word. It splintered through the television sets, as clear and sharp in our ears as breaking glass. Independence. Freedom. New Life. That is what the word meant to us. And although the dreams we had for our country have died in the years since then, killed by the things we continue to inflict on each other, nothing will ever diminish what we felt. Nothing will rob us of those stuttering sepia-washed images of Merdeka Day.

It was at this moment, after the third cry of 'Merdeka', that Father's would-be killer struck. We had driven in to Ipoh for the afternoon. Father attended to some business at CY Foo's and left me to wander the streets on my own. I killed time by sitting, as I always did, on the steps of the Hong Kong and Shanghai Bank. I enjoyed doing this because from here I could see all the streets spreading out before me. Everywhere was silent, deserted. I sat still and looked for movement; I saw only a stray dog trotting aimlessly round the block. It kept appearing in different places, half-heartedly sniffing the ground, before wandering out of view again. I could not work out what it was searching for. Occasionally someone would emerge from a doorway, break into a run and then vanish into another building. The whole town had, it seemed, shut itself away for that day, never venturing far from their television sets.

Father and I arranged to meet in our usual place, the nameless Hainanese coffee-shop on Sweetenham Street. Frankie, the old man who ran it, used to embrace Father whenever we walked into the shop. Father would raise his arms stiffly, bringing them round to touch Frankie's back lightly. After all these years, I remember Frankie because he was the only person I ever saw Father embrace.

On the way to Frankie's place I heard the crackle of wireless sets and caught a glimpse of the odd television screen. The parade had started; I realised I was late and quickened my stride.

By the time I got there I could see, over the heads of the many people gathered there, that the great celebrations were drawing to a climax. The Tunku was just leaving his seat and approaching the microphone; the Union Jack had already been lowered. The cheers rang out from the television, each louder than the previous one. A few of the men in the room raised their fists in unison with the people on the television. I looked for Father and found him peering intently at the screen. He was leaning forward, his chin resting on his upturned palms. From the back of the room I could see that many of those present were mouthing 'Merdeka' slowly, as if unsure how to pronounce this unfamiliar new word.

It was all part of this scene for me, part of these new and unreal images. A man stood up in the middle of the room with his arm outstretched. I thought he was pointing at the TV set. No one else looked at him; only I saw the gun in the man's hand. He stood there poised like a temple statue, calm and utterly still. As the third shout rang out from the TV, the man cocked the pistol and Father suddenly turned around. Perhaps it was to search for me, to make sure that I too was witnessing this occasion; or perhaps it was his instinct for survival, so deeply and mysteriously a part of him, which alerted him to the quiver of danger.

The gunman fired at virtually point-blank range, but Father had already begun to drop his body, pushing diving scrambling head-first into the mass of bodies around him. The bullet ripped off the epaulette of his shoulder before smashing into the TV set, exploding it in a colourful shower of blue lights and silver sparks. As he fell, Father pulled at the legs of a table next to him, obscuring the assassin's view for a split second. All around me, men began to run for cover. I watched them but could not hear their screams. I stood watching in silence as the gunman cocked the pistol again. This time I saw it clearly: it was a matt-black .38, old and well-worn. I also saw the man. He was Chinese, aged anywhere from 18 to 40, dressed in khaki trousers and a white cotton shirt. His hair was cut short back-and-sides and combed with a centre parting. In other words he was dressed like every other man in the room: I would not be able to recognise him if I saw him again.

He fired once more. I do not know how it happened, how the

bullet found its way to Frankie's stomach. I saw the old man collapse, doubling over and sinking to his knees before falling to the ground. The side of his head hit the concrete hard; the sound it made cracked loudly in my ears. The third shot was aimless and desperate. It shattered a glass cabinet full of coffee beans, filling the air with the smoky-sweet smell of rough Javanese coffee.

The gunman pushed past me as he fled. His arms were slick with sweat. His clothes smelled of ripe fruit and mud. I felt his hot, heavy breath on my face and heard the thin wheeze in his chest. In a second, the shop emptied. I watched as people disappeared into the bright dusty street, melting into the quiet afternoon.

I went to Father. His mouth rose in a half-smile.

'Did you see the Merdeka?' he said.

I nodded. Through the black blood and angry flesh on his shoulder I caught a glimpse of bone. It was pure, glowing white. I moved to the other side of him, trying to hold him and drag him to the front of the shop. He was heavy, immovable. His eyes closed and he chuckled the gentlest of chuckles. If my face had not been next to his I may never have heard it.

I don't know quite how I managed to do it, but finally I got him into the back seat of the Mercedes. I had just turned sixteen and I had never driven before. Somehow, though, I made it, stuttering through the white empty streets to the General Hospital. The nurses there put their arms around my shoulders and told me not to worry. They brought me warm bottles of Green Spot and stale curry puffs.

'Can you believe it, all by himself, you know. He got his father here all by himself,' I heard one of the nurses say in the next room.

'He's not his father's son for nothing,' whispered another.

Later that evening, as I sat waiting for news of Father's condition, a nurse brought me the blue batik shirt he had been wearing. It had been badly damaged in the shooting: only one sleeve remained and a few of its buttons were missing. But the people in the hospital had washed it and pressed it and folded it neatly. It was only when you held it up to the light that you could see the faint outlines of the washed-out bloodstains.

After the incident, Father's right shoulder hung in an odd way, stiff and unmoving, jerking from time to time with an occasional muscle spasm that made it look as though the shoulder was trying to bring itself level with the good one. Every time I noticed this twitch I remembered how, on that hot afternoon, I cradled Father's blood-flecked head in my hands. I remembered how he clung to my neck and shoulders with his left arm as I dragged him to the car, and how his hand felt on my forearm (damp, clutching weakly) as the nurses and I lowered him onto a bed. I realised then that I had never before known my father hug me or ruffle my hair, not even when I was a small boy. And as I sat waiting in the hospital I knew, too, that Father would never speak of that day again. Things would pass wordlessly, as they always did, and I would never again touch my father.

Of Noses and Feet
Chantal Schaul

The plants that Carmilla grew in her garden were all very tall, so that she could attend to them easily. There were lofty creepers, mostly beanstalks, peas, tomatoes, giant rhubarbs, berry bushes and fruit trees carrying plums, cherries, mirabelles, apples and pears. Carmilla did not cultivate any root vegetables or strawberries. The only flowers she could connect with were sunflowers.

Although Carmilla was graced with absolute beauty, she was profoundly unhappy because she was seven feet and nine inches tall. She cried herself to sleep every night. She hunched her shoulders and slouched her walk, in the hope of shrinking an inch or two.

Since her adoptive parents' death, Carmilla had led a very secluded life. Her parents had always done all they could to alleviate her height complex and protect her from the looks that people would invariably cast her. Her existence had always been in and around her parents' garden. But when they died so suddenly – in an agricultural accident – Carmilla found herself compelled to receive customers and go out into town on shopping errands.

One day Carmilla discovered the conveniences of the Internet and, little by little, rebuilt her life. She shopped only online and kneeled in the doorway when the delivery van arrived. To hide her tallness from her vegetable customers, she received them from behind a special desk which had the seating area sunk into the ground by half a storey.

But there was one aspect of her life that Carmilla had not

Chantal Schaul

solved yet, and that was her increasing loneliness. She had her daily work and felt safe within her house and garden, but she craved a soul mate and potential father for the children she so desperately longed for.

The answer came when Carmilla was ordering two identical pairs of trousers, which she would stitch together for double length. She stumbled over a dating website and jumped with joy. Now she would be able to search for an eligible male without ever leaving the house and with the additional benefit of knowing his height prior to meeting him.

For a few days Carmilla was fluttering with exuberance. She shied no effort to search the country, high and low, for a male match to her tallness. But as the days went by, her hopes shrivelled into dusty gloom. No man even remotely lived up to her elevation. The highest one was still only seven feet and five inches tall.

Carmilla did a world search. She ransacked every single country between the two poles. One hit popped up. Carmilla cried. He was Italian, his name Severino.

Severino was exactly the same height as Carmilla. His photo displayed a thoroughly charming and wonderfully good-looking young man with opulent dark hair, large and accommodating hazel eyes, and generously plump lips curved into a welcoming smile. He was a tax collector in Napoli.

Severino was the man of Carmilla's dreams.

Carmilla took extensive pains to compose an email to this Italian divinity. She went over it a million times, straightened out any blemishes in her prose, polished her uneven syntax, enriched her ideas. Finally, with a mixture of anticipation, fearfulness and devotion, she sent the message on its way to her god.

Waiting, waiting, waiting for an answer, Carmilla sought distraction in pea-grooming.

The reply took three days to arrive. It was worded in the most gallant and charming of ways, proving its originator to be a real gentleman.

'A million thanks for your enchanting message,' it began, and went on to weave metaphors around Carmilla's eyes, nose, lips and teeth, in an all-Petrarchan vein.

24

The words that Severino used to address Carmilla made her melt away. They were all taken from the world of vegetation: 'sweat pea', 'sugar plum', 'cherry blossom' and 'berry bee'. She fell for him completely and wrote back at once, using the most flourishing prose at her command, pouring out endless trickles of honeyed rhetoric and casting forth clustering clouds of sugar-dusted phrases.

At the end of a month's correspondence, Carmilla and Severino felt certain that they were meant for each other. They shared the same interests – landscapes and foliage; adored the same music – Mozart and Nik Kershaw; liked the same colours – rose and crimson; indulged in the same pastimes – wishful thinking and bird watching; and were both keen on having a whole horde of children one day.

They called each other 'darling', 'beloved', 'adored', 'wonderful', 'miraculous', 'enchanting', 'lovely'. They agreed on all matters, except for their attitude towards Liechtenstein, on which they sorely disagreed. But that remained the only point of dissent.

After three months of devoted e-mails, and a million portrait attachments, the virtual lovers were so eager to meet in the flesh that the tectonic plates of their respective countries could hardly withstand the magnetic force that emanated from their two souls. Severino finally got some time off his tax collecting duties and offered to visit the land of his inamorata.

The date was set, the deal was struck, and Carmilla's anticipation was of such vehemence that her soul almost fluttered out of her elongated ribcage. Her heart ached for Severino with such vigour that she feared she would wither away if she could not soon hold him in her arms.

She wondered which vehicle would deliver him to her door, knowing too well how difficult it was for a being of their height to fit into a car of any size. Would he be walking? Or would he tuck himself into a specially hired bus?

She peeked out of her window as a car pulled up outside her front door, and she was dumbstruck by the fact that it was an ordinary taxi. Had he, perhaps, reclined the front seat and angled himself into the boot?

When she saw the man who emerged from the taxi she wanted

to sink into the ground. He had the godly face of her beloved Severino, but a body of average height. She didn't give him more than five feet and nine inches. He almost looked like a weed. And yet it was unmistakably he, radiating divine beauty and emanating pure manliness.

Severino rapidly approached Carmilla's front door. In a panic, she fled into the garden. He must never be allowed to see her like this. In her trepidation, she grabbed a spade and dug a hole between the beanstalks, deep enough to stash her legs into. She threw her father's old mackintosh over her shoulders to cover up her disproportionate physique from her angelic visitor.

The bell had rung three times already.

'The door is unlocked,' Carmilla shouted in her sweetest voice. 'Come in my love, I'm in the garden.'

His steps approached.

'Where are you, my lovely?' His voice was more sublime than she had ever imagined it to be, mellow and yet alluringly masculine, rasping yet sweet. She almost lost consciousness and only just managed to keep her wits about her.

As soon as she glimpsed him, rushing towards her, her hitherto virtual love for him was drawn to a full circle and became overwhelmingly real. Their faces levelled, one set of eyes pierced the other, and both their hearts were welded together irreversibly and absolutely, heedless of their physical mismatch, in an eternal, if conflicting, unison.

Severino, yet unaware of the clash in their statures, tried to sweep Carmilla off her feet, but this proved an impossible endeavour. Instead, he kissed her for almost an hour. Her inflexible position stood in the way of any more audacious moves. She was dying to offer him tea or at least bid him inside the living room, but was unable to do any such thing. She felt awful.

Severino did not comment on her immobility and, instead, showered her with gallantries. When he asked for the toilet, Carmilla saw a loophole to escape. She quickly prepared tea, fetched a cake, sat down on the sofa, tucked her legs under a throw, slouched, and awaited his return.

They sat on the sofa for hours, chatting, gazing into each other's eyes, flattering each other, holding hands. The night came and went; they felt no hunger and no thirst, taking their sole nourishment from each other's company.

When Severino finally fell asleep, still tired from his journey, Carmilla sneaked away to the bathroom to freshen up. She returned unnoticed and placed food and drink within their reach for the impending breakfast.

Another day went by, consumed entirely by sofa conversations and kisses. Then Severino excused himself. He needed to go into town for an errand, he said, but did not enlighten Carmilla as to what this mysterious errand might be.

Mr Boscop saw Severino leave the house. He was a former lettuce customer of Carmilla's parents and one of the very few people who knew of Carmilla's tall existence. Ever since her parents' death he had been upset that she had stopped selling lettuce.

Mr Boscop followed Severino into town and caught him by surprise.

'Hey, Mr!'

'Si?'

'I saw you leave Carmilla's house.'

Severino gave no response.

'I don't know what went on in there, but don't you think she's a freak?'

'A freak? No –'

'You don't think so? You must be joking. Isn't she slightly too tall for you?' Mr Boscop laughed in a nasty way.

'What are you talking about?'

'Don't tell me you didn't notice she's about three times as tall as you.'

Severino was unsettled and gesticulated wildly. He lost his fake nose. Although he picked it up and put it back on very quickly, Mr Boscop did not miss his move.

'Have you got a fake nose?' He laughed.

'Excuse me, sir, it's a prosthesis. I lost my nose in an accident when I was a child. Now, would you kindly leave, I've had enough of your rudeness.'

Sniggering, Mr Boscop trotted off, right back to Carmilla's house. He barged in.

Chantal Schaul

'Carmilla, who's that strange fellow I saw walk out earlier?'

Carmilla was violently awoken from her amorous fantasies. She had always disliked Mr Boscop.

'I'm sorry, but that's none of your business at all.'

'Did you know he has a fake nose?'

Laughing, Mr Boscop stomped off.

When Severino returned from his errand, awkwardness installed itself between the two lovers. Carmilla was still tucked away underneath her throw, and Severino could not take his eyes off it, trying to assess the count of inches that lurked below. Carmilla, in her turn, had a hard time not staring at Severino's nose and trying to work out if the tiny difference in colour could indicate a fake.

Severino was the first to make an attempt at resolving the unbearable situation.

'My dear Carmilla, I wonder if there could be a difference in height between us?'

She reluctantly nodded.

'And does it cause you any trouble? Because, I remember, in the beginning of our correspondence you expressed your delight that we were both of the same stature.'

'Yes, I said that. But it seems to me now that we must have made some kind of mistake. How tall are you exactly? Not seven feet and nine inches.'

Severino took a deep breath.

'No, my lovely, I think not. In metres I am one seventy-six.'

'That's five feet point seven seven four two seven eight two one five two two inches.' Carmilla knew her height charts by heart. 'The website must have got the conversions wrong.'

They looked at each other in despair.

'And your nose?' she finally plucked the courage to ask.

He gingerly touched the tip of it with his forefinger.

'It is fake, my darling. The real one came off in a cycling accident when I was five years old. I'm sorry.'

'That's no problem at all, my dearest.' A tear trickled down her cheek.

'Would you stand up so we can compare heights?' he ventured.

Timidly, Carmilla pulled the throw off her folded legs and unravelled herself.

'Let's go outside into the garden, my darling. I can't stand up in here.'

Outside, among high-reaching vegetation, Carmilla straightened herself. Severino only reached up to her waist. He looked up at her like a little boy eyeing an alluring fruit tree.

Carmilla wished she could dissolve into thin air. From her lofty position she did not see that Severino was angling his nose into the concealing shade of a raspberry branch.

The lovers' realization of their startling insufficiencies crushed both their hearts. Perhaps they could have overcome their clashing physiques one day. But they did not get this chance. A harsh and cackling guffaw, laughed over the garden fence by Mr Boscop, shooed their clinging souls apart like a couple of bashful birds.

Severino ran off as fast as his legs could carry him and lost his nose in his galloping flight. A small red case followed the nose among the ridged earth between Carmilla's pea stems.

She found that it contained the most beautiful engagement ring.

He's Got Father Zang's Eyes
Dawn Marrow

'It's a boy,' Ba Ba muttered.

'No it's not,' said another voice.

No, what's not? thought Ma Ma, her heart pounding with worry.

There were mumbles and gasps, then Ba Ba cried, 'Turn it over. All of you lift at the count of three. One, two, three ...'

Ma Ma clutched the sheets. She twisted her head to see what was going on. The dirty gauze that separated her k'ang from the rest of the chamber obscured her view.

'It can't be . . .' cried Ba Ba.

Ma Ma grew hot, her breath rising up her throat like boiling water.

'. . . No. I thought you were dead.'

Ma Ma tried to hold on to what Ba Ba was saying, but his voice was drifting away.

'Is it really you . . .?'

'Wake up wife.'

Ma Ma inched herself up to a sitting position, confused as to where she was. She blinked as the sunlight made its way into her eyes. All the windows were held open with bamboo poles, letting the fresh scent of reed trees waft into the room. She could hear the sounds of scrubbing and the tinkling of bells. Gradually, she realised that her neighbours were attacking lotus stains on their plates and that Elderly Chu was walking his goats past her window. She stared at Ba Ba's sweating face, a lump of damp meat that sat squat on his shoulders as if he had no neck. He has no backbone either, thought Ma Ma in disgust. She stared at his limp body in the cart, at the arm that flopped over the side, and wondered why she hated him so much, even more so than usual. Not even the steaming bowl of soup on his lap could tempt her into tolerating him. Ma Ma leaned forward and, before he could wheel himself back, slapped him hard against his cheek. 'Husband, my lips are dry from screaming and only now do you come in with soup.'

Ba Ba looked down at the chipped bowl on his lap, his face wet with steam. He cleared his throat. 'Ma Ma, you know that we cannot afford soup. But not to worry, this hot water has been boiled eight times – once by each of your children. They spat their young chi into it to invigorate you. Even your new-born managed a lustrous bile that could be mistaken for a pearl.' Ba Ba held up the bowl for Ma Ma to see.

She looked at the floating froth. True enough, a pearl of spit spun in the centre. Grabbing the bowl, she took three deep glugs and threw the empty bowl against his head. 'Husband, did you not think to bring in my baby? Did it not cross your crippled mind that I'd like to hold him, let his little lips suckle on my breast?'

Ba Ba coughed, his hand uncertain whether to cover his mouth or rub his head. 'I'm not too sure about breastfeeding . . .'

'Why not? Are you suggesting that my milk isn't good enough for our youngest son? Well, it wouldn't be, would it? Since you can't even afford to buy Nourishing Belly Soup for your weak wife.' Ma Ma looked over his shoulder. 'Where is my baby? Bring him in.'

Ba Ba's eyes darted from side to side as if the answer to her question could be found knotted in the cobwebs.

'Hesgoneforawalk,' he mumbled.

Ma Ma wiggled her finger in her ear and stared at her husband. After thirty years of marriage, she didn't know whether she was deaf or he was dumb. Her head darted up as the main door banged shut. Her hearing was perfectly fine, she thought, wondering how she was so unfortunate as to marry a man whom all the earth's ailments found more attractive than she ever could. Drawing her tunic tight around her shoulders, she leapt over her husband's head and ran into the main room.

'Ma Ma,' her seven children chorused, their breath cloudy before them. She rubbed her eyes. The sunlight in here was sharper, making her children's faces appear like colourful flowers – large heads on thin bodies. She scrunched her eyes and blinked. Her eldest son came into view. Big Turtle, twelve years old, swung his legs beneath the table, his scrawny feet kicking his sister's ankle. Pink Lotus glowered at him and dug her chopstick in his arm. One by one, the other children reverted from flowers to faces. There were the Ding Dong Dang triplets; their soft hairless faces smiling angelically at her. Then came White Monkey Daughter whose snot made a round journey from her nose to her mouth and back again; and finally, three-year-old Clever Chu who could already read Chinese calligraphy even when reflected in their dusty mirror. Beside him was an old man, hunch-backed, staring at Clever Chu and licking his lips.

'Who's the guest?' She whispered to Ba Ba who had wheeled up quietly behind her.

'What guest?'

'Don't be a fool, husband. That beggar there . . .' She pointed at the toothless old man, who stared at her with his black eyes. Ma Ma shuddered, reminding herself to whip her husband later for inviting strangers into her home.

The old man looked as if he were suffering from mountain disease. His white hair grew in clumps on his bulbous head, and was littered with leaves from his morning walk; his eyebrows reached down to his gnarled knees, and the hair on his knuckles rose up into the air like twisted threads of smoke.

'Husband, I want you to get rid of this beggar immediately,' she muttered through clenched teeth.

Ba Ba coughed. 'Wife, he is no guest.' He hesitated. 'Can't you recognise your own father-in-law? It's a blessing. He's come back as our son.'

Ma Ma turned to Ba Ba. She grabbed the handles of his cart and pushed forward. Feeling the jolt as the wheels caught between the doors, she shoved him through and tilted it up. He slid into the other room and fell whimpering to the ground. Slamming the door behind them, she screamed. 'Husband. I cannot stand you any more. Do you realise our neighbours laugh

33

at you? And how can I defend you, such a weak man, refusing to work because you claim . . .' she spat out the last word, '. . . claim that you have a bad back.'

'It was you that broke it,' muttered Ba Ba from the floor.

'And now you invite your beggar friend into my house and pass him off as my son . . . as your father.'

Ba Ba lifted his head a little way up from the floor. 'Although it was unfortunate that Father died on our wedding day, surely you must remember his lucky face? I hung a scroll of him on our wall.'

Ma Ma remembered the scroll, those painted black eyes that used to wink at her each time she got undressed. She had to rip it up when she saw those thin lips move, fearful of what he might tell Ba Ba. But it couldn't be the same man, thought Ma Ma shuddering. She looked at Ba Ba. 'You're a hateful chicken head, husband. Reminding me of such a bad Feng Shui painting. Next life, I will be born an empress, for I have suffered enough in this life.'

'And how about you, wife? I haven't been in your bed for sixteen years. None of those children are mine.'

She stared at him, her mouth open. How could Ba Ba accuse her of such a thing? The several men and what looked like a man (it had been too dark) whom she'd taken to bed, had only been there to keep her company and play mah-jong. What they did to her when she was feigning sleep was a different matter. Besides, it was no secret. She had always wheeled Ba Ba opposite her k'ang so that he could watch.

She looked at Ba Ba. He was clutching the floor's splinters, dragging himself forward. One of his shaky hands grabbed hold of her ankle.

'How dare you?' she screamed. She pulled her foot away and kicked him in the face. He flipped over like a fish in a puddle. Ma Ma stared at him groaning on the ground, his bent hand twitching beneath his chin. Not wanting to see his face any more, Ma Ma tipped the cart over his body and kicked his limbs so they fitted tightly underneath. She walked away, ignoring Ba Ba's dull knocks against the wood.

Pressing her head to the door, she listened for her children's usual hungry cries. Silence. She slammed open the door and stepped out into a pile of rubble. She looked back, convincing herself that her mind wasn't playing tricks; this door should lead to the main room and not to the courtyard. But if so, then why were there no walls, no furniture? And why could the sun be seen as whole as an orange, not the normal spray of light that found its way through the holes in her roof? The unrestrained scent of market air wafted towards her. She ran to the end of her courtyard, disbelieving the sight of the road that normally held market stalls. She stumbled over a heap of bricks – the last remnants of the wall that used to stand proud, deflecting the smell of the outside into her home. There were holes in the earth where her reed trees used to be. The bamboo poles that propped open her windows lay discarded on the ground like giant toothpicks. Even her neighbours' huts had collapsed, exhausted, to the ground. Ma Ma listened for the usual sounds – the slapping of children's backsides, the scrubbing of dishes, the occasional smash. Not even Big Throat Lily could be heard screaming her aubade. And what had happened to all of her stolen pottery, thought Ma Ma, biting down on her knuckles. Not even her precious dining table remained. All gone. She cursed her seven children. They must have collaborated with that old man and stolen her out of house and home.

Ma Ma stumbled forward in shock. She rubbed her hand along the edge of the jagged wall. Moist. Bite marks. A string of spit dangling amongst cobwebs. The sound of chewing and a loud grumble came from behind her. She peeped over her shoulder. The door creaked shut, revealing the old man behind it, his body flattened from being pressed between the wall and door. He wiped his mouth and stared at her with his dark eyes. She stepped back with a yelp as he shifted forward. His hand came away revealing cheeks puffed out with the shapes of heads and lanterns, angles and edges. A table leg jutted out between his teeth. He sucked in the wooden leg as if it were a noodle. Her precious table wasted as dessert. She watched him lick his lips, and balled her fist, ready for Iron Punch. The old man gulped, his cheeks emptying, the shape of a table stretching down his throat. A blink and he stood before her.

'Mummy,' he whispered.

She choked; his breath held flecks of bone and blood, spraying out with each exhalation.

'Mummy,' he whispered again, only louder, his arms coming around to hug her.

She swept her fist upwards. In the moment that her knuckle was about to collide with his nose, his face opened into a gaping hole. Teeth closed around her.

Her family had saved a place for her at the table.

Like It's The Truth
Philip Craggs

Y ou try not to look at your watch. It doesn't help, seeing how little the hands have moved since you last checked, knowing how long you will have to wait until you reach your destination and can get out of the ache-inducing seats. (Noughts go first.)

(Centre square).

You sit, knees painfully pressed against the seat in front, note pad on thighs. You think there is something distinctly odd about playing noughts and crosses against yourself, but you need to be distracted from:
'I want me wiiiiiiine, gimme me wiiiiiiine nowwwwww.'
'No, shut up, you're not avin it.'

(Block off a diagonal line and leave two potential lines across the top and down the right-hand side of the grid for the crosses).

'It's my wine I can av it whenever I wannit.'

Philip Craggs

(Cuts off right-hand-side line for crosses, and sets up top left to bottom right diagonal).

They've been arguing for an hour, punctuated every few minutes by the woman loudly announcing the tacky TV chat show they have just been on so everyone would know. She tries to stand and reach the baggage rack but she's in the window seat and can't get at it. Her companion, whose hair is the same length as his stubble and whose cheap tracksuit hangs off his bones like old, loose skin, grabs her arm and pulls her back into her seat. Everyone else in the carriage pointedly ignores them. Or tries to.

(Blocks other diagonal, sets up line across the top).

'You can't drink in 'ere. You're not getting pissed in 'ere. Just siddown will ya?'
'Don't you tell me what to do. Deceptive, that's what you are. They said so on the programme. *Deceptive.*'
'It was fucking wrong.'
'You took the test! You admitted it. *Deceptive.*'

(Blocks crosses top line. Sets up noughts line vertical centre).

She pulls a fag and lighter from her pocket.
'It's *No Smoking,*' says the man.
'How long till we reach Sheffield?'

'Three hours.'
'Three hours? I won't go that long without a fag, and you know I won't.'

```
X | o | X
--+---+--
  | o |
--+---+--
  |X| o
```

(Purely defensive move).

'I'm going to smoke it in the loo.'
'There's no need to fucking announce it to everyone. They don't care.'
'I'll talk as loud as I like. *Deceptive.*' She fires the parting word and walks down the aisle.
'Mouthy cow,' says the man when she is out of ear-shot.

```
X | o | X
--+---+--
o | o |
--+---+--
  |X| o
```

(Going for a horizontal line across the middle).

```
X | o | X
--+---+--
o | o | X
--+---+--
  |X| o
```

(Result: draw).

The carriage suddenly feels silent and you look around at your fellow passengers. Opposite you sits a man of around sixty, bald on top with short white hair starting at about eye-level. Next to him a boy, maybe eleven. The boy is drawing something in blue biro.

Stuart used to sketch when he was young. You remember being forced to decorate the margins around your work at primary school. You were always OK with the written work whereas Stuart's handwriting looked like a spider had been

Philip Craggs

dipped in ink and sent scurrying across the page, but his margins, whether colourful patterns, drawings of wild animals, or whatever else had caught his imagination that week were always lavish.

The branches of a passing tree scrape against the window, surprising the boy. He drops his pen. It bounces off the floor and into the aisle.

'Get my pen back for me Granddad.'

'Can't. Got a bone in me leg.'

You reach down, pick up the pen and throw it into the boy's lap.

You draw another grid but the train needles into a tunnel. The noise of the engine bounces off the walls and batters back against the carriage.

You glance out the window into the sheer black of the tunnel and see your face. Behind you the rest of the carriage exists in photo-negative, as though two trains were running side-by-side. A black-eye dimension where the laws of physics are different and photons create the dark, where the night sky is blade-sharp white and the moon the most void shadow rather than the sliced-open apple of our own.

Maybe in that universe silence is the roar of the engine, Betamax has taken over from VHS and birds fly underwater. Maybe Stuart is still alive.

The void is suddenly replaced by green landscape. You look down at your note book and start a new game. You end up with noughts top right, top left, bottom centre, centre left, bottom right. Another draw.

'Someone's taking ages in there,' says the woman, returning to her seat, lit cigarette in hand. 'I bet you cheated the test anyway. I did.'

'You what?'

'I lied. When they asked us if I'd slept with anyone else you dint know about. I said I ant, but I ad. And you're as clever as me, you could av done it too.'

'Yeah, but ah dint though.'

'Yeah, right.'

'Ah dint!'

'Lying bastard. I know you lied, like you're lying now.'

A mobile phone rings, answered by a young woman on the other side of the carriage with long dark hair and overcoat to match. The same ring-tone as yours. You remember the last time it rang, a couple of days ago. *It's about Stuart.*

Start with the nought top centre this time.

'Anyway, you can't cheat them tests. Not on the telly. They've got experts.'

We thought you should know.

Cross top left.

'You've just gotta make yourself believe the lie. Piss easy.'

Seeing as you used to be such friends.

Nought centre square.

'You dint cheat it, you can't. Stop showing off.'

And we hope you don't mind . . .

Cross bottom centre.

'It's dead easy. Think about the lie like it's the truth and you convince yourself. When they was asking me whether I'd slept with Steve or not I caught meself thinking "I wish I ad!" An' I ad!'

. . . only we didn't know who else to ask.

Nought bottom right.

'You're talking out your arse. I didn't cheat that bloody test and neither did you. Now shut up for fuck's sake.'

We know you used to know more about his painting than anyone else.

Cross top right.

'Say what you like. I know. Deceptive.'

And we don't really know his new friends, so we can't ask them.

Nought centre left.

'You're pissing off everyone in here. If you don't shut up I'll fucking slap you.'

We'd do it ourselves but . . . well, you know how it was between us and Stuart.

Cross centre right.

'You do an I'll slap you back harder. You better watch out when we get home.'

He didn't make it easy.

One square left.

'You're coming home then? Not going back to your Mam or something?'

Philip Craggs

We did love him you know. I know he didn't think . . . and we, we didn't always act like . . .

It's too late now for any other result: nought bottom left. A draw, stalemate. No winners.

'I'm not leaving our Becky wi' a no-mark like you, not without her Mam.'

We did love him.

At every station you watch the platforms as just-freed passengers meet those waiting for them. The man and his grandson met by the boy's parents with smiles. The girl whose mobile went off earlier met by her boyfriend, hugged and lingeringly eyes-open kissed. You should turn away and allow them their moment free from staring eyes, but you can't, and you keep watching them as the train pulls away and they stand there still, bodies together, time stopped.

You pass through Sheffield, where the couple with the loud voices finally disembark. At Nottingham the train is filled with students. A group of sportily-dressed lads sit opposite you. A woman, maybe mid-sixties but with dark hair barely touched by silver, sits in the vacant seat next to you, shopping bag on knee. You draw another grid and act invisible.

'I was stood right behind it – it hit his hand.'

'I reckon he left his cards in the dressing room.'

Hang on, that can't be right. You narrow your eyes and stare accusingly at the grid. You prod each square with your pen, trying to remember the order of the moves you have made. Even when you have done that you don't feel satisfied. You glance at the woman beside you, who notices your attention.

'Yes?'

You pause to consider pleasantries. In the end you open simply with:

'Should you be able to beat yourself at noughts and crosses?'

'I don't know, love. Can't say I've ever tried.' You recognise the northern vowels in her gentle voice. It seems like everyone on this train is going home.

'Well . . . I've just done it. Prob'ly doesn't mean oht. Just weird.'

You pass her your notebook and she examines the grid carefully.

'I wouldn't worry about it. You're probably just tired. I always get tired on long journeys. One day I'll fall asleep and miss me stop! Me son'll have a search party out for me.' She reaches into her pocket. 'Would you like a sweet to suck? I've got some Mint Imperials. No? Oh well, just ask if you change your mind. Have you got far to go?'

''Bout an hour, I think.'

'I'm visiting me son and his family. See me grandchildren. They've just had a little girl, a right bonny bairn she is. Staying over Christmas. Is that why you're travelling? Christmas?'

You don't want to dampen her spirits with the truth, but you can't think of a decent lie. 'A friend died. His parents want me to sort his things out. Possessions and stuff.'

'Shouldn't they be doing that?'

'Yeah, well, they're . . . not up to it.' You think about the things you're going to have to do; go through all Stuart's cupboards and drawers. To tally up everything that he left, to tally up the ashes of his life and help decide where to scatter them. 'He was me mate. I don't mind.'

'When me husband died,' she says 'I sorted out the house. I told meself that it wouldn't bother me, didn't expect to cry. But I think part of me knew how hard it was going to be; I wasn't surprised when I cried. I just hadn't noticed the signs. I'd been a bit clumsy, dropping things. Like I was distracted. Surprising what you find when you really look. Not belongings, or possessions or things like that. Memories. Feelings you thought you'd lost, or didn't know you had. He was a miserable bugger most of his life, but he meant something to me even then. It was only when I had to tidy his things up that I remembered why I loved him in the first place, no matter what me Mam said about him.' She chuckles. 'Always listen to your mother. She really does know best.'

'Ladies and gentlemen we are now arr&^ing at %&^($£* st**ion. Please make sure you take all lug&*ge with you when y*& &&^^rt the train. We hope you have had a &^*sent journe&.'

'Oh,' she says, 'is it my stop already? Well, take care, love. I'm sure you'll be fine.' She stands, reaches into her pocket and pulls out a crumpled paper bag which she drops in your lap. 'Mint

Philip Craggs

Imperials,' she says, 'in case you feel peckish later.' And with that, she walks down the aisle.

'Yeah', you say to yourself, 'I'll be fine.' You decide to play another game.

Start in the centre again. For some reason it is important to you to start as you did in the first game. Cross: top centre. Nought: top right. Cross: bottom left. Nought: bottom right.

Stop. You look at the grid in front of you. You've done it again. Cross: centre right. Nought: top left.

```
 o │ X │ o
───┼───┼───
   │ o │ X
───┼───┼───
 X │   │ o
```

You find this strangely disturbing but can't put your finger on why.

Room Eight
Michael Miller

The woman appeared at the front desk in the corner of Daniel's eye. She wore a dull grey coat and slacks and had a face that seemed to sag below the lines of her cheeks. Juan, looking up from his crossword puzzle, pocketed his pencil and asked how he could be of service.

'I'd like a room for one night,' the woman said.

'OK.' Juan searched for the list of numbers.

'By any chance, is room eight available?'

'Room eight?'

'Yes.'

'Any reason?'

'Just the view.'

There was a brief silence. 'Hold on a moment.' Juan excused himself to the office next door, where Carl sat with Daniel at the table. Daniel's shift started at ten, and he had arrived early to collect his pay check.

'Are people allowed to request rooms?' Juan asked Carl in a low voice.

'If they want,' Carl said. 'Why?'

'A woman's here asking for room eight.'

'So give it to her.'

'Wasn't it a year ago today? I mean, should I ask her any more questions?'

'She wants the view, she gets the view. Don't leave her waiting.'

Juan went back to the desk, retrieved the key for room eight, and told the woman to enjoy her stay.

'Could one of you escort me there?' she asked. 'Just a general precaution.'

Carl nodded to Daniel. 'Will you take her?' He continued filling out the check as his night clerk left.

The woman smiled shyly when Daniel came around the desk. A single suitcase, lightly packed, dangled from her hand. Daniel took the key from Juan and led the woman around the side of the building, cautioning her to step over a puddle of oil that a car had left on the pavement. Three cars now remained in the lot and the desert stretched out flatly behind them. When Daniel unlocked the door of room eight, the woman touched his arm softly and went inside. He stood on the threshold, waiting for an order, while she turned on all the lights, looked inside the bathroom and opened the closet. Finally, she returned and collected the key from him.

'Good night,' he told her. The door closed in front of him.

The sun still hovered low in the sky. Daniel slid his hands into his jeans pockets and walked slowly around the motel, spotting distant cars on the road and wondering if they were going to pull into the lot. The diner and gas station across the street were surrounded by empty spaces. He had wished for a quiet place like this, a warm stretch of land where he could step outside at night and not have to put long sleeves on. The motel sign, with the words 'April Flowers Inn' in red, was the only bright colour on the horizon.

Three more hours waited until the night shift. Daniel stepped into the office for his check and then wandered across the road to the diner. He ordered a cup of coffee, drinking it in slow sips while he watched two old men on the other side of the room. A waitress with a heavily made-up face drifted around the tables with a rag. When the sky began to grow dark, Daniel paid his bill and returned to the motel lobby, where he had left a thick stack of magazines to keep him occupied during the night.

Juan sat behind the front desk and handed a key to a tall, bearded man, whose motorcycle filled one of the parking spaces outside. 'Room two is just on your left,' he said politely. When the man left, Juan winked at Daniel and added, 'Trick of the trade. Never put a creepy man next door to a single woman.' He looked outside to make sure no one else had heard him.

At ten o'clock, his shift ended. Daniel took his place at the desk and laid his magazines on the nearest table, in hopes of going at least a few hours without having to open one. His eyes drifted from the water cooler to the interstate map on the wall and finally to the spread of dark sky outside the window. The sounds of car engines rumbled occasionally on the road. As he sat alone in the room, he thought back on the woman who had come asking for room eight. Her silver blond hair and soft face glinted in his memory, and he wondered if he would see her again before the sun rose. He wondered if she was still awake.

The hours passed slowly. Another single man arrived after midnight and asked for a key; Daniel remembered Juan's words and assigned him to room four. The pre-dawn hours took him halfway into the stack of magazines, and then the telephone rang on the front desk. He picked it up before it could sound twice.

'April Flowers Inn,' he said.

The woman's voice came on the line. 'Are you the man who escorted me?'

Daniel sat up straight, clutching the wire. 'Yes, I am.'

'Would you mind coming down here for a minute? I want to ask you something.'

'Certainly.' Daniel looked around for anyone to take his place, realized that there was no one, and locked the front door behind him on his way out. When he knocked on room eight, he heard the woman pause for a few seconds before she opened the door halfway. 'Come in, come in,' she whispered.

All the lights in the room were out. The woman wore her clothes from the previous day and her suitcase lay unopened by the wall. As she went across the room and sat on the edge of the bed, Daniel reached for the light switch, but then drew back his hand. 'Is everything all right?' he asked.

'Fine,' the woman answered. 'Come, take a seat.' Daniel pulled out the chair and sat down, keeping a distance from the bed.

The silver in her hair stood out in the moonlight. 'You know that my son died in this room a year ago today,' she began after a pause.

Daniel bit his lip. 'He was yours?'

'Yes.'

'What was his name again?'

'Kyle. My only one. I hadn't seen him in two years when I heard he had passed away. I didn't even know where he was.' She ran her finger along the fold of the quilt.

Daniel sat in the dark, stilled, waiting for her to say something else.

'But it was right about this time, wasn't it?' the woman continued. 'The coroner said they found him after noon, and they guessed that he had gone right before sunrise.'

'I think so.'

'I never saw the room myself. Not until now. They just told me the number and the name of the motel. I thought it sounded so far away from everything.'

'He may have wanted a place like that,' Daniel said. 'Some people look for calm areas. That's why a lot of us come out here.'

The woman strained a laugh. 'I always wondered where he would end up. We couldn't keep track of him. One month he would call us from New York, the next he would be somewhere down south. He wasn't a homebody, you know? When we heard about his death I was actually a little bit relieved. I felt like he was finally somewhere I could reach him.'

'You waited until today to come see the room?'

'Just a personal thing. I don't think the weather here changes very much from one year to the next. I wanted to see it just the way it was to him. Were you one of the ones who found him here?'

'Yes. I was.'

'Do you remember what it was like?'

'What it was like?'

'How the room was? He just had the one suitcase with him, and they told me he checked in alone.'

Daniel rubbed his hands together. 'The window was open. The blinds were drawn and he had opened it just a crack. And his suitcase was right by the wall, about the way you have it.'

'He was in the bed, wasn't he?'

'Yes.'

'Under the covers, or on top?'

'On the mattress. But he had thrown the covers back over his feet.'

'How was he laying?'

'On his back.'

'Looking straight up?'

'Toward the window.'

'Were his eyes closed?'

'Yes.'

The woman rose slowly and walked over to the window. Drawing the curtains back, she undid the window latch and gently moved the glass a few inches. 'Was it like this?' she asked.

'Yes.'

'And the bed? Can you put it the way you remember it?'

Daniel stood up and presided over the bed for a moment, then took the covers in his hands and peeled them back. 'About like that,' he said.

The woman came over beside him and examined the mattress. 'Where were the pills?' she asked after a moment.

'On the floor next to him.'

'Then he wasn't looking at them?'

'No.'

She sat down on the edge of the bed and fixed her eyes on the window. The sky had begun to turn dark blue. 'It was probably right about this time,' she muttered to herself. Daniel placed his hand lightly on her shoulder, and when she didn't shake it off, pressed it more firmly.

'Do you remember anything else?' the woman asked him.

'No. This was it.'

'This was it,' she repeated to herself. The two of them looked at the window in silence for a few minutes, and then the woman patted Daniel's hand. 'Well, thank you,' she whispered. 'That's all I wanted to know.'

'Is there anything else I can do?'

'No. Go back to your desk. I'm sure you've got other customers.' Daniel walked across the room to leave, but lingered for a few seconds, watching the woman silhouetted against the window. Her back was turned to him. When he went out, he closed the door behind him as quietly as possible. Then, not having kept track of the time, he ran back to the front desk. A young couple waited with their bags under the sign, and sneered at him as he fumbled for his key and let them inside. After he had assigned them their room, Daniel ignored the stack of magazines and sat with his hands on the table, following the rising sun an inch at a time.

At half past six, Carl returned. A dark-haired woman followed him a step behind, slowed by her pregnant stomach.

'Good morning, Daniel,' Carl said.

'Morning.'

'How did everything go?'

'Fine. A few customers.'

'Good, good.' Carl began rustling through a stack of paperwork.

'Is this the new boy?' the woman asked.

'Yeah. Daniel, this is my wife, Alice. Alice, Daniel.'

'Hi,' Daniel said.

'Nice to meet you,' Alice replied. 'Enjoying your first week on the job?'

Daniel smiled. 'So far.'

'Second week now,' Carl cut in. 'Daniel, would you mind holding down the fort for another half hour or so? Alice and I have to run one quick errand.'

'I don't mind.'

'All right. See you then.' Carl left with Alice behind him again.

When they were gone, Daniel walked outside and sat down on the curb with his arms folded over his knees. The sun had risen over the mountains now. A single car sped by, sweeping clouds of dust off the pavement, and after its engine faded away Daniel realized that he couldn't hear a sound. All the rooms behind him, his rooms, lay silently behind closed doors. A hand turned the 'open' sign in the window of the diner. Daniel looked out at the flat road, putting his mind to a state of calm, and thought again about how the weather never changed in the desert, and how the April Flowers sign was the only color visible a quarter mile away.

Class
Tom Rowson

I 'll give a star for the best one says Miss Hadlee sitting down in her chair. She just wants to read her book again. She always gets us to draw things when she wants to read her book. Mrs Jeffers nearly caught her once when she came into the classroom but Miss Hadlee pretended to rub her foot and put the book in the bottom drawer of her desk. But I saw her. Now Miss Hadlee reads with her back to the door and with the drawer open.

I look to see if Si is writing the note. He is so cool. He never lets anyone touch his hair cos he is scared people will push his spikes down. I hope he wants to be my boyfriend. Amy said he will pass me a note in class to tell me if he does or not. I got Amy to go and tell him I fancy him in lunch time. We were sitting on the steps of the Year 3 block and talking about how nice Si was when Amy said I should go and tell him that I fancy him. I didn't want everyone to know so Amy said she would go and do it if I swapped my Snickers bar for her apple. I gave her my chocolate and she went over to tell him. He was playing football with Adam trying to keep the ball off the ground. I think he looked over when Amy spoke to him but I couldn't tell cos the sun was in my eyes.

Rob pokes me in the side. Hey Abby he says can I borrow some pens? No get your own I say. I let Rob borrow my felt tips once but he broke the tip off my purple one and sucked the ink out of the red one so his mouth went all red. In break time he ran around pretending to be a vampire and trying to bite people's necks. He's a right idiot. I don't like him. He smells like the cupboard at home where mum hangs up the washing and inside his ears are bright yellow.

I try to get Amy's attention by looking at her but she is busy trying to straighten her hair. She is always pulling her hair to try and get the curls out. She hates curls and thinks they make her look like she lives in a dump like Stig. Her mum says that if she wears her hair in a ponytail then it will stop being curly. I don't believe her but Amy does and always has her hair in a ponytail. Some of the boys pull it when they want to annoy her. Amy's not looking at me. I throw a ball of paper at her and she stops playing with her hair and looks at me. What? she says. I quickly check that Miss Hadlee is still reading and she is so I turn back round again and really quietly ask her when Si's gonna write the note? I don't know says Amy he said he would do it in class. But class is nearly over I say. Don't worry he'll do it soon says Amy you'll just have to wait a bit longer. I don't know if I can I say. My mum always says good things are worth waiting for says Amy. She smiles at me and then goes back to drawing and playing with her hair. I start to draw. Miss Hadlee said the castle has to have a keep and turrets and a drawbridge and a moat and they all have to be marked. I like drawing but castles are boring. They are just old houses without windows. I like drawing animals instead. In English when Miss Hadlee was reading us Tarka the Otter she made us draw him for homework. I got a star for my picture. Miss Hadlee said I drew his fur really well. I'm never gonna get a star for this picture. It's rubbish.

Si's still drawing. His tongue is stuck out the corner of his mouth cos he's working so hard. He looks even cuter like that. When he becomes my boyfriend I wonder if he will let me touch his hair. I hope he does. We will go to the cinema together and he will buy me loads of sweets and popcorn and stuff. And he will say lots of nice things to me like Amy's sister's boyfriend says to her though I don't think Amy's sister deserves to be told nice things cos she's not very nice to Amy. She always shouts at her and doesn't even let her into her room.

Out of the corner of my eye I see Si rip a piece of paper from his book. I stare at him as he writes something. I think he has written about five words. He folds it over and writes a name on it but he is on the other side of the classroom so I can't see whose it is. It must be for me though. It has to be. I think I can hear my heart beating through my shirt. Si leaves the note on his desk.

I have to tell Amy that he's written the note but she's busy drawing and I don't want to throw anything at her in case Miss Hadlee sees. Amy keeps taking out pens and then putting them back into her pencil case. She loves her pencil case. It's got a picture on it of Britney Spears riding around in a buggy with her hair flying out behind her. Amy thinks Britney is the coolest person in the world. She was the first person in school to have her album and know all the words to the songs. I think Destiny's Child are better. They wear nicer clothes and dance really well together. Also whenever they're on TV they always have different hairstyles to when they were last on.

Amy wants to be a singer when she grows up. She practises in her bathroom all the time. When we were in IT class once me and Amy were sitting together at the computer and Amy went to the Britney Spears website cos she's a real whiz at computers and can do things like that. She turned on the speakers and made the computer play Hit Me Baby One More Time and she sang along to it and danced. She was really good. Her voice sounded wicked and she could dance at the same time without getting out of breath. Everyone laughed and cheered except for crusty old Mr Bilcone who got really angry with her. He sent her out of the class and made her spend the rest of the lesson in the corridor facing the wall.

Si puts the note on the table behind him without turning or looking around. Vicky is too busy drawing to notice it even though she's wearing glasses. I want to shout at her to pass it on but I have to stop myself. She would probably cry if I shouted at her anyway. She cries all the time. At the end of Tarka the Otter when Deadlock died and Tarka went under the water and there was three bubbles and then nothing she burst into tears and Miss Hadlee had to look after her. I don't know why she cried though cos I think Tarka lived. No one said he died. Darren who is sitting next to Vicky sees the note luckily and passes it on. My heart feels like it's gonna explode.

Miss Hadlee looks up at the clock above the door and says you have 10 minutes left and then goes back to reading her book.

Tom Rowson

Mark is attacking his desk with his compass. Scratching lines up and down. He looks at the note but doesn't pass it on. When we were in Year 4 Si got in a fight with Mark cos he was saying nasty things about his mum. Mark is always being horrible to people and nicking stuff out of everyone's bags. Once he got suspended from school for a week for saying the F word to Miss Andrews. Si calls him Skid Mark which makes him really angry. Mark picks up the note and looks like he is gonna put it in his pocket but then he throws it onto the next table.

Rob hits me on the arm and says please can I borrow your pens? I only want the grey one. No I say moving my box of felt tips to the other side of my book. I've hardly drawn anything. My picture looks like a block of concrete. There are no turrets or anything on my castle. Rob's done a moat with little people being eaten by crocodiles and sharks and people firing guns from the turrets and everything. Even his picture's better than mine and he's useless at drawing.

Ben hands the note straight over to Adam. Adam doesn't even look at the name but gives it to Julia. He must know who it's for already. Him and Si must have talked about me together. I wonder what they said? The note's really close. I hope Si wants to be my boyfriend. I think he fancies me. Last week in gym he picked me for his team and at the end of the game he said I throw really good. And then a couple of days ago he told me that my trainers looked mega cool. He made me feel well happy cos Amy said she didn't like the blue flash down the sides or the yellow laces. She said they looked like football boots. I think she was just jealous though cos she has to wear normal shoes cos her mum won't let her go to school with trainers on like my mum. My mum says that she's not forking out for two pairs of shoes for school when my feet are growing so fast and the teachers will just have to like it or lump it.

Julia gives the note over to the new kid Kate. I hope she knows what to do with it. She looks at me and leans forward. I grab the note from Kate's hand. She says pass it and then her face freezes like when you press the pause button on the video.

I'll take that young lady says Miss Hadlee snatching the note from my hand. Stay behind after class and I'll deal with you then.

She rips up the note and puts the little pieces of paper in her pocket. Rob that's a very good picture she says peering down at his book. It looks like you've put a lot of effort into it. I think you deserve the star for today.

The bell goes and people start packing away their things. I wonder what Kate meant? Miss Hadlee walks over to my desk. Right young lady she says let's see how much work you've done. She picks up my book. I watch Si put his bag over his shoulder and walk out of the classroom. Amy follows him.

The Butcher's Daughter
Claire Sharland

Emma dressed carefully for her first day back at school. She put on her favourite skirt, with strawberry motifs on its pockets, and her father brushed her hair into a ponytail. He was clumsy at it, and pulled, but she didn't say anything or squeal. She liked it when he brushed her hair. She passed him the ruby-red bobble she had been clutching in readiness, and watched in the mirror as he fastened it. Her shoes were waiting, neat and shiny, underneath her chair. She had cleaned them the night before. There was still a smear of black polish on one of the buckles.

Sitting down at the kitchen table for breakfast, she felt like a stranger. Wordlessly, her father placed a bowl of porridge in front of her. Heaping sugar over the grey mess, she wondered if he was still angry with her for taking the silver-cased lipstick from Alice's mum. It had been so easy just to take it from her dressing table that it didn't seem to Emma that she could be doing something wrong. Alice's mum hadn't even known it was missing until Emma's dad made her take it back. It had been such a small thing; even Alice's mum had said so.

Emma struggled to swallow the lumpy porridge, hiding as much of it as she could underneath the spoon. He took the bowl away to the sink without seeming to notice. She wished she could stay at home with him, and help him in the shop so he would like her again.

Alice wasn't at the corner where they always met before school so they could walk together. Clutching her school bag, Emma stood facing the direction from which Alice would come, expecting to see her appear at any second. After a while Emma set off to school alone, watching the pavement as it passed beneath her feet. It was strange, Emma thought. Maybe Alice had been early and she had simply missed her.

Emma was just in time to join the end of the line as her class filed into the sports hall for assembly. There was excited chatter up and down the hall, about the long summer holidays just gone, and how it was to be back at school one year up. Alice was sitting in the same row, just a little further down. She caught Emma's eye, but looked away quickly, saying something into the ear of the girl sitting next to her, who gasped and looked at Emma in mock horror. Emma shifted uneasily on the hard wooden floor.

In the dinner hour, Emma hid in the girl's cloakroom. It was a better refuge in the winter, when all the coats offered protection. In summer, the mustard coloured walls were bare, but at least she had escaped the sunlight which exposed her to all the eyes in the playground. It was as Emma had suspected, Alice was shunning her. She sat next to someone else, and they giggled and whispered to each other all the way through Maths until their new form teacher, Miss Williams, told them to be quiet. But still Alice cast sideways glances over at Emma, only to look away again with a toss of her head, so that Emma knew it wasn't just that Alice had forgotten her, but that she wanted her to be miserable.

Emma had stared down at the page of her exercise book, and into the cool interior of the figure zero, wishing that she could step inside its pencilled line and curl up and go to sleep. But here she was safe. Nobody would come into the cloakroom. The old-gym-kit smell was ripening in the heat, and she welcomed it, because it would ward off everybody else but her. She sat on the narrow bench and drew her legs up beneath her, cloaking herself in the solitary raincoat that hung up red behind her.

'She's in here!'

Emma looked up, surprised by a girl in the doorway. Alice appeared behind her, followed by another girl. It was hard to see their faces in the gloom with the sunlight outside. Alice was carrying something behind her back, careful to keep it out of view. Emma uncurled her legs from under her, and stood up slowly.

'Get her!' cried Alice, and the three of them were on Emma so quickly that she didn't have time to move. She thrashed from side to side, but they had her arms pinned down to the floor.

'Make her open her mouth.' Fingers prised at her jaw. Emma turned her head from side to side to avoid their grip. She closed her eyes to block out the sight of Alice standing over her, holding a glass bottle.

'Hold her nose.' Alice's voice was closer now, and Emma opened her eyes to see that Alice was kneeling down as if to tend to her, and that it was a bottle of milk she held, maybe somebody's milk left over from break, though it must have been left out in the sun a long time because it had separated, the top half water and the bottom thick and yellow. Emma could smell it, and it was evil and it came closer, so at first it seemed a kindness when somebody pinched her nostrils together.

But then the pressure built up in her head and she felt something hard, glass being pressed against her lips, and she understood. She fought as long as she could, though she knew it had to happen or she would die, and in the midst of it she heard somebody call out: 'Thief! Thief!' And her mouth shot open and she gasped for air, but instead she breathed in the slip of rancid curds. Then somebody released her nose, and it got worse because she could taste and smell. She sat up and was sick. It came up though her nose so she thought she'd drown, and down her windpipe, over her clothes, and into her hair. A bell rang from what seemed to be very far away. Emma dimly saw the three of them run outside into the light, and for an instant she was sorry because they left her so terribly alone.

Emma lay back down, and turned on to her side. The tile floor was cold against her cheek. She closed her eyes. Her eyelids were like tissue paper. After a while she felt a gentle touch on her shoulder. She rolled over and recognised Miss Williams looking down at her. Miss Williams helped her to her feet and led her to the sink. She wiped Emma's face and hands with wet paper towels. It felt cool and nice to be made clean again. Miss Williams dabbed at the streaks of sick that were already drying on her skirt, though the paper towel left bits of pulp sticking to the material, so she stopped. As Miss Williams led her out into the clean air, Emma caught sight of the empty milk bottle where it had rolled away underneath the bench.

Claire Sharland

She sat in the staffroom whilst Miss Williams rang her Dad. When she came back she held out her hand. 'Come on, Emma,' she said. 'I'm going to drive you home.'

The drive was quick. Miss Williams pulled up outside the shop, and got out to open the door on Emma's side. As they came into the shop, her father came forward from behind the counter to meet them in his bloodstained apron.

'Silly girl,' he said. 'You should have said this morning that you were ill. No wonder you didn't eat your breakfast.' He bent down, and grasping her underneath her arms, gathered her up to himself. She could smell coaltar soap, and see the tiny, raw place where he must have nicked himself shaving. She couldn't keep her head up anymore, and leant forward into his neck. 'Thank you,' he said to Miss Williams, and carried Emma up to the bathroom where he ran a hot bath and then left her alone so she could slip into the steaming water and soap away the sourness.

After her bath, she put on clean clothes, and lay down underneath her green candlewick bedspread. Its gentle weight over her was reassuring and she felt much better, only very tired. Later, there was a gentle tapping at her door, and her Father looked around the door.

'How are you feeling?' he asked. Nodding, she sat up sleepily in bed, and wondered how long she had been asleep.

'Would you like something to eat?'

Emma smiled.

'Righty-ho then,' he said, and withdrew downstairs.

She had her supper on a tray on her lap in front of the telly. He had brought down the old eiderdown from his bed, and she was cocooned in it, loving its familiar smell. She was forgiven everything. A boiled egg rested, self-possessed in a white porcelain egg-cup, and a second rocked gently beside it on the saucer. She admired its peaceful curve. There was a plate of hot buttered toast, cut into triangles so she could dip it corner first in her egg, and a glass of milk. She put the milk out of reach on the coffee table, and regarded it there while she ate her egg.

The Torture-Chamber
Tom Lewis

One Wednesday when we came into the classroom there was a new boy sitting at the front. His blazer was stretched tight across fat shoulders. His hair was greasy and black. He was sat all slumped in his chair, staring at the wall with his little eyes. It was a funny time for a new boy to arrive, in the middle of the week, in the middle of the year.

Of course he was bullied. They crammed his mouth full of sandwiches. They used his bag as a toilet. They made him lick water from the drain. Then, one lunchtime, he came and found us at the place where we stood between the wall and the fence.

'I've got a torture chamber,' he said. His eyes swivelled across us, from face to face.

'A what?'

'A torture chamber.' His voice was triumphant, as though he had just won an argument. 'Do you want to see it?'

'No.' We didn't believe him. His face screwed up, sour.

'Why? Are you scared?'

'Of course not.'

'Do you want to see it, then?'

'No,' we said. 'Piss off.'

At that the fat boy clenched his fists so his knuckles stood out all white. For a moment we thought he might hit out, or start crying, or something. Then his shoulders dropped and when he spoke his voice was calm.

'It's got a rack, and a guillotine. My dad made that.' He looked at us through his glinty little eyes. 'It's only up the road. I can take you after school, before my dad gets home.'

Tom Lewis

'All right then,' we said. The fat boy didn't have a dad. Teacher told us that. The fat boy was nodding as though we'd signed our names to some important contract.

'It's only up the road,' he said again. 'I'll take you after school.'

We met at the back gate and followed the fat boy. The sole was loose from his shoe, and it flapped as he walked. It was further than he'd said. He led us down to a road full of houses that looked like they were about to fall apart. The fat boy's house was all crumbly and cracked. He opened the door with a key that looked lost in his fat hand.

'It's down here,' he said.

We followed him inside. All the walls were bare and there were no pictures anywhere. He led us along a narrow corridor, and down some steps to the cellar. His hand fumbled against the wall and then a dim bulb buzzed on. The fat boy's eyes shone. 'See?' he said, and there was a sort of tremor in his voice.

The cellar was large and dark. Bits of newspaper were all strewn across the floor. Dolls hung by their necks from the low ceiling and the whole place reeked of the fat boy's strange, biscuity smell. We looked at him and shrugged.

'This place stinks,' we said. 'This place is a pigsty.'

'It's not a pigsty,' said the fat boy. 'It's a torture chamber.'

He picked up some rope like a whip and showed us how to aim and hit the dolls. The fat boy could aim and hit the dolls ten times in a row. Their eyes stared as they swung and bounced against the wall. Then the fat boy picked up two or three small objects from the floor. 'Thumbscrews,' he said, turning them over in his fat fingers. 'You can try them, if you want.' He held them out to us, and we took them from him, one each. They were slimy with black grease.

'Those aren't real thumbscrews,' we said. 'They're just old nuts and bolts.'

The fat boy frowned. 'Look then,' he said. He slipped one over his thumb. Then he found a spanner on the floor and gave it a few twists with his free hand. The thumbscrew squeezed into the flesh of his thumb.

'See?' The fat boy's eyes glinted.

We shrugged again.

'That's nothing,' we said.

'Yeah,' we said. 'That's nothing.'

'Yeah,' we said. 'That wouldn't hurt at all.'

The fat boy looked at us scornfully. 'Alright then,' he said at last. 'Test them.'

'What?'

'Test them. Try them out. Then you'll know.'

We laughed. 'We're not testing those.'

'Why not? If they're not real?'

'If they are real,' we said, 'prove it.'

'Yeah,' we said. 'If they are real, you show us.'

Suddenly it was so quiet you could hear the fat boy's heavy breathing. His chest pulled and heaved, and funny little wheezy noises came out of his throat. But when he looked back to us his eyes were hard and dark as coals.

'All right then,' he said.

At first we couldn't tell if the fat boy was joking. But his face was dark and red, and as we hesitated he said, 'Come on! Unless you're scared.' He held the spanner out to us, and we took it and held it in our hands, measuring its weight. 'You'll have to fix my hand still,' said the fat boy. 'It's best if I lie down, and you can hold it against the floor.'

So we pinned the fat boy's arm to the floor with our knees and our feet. He didn't struggle or shout or anything. He only watched us carefully with his little eyes. Then we started turning on the screw. The fat boy's thumb turned red, and then white, and then we heard him sharply suck in his breath.

'Come on!' he said. 'I'm not worried.'

So we kept turning on the spanner, until there was a sort of splintering noise like a snail crushing under a shoe. The fat boy yelped and we saw that his nail had cracked, and suddenly the air felt all thick and warm so you thought you were going to gag. But when the fat boy looked up at us his eyes were bright, and when he spoke his voice was trembly with excitement.

'You thought that was good?' he said. 'That was nothing. That was nothing at all. You haven't even seen the rack.'

He led us over to an old bed in the corner of the cellar. It was made of wood that was going soft in the damp. The fat boy had taken the mattress out so you could see the wooden struts underneath. We looked at the soft wood, and the broken struts, and the old leather belts that hung from each corner, and suddenly we remembered that it was only the fat boy, and only a dirty old cellar, and not a real torture chamber at all.

'That's not a rack,' we said. 'Racks have cogs, and winches and chains. That's just an old bed.'

'It is a rack,' he said.

'Not a real one.'

The fat boy glared at us. He lay down on the wooden struts and looped the belts around his ankles and wrists. 'Come on then,' he said. 'Come on! I'm not scared.' So we fixed the belts tight around his ankles and wrists, one of us at each corner. The fat boy lay quite still, waiting. 'On three,' he said, while we were adjusting our grips. 'One. Two. Three!'

We pulled on the belts, and the fat boy's arms and legs came straight. He didn't make a sound but his shirt came untucked so you could see his flabby belly. 'Come on,' he said. 'Harder!' So we leaned right back and pulled on the belts with all our weight. The fat boy's face turned red and his fingers turned white. The belts were biting hard into his ankles and wrists. 'Harder!' he said through his teeth.

The belt straps were all slippery with sweat so we wrapped them round our hands before we started pulling again. Now the fat boy's shirt was high around his waist so you could see the whites of his armpits. He had pulled his face into a grimace and our faces were shiny with sweat.

When the fat boy got up from the bed his wrists and ankles were all raw and red. He rubbed them absent-mindedly while we kept our faces hard and cool.

'That's it then?' we said. 'That's it? That's not like a real rack at all.'

You could see that the fat boy was getting mad. He screwed up his face and clenched his fists, and again we wondered whether he might strike out, hitting. Then the colour drained away just like before, and his eyes turned dull and grey.

'All right then,' he said at last. 'What about the guillotine?'

'That's not real either!' we said. 'It's all stupid.'

'Not the guillotine,' said the fat boy. 'My dad made it. It's got a sharp blade, like a razor.'

He led us to another corner of the cellar, where a dirty white table cloth was draped over something tall. 'My dad made it with a plastic blade,' the fat boy said. 'But I fixed it with a real one.' He pulled back the cloth and we looked at the guillotine uncertainly. It was a lot smaller than we'd expected. There was a wooden frame with a small hole drilled through the base. Above that was the blade, shiny and sharp. The fat boy had weighted it heavily with a brick. All this was sitting on a little table and underneath was a basket full of carrots.

'It's for fingers,' the fat boy said. 'Look'.

He picked up a carrot from the basket. The carrot was old and green and it looked pretty soft. The fat boy slipped it neatly into the guillotine and drew up the blade. When it dropped there was a thud and the carrot fell away in two separate pieces.

'See?' he said.

We looked at the mouldy carrots, and the makeshift guillotine, and the fat boy's eager face, and suddenly we all started to laugh. 'That's no good!' we said. 'It would never get through bone.'

'It would.'

'It wouldn't! It hardly got through that carrot.'

The fat boy fell silent. Then, before we could say another word, he slipped the little finger of his left hand into the guillotine, lifted the blade as far as it would go, and let it drop. We all heard a sort of click as it nicked his bone. The fat boy looked down and pulled his finger from the guillotine. We stared at him in horror. He wrapped his finger in his untucked shirt and the red sprawled lazily into the white.

'Wait.' The fat boy's voice sounded strange and swollen, like he was talking through a mouthful of bread. 'Wait.' As we stood watching him he took his finger from his shirt and put it back into the guillotine. He lifted the blade and dropped it again, and again there was that click. We stood absolutely still. We could not look away. He lifted the blade again, and the cellar swam slowly around us.

'This place stinks!' we said.

'Yeah,' we said. 'This torture chamber stinks!'

'Yeah,' we said. 'This torture chamber isn't real at all!'

We made our way back up the steps into the house. Through an open door we saw the fat boy's mum. She was all tired and pasty-looking with her sleeves rolled up to her elbows. We didn't say anything, but turned and ran, and once we were running I didn't stop until I was home.

Logical Value
Alex Watson

I have realised; Holbein is scared of me. I can hear him at night, in the hallways; scared to open the door; treading water in the darkness. He catches himself with sharp breathfright; hand still frozen on the handle. It is as though he never quite knows who is in here. Even though it is always only me. Either side of the door, he tells me quietly, while everyone else sleeps, he sees ones long gone. He sits at the desk working on calculations; and he sometimes catches his bowed head in his clasped hands; and I watch the tears gather on the inside of his spectacle lenses; as if they are being collected in two Petri dishes.

This sea air carries the licked salt of many wounds. It hurts me when it blows through the cracks in the window frames; splinters and cuts my hands and joints. But Holbein likes working in this little house on the North-West coast; where the sea coats the glass.

I can see grey storm clouds gathering over the sea; they darken the study. Holbein sits at his desk under the window; rain spots form on the huge glass panes. I am sitting behind him, on a chair against the far wall; watching him read a letter. It is not long; he reads it twice and looks up, staring out, over the waves. I have watched him stare like this for hours; hours and nothing; he called the two his second twins once. He glances down at the letter again; I cannot guess what it says, though I know the date; I stamp that on the flow of time habitually; and he is not due to be sent anything today.

Alex Watson

They say little to each other, but Holbein will tell Helena this. He leaves the study, and I can hear them downstairs, echoes of their stiff movements reflected through the house by the floorboards, borne awkwardly together by the front room.

Holbein: I've received a letter. From the Palace – the King wants to see me. It's a special invitation to the celebrations, for the anniversary of the end of . . . He wants me to be there.

He slows as his words seize up; there is silence as he waits for her. Up here in the study, I can see the dusty wooden head of one of his old inventions lying in the corner shadows, on a pile of long unread books. There is still enough light outside to project the rolling shadows of falling rain onto his face.

Holbein: Will you come? I would like you to.
Helena: After all these years, he wants to see you. And you're going to go. (She weighs each word slowly, sharpening the edges). Well, it is too far for me. Go alone, Johannes.
Holbein: Your heart is not in a trip to the capital? It will be a bright and busy place at this time of year.
Helena: (Her voice is brittle). My heart would be too much in it. I need to have time to myself. I do not think I could be in the same room as him.
Holbein: I do see what you mean, I do Helena, but I –
Helena: You should go Johannes, but I cannot bear it at the moment.
Holbein: We are fortunate to retain royal favour, you know, we're lucky to have this place, we are –
Helena: His good fortune still seems pitiable to me.

Helena's last comment comes poltergeist-hurled from her throat; then she is silent. Holbein comes back upstairs. He takes his glasses off. He is unused to wearing them; forgets they are transparent; forgets his eyes wander behind them and that Helena always sees this disconnection. He hasn't spoken to her as he'd planned; I can see he is frustrated. Distracted; he winds up a little music box that lies on the desk, weighing down a pile of papers. Two dancing figurines twirl stiltedly on the top; it cranks out its star-sparkling tin notes, clicking and desperate. I wonder that he is so interested in such a simple thing; but he listens attentively, and then flexes his own fingers; the engineer in him watching the 'marvellous complexity' of the joints moving and the bones sliding under the skin. Still working after almost fifty years. I wait silently; eagerly: now Holbein begins fervently drafting designs; drawing out ideas again and again; new mechanisms.

Holbein starts to work with a driven regularity; combing pages of equations, left to right; pushing the numbers through. Columns of problems and solutions. It is a regularity I envy. He seems to forget the things that cloud his mind. But some things, it seems, never forget him. It happens suddenly; he turns from the desk and gazes at me; staring at my unblinking eyes; he breathes heavily; each lungful of air squeezed through gauze, as something presses on him. I can feel the intensity with which he concentrates on me; pushing down. I would like, most of all, to ask him what it is that he sees in these moments; he has never told me. Perhaps he is thinking of how difficult I will be to complete, for I am not yet finished, and I do not work; I know that; I think of lists of all that I cannot yet do, for I am constantly reminded; I never make any noise because my jaw cannot move, and my limbs are all locked in silent stasis. Eventually he turns back to the desk, and we continue to spend our time silently together, as he thinks and thinks of me; what I am; what I need.

It is evening; the storm has passed. Holbein has left the study to eat downstairs. I can hear him clanking pots and plates in the kitchen. Helena will be in the front room. The two of them move about the house so separately it is as if they forget the other is there. They talk in echoes; sending sounds to each other distantly. He tells Helena he is going to bed. She tells Holbein she is going to read. He climbs the old staircase, climbing up through the echoing core of the house.

Alex Watson

It is night in the study; Holbein has left one of the lamps on low, so the room is dim and shadowy. I sit and stare doubly at my window; out of it, seeing little, and at it, seeing the hardness and immobility of my reflected glass expression. I hope that he will come and talk; perhaps about the letter and what celebrations he has been invited to. I wonder when he will go to the Palace; if perhaps he will take me. But even though I have never left this room, there are still things to be seen and sought in here. I observe how strangely different my window likeness looks when lit by just one lamp. Light chooses where to go and can make a shadow out of anything. The house is quiet. But now: I can hear the doors closing. One by one.

I listen and now: I can hear Helena beginning to play her cello; a piece from a subdued solo suite. For the first ten to twenty minutes, she plays with calculated accuracy, her elbows and wrists locked, moving only in tiny gradations; she tries to keep the cello quiet; pulling the bow and the strings apart the moment they meet. Holbein would find such precision admirable; but she does not want us to hear; with all the doors shut she can imagine I do not and she plays only to her dark audience. But I always hear; because what is quiet and subtle must find an equal and opposite reaction; an underscoring; so Helena always goes with the music and so the cello's dark resonance swoons and sways through the house's wooden frame.

There is a huge explosion. I do not know the sound, but I can estimate. It will be the naval defence battery, two miles away, on the headland. A ringing, double cannonade. The wall of sound barrels out to sea, booming over the dark water. Silence tremors in its wake. I count; there is no response. It must be a salute, rather than a warning. Our house is quiet too until I can hear Helena moving downstairs; putting the cello away; the way she struggles to move it quietly; the way it groans as it is closed into its bier; put to the back of the closet, coats and cloaks pulled over the box. Three minutes later; the sound of the front door; I strain to see her moving up the path. Then the dark walls of my study echo with colours, red and green all over. They are letting off fireworks in the town square. Underneath the royal gold and blue shower, I can see Helena's fragile shape, hands thrust in pockets, walking to the lonely coast path, standing just by the cliff edge. She is so strange; watching the waves . . . No, she must be listening, she cannot see much of the ocean at night. With her black coat and black hair she preserves a little piece of the night sky underneath the exploding colours. I would like to talk to her, but she never talks to me. I do not think she likes the study; it is as if she finds it repellent.

Late at night; I hear Holbein in the hallway again; waiting at the study door; thinking of the darkness on both sides. Holbein enters the room, and slowly walks right up to me, staring at my face. The wind blows through the winter trees outside, shuffling the few dead leaves, shadow pillars on the wall. Their scratches at the window glass sound like Helena's nails when they nick the cello strings. Holbein does not seem sure who I am; how he should be. He looks deep at my unblinking, painted eyes, and I look back at his, painted with tears. It is for me he cries, then. He is so close to me; I can feel his thoughts; he cannot contain them; he wrought me and now he wreaks them upon me. He is afraid for me; he knows I could take years to finish, as I have taken years to come this far. But he is afraid of me, too. Yes, he is afraid of me.

Holbein: I thought you would – could – be just like your brother. Because you wouldn't age, because you'd be an unchanging memory for the years ... But you're only as present as he is gone and lost.

Outside it is raining again and the sharp smell of salt fills the room, leaking in through the open window. Papers blow about, designs shuffled randomly by unseen hands. I cannot tell what it is I am supposed to do.

The Bayswater Coven
Helen Gallacher

'It must be her.'

'What must be her?'

'The things that have started happening. In the houses.'

'Ryan. Come on. What is actually happening?'

'Things.' He shook his head, and – well not exactly smiled; it was more as if he had tried to smile but his mouth had gone dry and one lip had stuck to the top of his teeth.

'Stuff. Things left in the houses I show people. Then other – events.'

'What kinds of things?'

'Disgusting things, Paul. Horrible.'

'Like what?'

He got up, strode over to the windows and moved one of the blinds just enough to be able to peer out into the square.

'What are you looking for?'

He turned back to face me and shrugged, his eyes fixed on the ground.

'Once I thought I saw her out there at night, standing across the road by the railings.'

'Doing what?'

'Looking up at these windows. I waved at her to come up. She ignored me – just carried on looking at the windows. She was staring – as if she were in a trance. I went downstairs to the main front door but by the time I got there she'd gone.' He said this fearfully, as if her presence had been a threat.

'You sound like you're almost –' I thought it better not to finish the sentence but it was too late.

Helen Gallacher

'Almost what?' Looming over me, he looked like a minotaur. 'Almost afraid.'

I flinched. I had expected him to be angry at my implication that he could be frightened by this woman he fucked for lunch, but he seemed unsurprised, as if he had been living with the fear for some time and was relieved to be able to share it.

'Well why would she do that, Paul? Why would she just stand there, staring at my windows, then go away without saying anything, when earlier that day she'd been groaning all over my bed?'

Maybe she'd lost her voice, I wanted to say, having heard how much those groans took out of her, having imagined her staggering sated and dumb down the stairs, having dreamed of kissing her throat. But I wasn't sure how Ryan would react.

He picked up the mini DV cassette marked 'R Oct 02' and absentmindedly held it to his nose as if to sniff the remnants of her scent.

'I met her when I showed her round a house. I'm known as someone who can sell houses. Not everyone can do it. There's a certain way I walk through a house . . .' He paused, as if considering how to nail down his own magic, then seemed to give it up as if such a task were impossible.

'I can evoke sumptuousness. My mouth can perform miracles, verbal Heimlich manoeuvres. I can talk a house to life, to grandeur. I can fill an empty dining room with golden candelabrae using nothing but my own tongue. So they give me the things that are hard to shift: gutted shells, dirty bedsits, filthy, rotten, rat-infested, stinking mansion flats where incontinent old men died crapping their underpants; because I am a visionary. I can see these places for what they are; sackfuls, millions of pounds.

But I also know the rules. You see, there are certain things that put people off buying houses. A purple door, for instance – you'll never sell a house with a purple door. Or a house where a murder was committed. That's number one. People think somehow the horror of the events are recorded in the house walls . . . it's an influential belief. Fred West's house was pulled down. After the bodies were found at 10 Rillington Place they demolished the entire street . . .'

He drifted off again. His voice had faded to nothing.

'Is that what you think?'

'No. I think it's a load of bollocks. Intelligent walls? Sensitive paint? What a load of crap. If paint is so sensitive why doesn't it complain about being stuck inside a tin for most of its life? Can we hear it crying *"Please Mr Decorator – let me out!"*? Can we FUCK.'

'But the trouble with beliefs is that they do influence people. Even I, devout believer in nothing, am beginning to be influenced – by –'

'By what?'

'It started in this one building – a gothic monstrosity near Orme Court. A run-down redbrick block of old mansion flats. Solid enough but funny-shaped rooms, long corridors, badly lit. Communal hallways and stairs not very well maintained. No evidence of service despite expensive service charges. Apartments there come up regularly; people seem to move in, regret their decision, then move out as fast as they can. But actually some of these flats aren't bad: quite spacious. Plus the vendors may have made all kinds of improvements. Recently a place there came up that I thought I could do really well out of; a huge basement with a walled garden. It had a spectacular bathroom, one of those walk-in wet rooms. You go in and it's raining indoors! Amazing – this isn't a bathroom, it's a theatre. You won't have seen anything like it.'

Despite resenting Ryan's snobbish assumption that I would not be familiar with state-of-the-art plumbing, I inwardly acquiesced, for it was true that none of the hovels my few friends inhabited were ever likely to be featured in *The World of Interiors*, though I had once squatted a place where it rained indoors (there was a hole in the roof).

'There was also a huge master bedroom that led out to the garden – potentially a great room in which to shag, though it would have to be talked up as such, as it hadn't been redecorated for some reason (I think the owner had run out of money and been forced to sell before he'd finished renovating). I'd arranged to show the place to a married couple – trendy designers, both good-looking. The woman was quite fuckable. Italian bird. Black

75

hair, big lips, huge arse. I think she fancied me quite a bit. They'd heard about the bathroom, but as a means of flirting with her as much as anything else, I try to get them interested in the bedroom. So I start mentioning it as soon as I unlock the front door, this amazing bedroom, how relaxing, how liberating a space it might be, how they could really unwind in there.

I lead them into the hall – immaculate; the living room – beautiful; the kitchen – okay, if nothing special. And I completely forget about the bathroom; all the time I'm going on about how they must see this bedroom, as if I've been hypnotized into talking about it.

Only the nearer we get to the bedroom, which is at the far end of the hall, the more I notice a smell. At first it's faint, like a trace of something bad that's been removed.

But as we move closer to that door, it gets stronger. The stench really hits me as soon as I open the door; I don't know what it is but I reel from it and I try to persuade the couple to come back another time. They say no, they're here now, maybe it's something in the garden, it won't put them off. But when we go into the bedroom the windows are closed – it must be something in the room. There seems to be only one thing in the room, and it's right in the middle of the floor – a square wooden trunk about a metre tall, with holes punched into its lid. Apart from what's on the wall of course.'

'What's on the wall?'

'A load of photos – mainly of women – all women I think. Covered the entire wall. Most I didn't recognize, but some are well-known women – Lady Diana, Karen Carpenter. All their eyes have been cut out, or ripped out, and nailed to the opposite wall, as if they're blindly staring at their own impaled eyes. And someone has painted one word above the door into the garden, in massive dark red letters : PANIC. I suppose the sight shocked me, but for some reason I just carry on walking towards the middle of the room as if this were any old wallpaper.

The nearer I get to the box the stronger the smell becomes. There's something about this box; you wouldn't want to touch it. It seems well made, possibly satinwood, but the surface has been scratched with signs.'

'What kinds of signs?'

He laughed, a desperate kind of a laugh, then stifled his voice with his hand, which he held over his mouth for a while before rubbing his eyes.

'Pentangles. Inverted crucifixes. Writing. Oh, and did I mention, there were white stains over the lid of the box, thick spurting marks angled inwards, as if about seven men had all stood round this thing and wanked over it? And the icing on the cake was what seemed to be a large blood stain that had seeped out of the bottom of the trunk and soaked into the floorboards.'

'Did you open the box?'

'Did I fuck. It freaked me out. I told the couple they'd have to come back another time. They didn't want to leave – the man thought it was a hoot and the woman seemed almost turned on by it! They weren't afraid at all – for so-called designers they displayed very little imagination, I have to say. Seeing him laugh made me really angry – I screamed at them to get the hell out of there, called him an idiot and her a spaghetti-arsed slapper. I was – unprofessional, I admit. I think at some level I was ashamed not to have shown more cool about this thing. Anyway, they storm out, shouting how they're gonna complain to head office. I shout back, telling them they can fuck themselves up the arse for all I care. But when they're gone and I'm alone in this room, I'm strangely attracted to the box. I still can't touch it but I begin to study it, and I notice that some of the words are names. Men's names. Charlie; John; Alex; and Ryan. Someone had scratched my name into this box. With a knife.' He looked at me, nodding slowly, waiting for some wise comment.

'Ryan's not that unusual a name,' was all I could think of.

He sneered at me.

'Isn't it? Who else do you know called Ryan?'

I was stuck, for a while; then I remembered.

'There's that –'

'That footballer. That's what you were going to say, isn't it? That underachieving, hairy-backed footballer.'

I nodded.

'Apart from him – who else? Who else d'you know called Ryan?'

Helen Gallacher

I couldn't think. His rising voice, his reddening face had flustered me. I tried to sidestep him.

'I don't know many people, full stop.'

'You do surprise me,' he snapped, then abruptly dropped his head into his hands, covering his face.

My Favorite Marxist
Jennifer Kabat

How was I supposed to tell her? I mean, how do you explain to your new girlfriend a ten-year-long friendship, relationship really, with an ex-stripper? What do you say? I still have no idea. Should I have said that we met when she was peeling out of her clothes and quoting tracts of literature?

Okay, to be precise that wasn't the exact moment. I made Amy's acquaintance at 7.15 in the evening, nearly ten years ago this fall. I was cradling my scotch, trying to avoid bogarting in on someone else's table dance and looking down at my shoes when I saw her feet in front of me. Black patent stilettos with bobby socks.

I started up her legs, taking in her dainty ankles, firm calves curving out, that sexy knot at the back women get from wearing heels. I ran my eyes up, scaling her body, knees, thighs hidden halfway up by the hem of a dust blue kilt.

She was wearing a school uniform. My heart pounded.

Perhaps it was a natural outgrowth of the faith in which I'm lapsed, going hand in hand with a perpetual sense of guilt and an inability to cry, but that Catholic schoolgirl look has always done it for me, way before Britney Spears.

Her white blouse was tucked in at the waist, smoothed over her breasts, the pressure of them pulling at the third button in the valley between her tits because the shirt was a touch too tight. A velvet ribbon encircled her neck, and she had the palest skin, thick red lips, high cheeks and dark hair cascading down her back. I caught my breath. I didn't say anything. I don't think I could.

'Can I join you?' she said. Her voice was a bit rough at the edges. It sounded like sweet wine with a whiskey bite.

'Of course, of course, please do.'

The club was empty, a few guys at tables, another six at the bar, and the dancers milling around waiting for their shift to start. To think out of the handful of men here, I rated a dancer coming to sit with me. Me?!

She flopped herself down on the leather banquette, probably in fact not genuine cowhide but some other animal like a pleather or a vinyl or nauga, and perched forward on the bench. She crossed her legs. I stared at her skin, her thighs pressing on each other. I spun my ice cubes around in my glass.

She adjusted her bag so it sat up straight. 'So are you enjoying yourself? What's your name?'

I wasn't sure which question to respond to first, so went for the latter. Its answer was more straightforward. In terms of actual enjoyment I would have to say no, in fact I wasn't, not yet at least. That's why I was there.

A drum-roll pounded through the club. My eardrums throbbed, a light flared and a slash of white reflected off the mirrors. A strobe kicked in and fractured Amy's movements. She'd lift her wrist, touch her hand to my shoulder, bend close to me, each gesture isolated by darkness. The music cranked up decibels, our table shook. I hadn't realized we were sitting beneath the speakers. A disembodied voice with the intonation of a bingo caller said, 'Tonight Hudson Beaverz presents the best in sensual entertainment. Thirty of New York's best Beaverz for your pleasure. There's evanescent Eve, or exotic Annick, the lovely Lily, our naughty . . .'

I turned back to her. She fished a cigarette from her purse, lit it and looked up at me. 'So you were going to tell me your name?'

'Yeah, of course, Barry. Barry McGovern.' I tried to punctuate it with a definitive nod of my head.

'As in George McGovern, the presidential candidate?' She flashed me a crooked little half smile. Her earrings sparked with a blaze of red lights.

'Yes, I mean, no, no we're not related, but it's the same spelling. I did, however, volunteer on his campaign when I was twenty.' The smoke machine belched a cloud of acrid gray air. Chemicals seeped into my lungs. I coughed. The music was so loud, Amy had to lean in close and shout for me to hear her. Her hand was held against my ear to amplify her voice.

'And I worked on Carter's.'

I gave her a puzzled look.

'Campaign that is. Handed out buttons at the polls on election day when I was like six or something. I have a thing for liberal losers. He's still my favorite president.'

I smiled. I was just tickled by this, by her. I had no idea I might get this in a topless joint. I hadn't even intended to come in. I was just walking up Church Street looking for a place to eat, and now this. I didn't even notice our age difference. Not then at least. How could I? This was not the sort of chit-chat I was expecting from a stripper.

I studied her face for a second, her eyes smudged black behind smoked mascara and lips so big, they were nearly fishy. They were the sort that for years have inspired me to a lust that's almost violent. She cleared her throat, and I realized I'd been silent too long. She was facing me, her head tilted to the side as if my very words held her rapt attention.

'Hey, I didn't even ask your name.' I chuckled, hoping laughter would convey my embarrassment for not inquiring sooner.

'Lily.' She paused for me to register it. 'So what do you do, mister-no-relation-to-George-McGovern?'

'I'm an architect.' I was going to say more, but her eyes were wide and blazing. It looked like shock. I wondered if I'd said something wrong.

'An architect? Really? That's cool. I did architectural history in school.'

'Oh, where?' I expected NYU or Hunter, nothing too academically challenging. I don't know why; it wasn't that she didn't seem smart, I just didn't, well, she was a stripper. She laughed and glanced down like she was embarrassed to tell me.

'Columbia,' she said, 'but I dropped out of my Ph.D. program. It was too conservative.' She was looking at me from under her long lashes.

'Columbia, eh? It was way too conservative for me too.' I

slapped her knee like we were old pals. My scotch sloshed over the side of the glass. Clearly I'd had a bit too much to drink. She gave me a strange look, creased her brow and shook her head at me.

'I'm serious. Really.'

She thought I was making fun of her because, of course, it was uptight, it was the Ivy League. I forgot to mention though that it was also my Alma Mater. To try and get things back on a good foot again, I hurried to explain. 'I went there to study architecture but I was a bit much for them. They weren't big on Marxists. Christ, I didn't even want to build buildings.'

'So wait, like, who's your favorite Marxist? Mine's Althusser. Don't you just love him? So pragmatic even though he offed his wife.' She threw back her head and laughed.

'Ah, yes, Althusser,' I said even though I couldn't remember a thing about him. She took my hand in hers.

'You have to let me dance for you.'

'Uh, OK sure.' I wasn't going to decline. After all that was what I was there for, but I worried that I'd bored her, that that was why she wanted to dance or else I'd misinterpreted some Hudson Beaverz rule, like if she sat with me for fifteen minutes or more she had to dance. But no, it wasn't that at all.

I handed her twenty dollars. A motorcycle revved, and a chorus of 'Girls, Girls, Girls' kicked in. She propped her foot on the banquette next to me, lifted her leg up so I had a good view of her inner thigh and slid the bill into her garter.

'Can I move your briefcase?' she said. It was sitting between my feet. She swooped over, picked it up and deposited it on the far side of me. She took my knees in her hands and spread my legs. 'There, there, that's better.'

I hadn't realized they were clenched together. She stood between my knees and smiled at me.

'Should I start now or wait for the next song?'

'Oh, now, by all means. That is if that's what you'd prefer. I mean, you might catch a chill standing there.'

She smiled a closed mouth grin and laughed through it. A chortle. It was a chortle that managed to say, 'Oh, isn't that just sweet,' meaning she really just thought it was stupid, that same stupid joke. She must have heard that one before, then.

A light shot through the bar, and before it went dark again, I could see she had red hair, not brown. I'd thought it was auburn.

She ran her hands over her blouse, thumbed the Peter Pan collar and writhed. Every move was a writhe, a roll of the hips delivered with a slither and wiggle, all so slow the seduction of it sucked me in. She bent over. Her back to me, her ass in my face, her hands planted on her thighs, she gyrated. With each undulation her rear bucked and swayed. It was round and plump, giving just a little quiver with each move, just the way I liked it. Oh, her slender legs and womanly buttocks . . . All the while she was looking at me over her shoulder, a cheeky grin on her face like she couldn't take her eyes off me. She turned to face me and leaned in close. Her cheek brushed mine, and she whispered in my ear, 'The commodity fetish is a strange and mysterious thing.'

She undid her top, fingering every button. The shirt fell open in a V to frame her breasts. She pulled them out, pushed the blouse out of the way so it cradled her tits, pushed them up and out at me. They were gorgeous. Pert, perfect. We're talking a Greek statue here. Exquisite, she could have been one of the Elgin Marbles or Diana in the Louvre, with flawless circles, nipples smack in the center and just enough weight to them that you could cup them in your hands. She laughed. My eyes must have gone very wide.

'As soon as it steps forth as a commodity, it is changed into something transcendent.' She was stripping and quoting Marx. *Das Kapital.* It all almost didn't compute. I couldn't blink, I couldn't move. My mouth was open, my breath suspended.

She slowly peeled off her shirt, draped it around my shoulders. Lily put her hands on my knees and arched towards me, her tits only inches from my mouth. She pushed herself away and whipped her hair around. Her tresses trailed down my shoulder. 'Whence then arises the enigmatical character of the product of labor so soon as it assumes the form of commodities? Clearly from this form itself.'

She tore off her skirt and circled it overhead like a lasso. She slapped her ass. 'A commodity is a mysterious thing.' I was coated in her smell – musky, rich. It was so familiar. I couldn't figure out where I knew it from. I bent in to get nearer to her.

'Hey, the bouncers won't like that.' She stopped and glared at me a second. I sat on my hands.

'Sorry, sorry,' I said. She started dancing again. One of the bouncers appeared. He lumbered over me. He wore a blazer and had an earphone. His arms were crossed against his chest. Her head on my shoulder, she angled her nipples towards my face. It was patchouli. I chuckled. My first girlfriend wore patchouli oil. Amy rubbed her hands over her breasts and down to her G-string.

I shifted my weight. I wanted to touch her. The bouncer watched for any moment of contact. It wasn't hard to complete the equation and imagine fucking her.

'Its value does not originate in its use.'

She crashed next to me laughing when she was done. I stood up and applauded. 'Bravo, bravo!'

People stared. The heavy looked like he was about ready to throw me out.

'I'd always wanted to do that,' she said.

'Me too, I'm sure, even if I never knew it.'

I left the club that night wanting to tell all my friends about her. *You can't believe the woman I just met* . . . Only what would I say? I didn't even know her real name. And how would I even start to explain to Carrie that Amy was coming to stay with me in three days' time?

So She Had Been Having Sex with an Artist
Alyssa Russo

There had been so much Nora had wanted to say to Gabriel at his funeral.

As he was lowered into the grave, she wanted to tell him about what he had done so effectively in those two brief months that they had dated, things he would never even know: the fact that she ate steak now, and could identify key members of the Fluxus art movement. She wanted to be there beside his coffin more than just physically, wanted to be more than just adjacent to his garishly blonde mother and anorexic sister, watching them as they sobbed and held each other's sympathetic wrists. She had been tempted to fall forward onto her knees and claw at the coffin's lid like in movies, to be conspicuously *sad*.

There was a faint trail carved into the green of the grass that Nora followed slowly, looking down and watching her feet as they moved, one in front of the other and trying not to think of the thin, ginger-colored trail leading from his navel downward. Instead she lifted her head towards the sky and walked rather clumsily, her eyes stuck on the immense expanse of gray.

It began to rain. Nora scoffed at the appropriateness and threw her shawl over her head, her fingers hovering around her ears. Nora thought she must resemble a sort of perverse nun: her nails were neatly cut and contoured, painted bright red. She had gotten the manicure a few weeks before, in a raging fit of self-indulgence, when she had also gotten her bikini line waxed, and bought an entire set of Shane Taylor knives from the Internet. As she washed the knives before using them, she had sliced her thumb on the fillet knife. The purplish scar below her crimson thumbnail was just beginning to heal.

As she walked forward she came to the gravedigger's tiny shack. A shovel rested against the crumbling side of the building; Nora noticed how the rust and mud stuck to the handle, turning it brown. Flecks of damp earth were congealing around the shovel's head. Nora knew she was near, and her breath quickened. She wiped her eyes. The rain had let up but a cool mist was still falling and clinging to her face.

There was a tightly landscaped hedge that punctured the clearing near the shack, leading out towards the graves. She followed the hedge straight along the path to where it stopped suddenly. Nora felt her heart beating in her ear. She rounded the corner hesitantly. There it was, as she remembered it: gray, tall, stone.

She walked towards it. As she was about to face the slab of stone head on, she saw a figure intrude into her sphere of vision, screwing up the symmetry of the landscape and the gravity of her solo visit, marring the ceremony of her arrival.

It was Allison McGuire.

Gabriel's sister had her light brown hair in a haphazard bun low on her head, about to unravel. She still looked unnaturally thin, and the circles under her eyes looked deeper, more crater-like, unnerving. She turned to catch Nora's surprised gaze, swaying slightly on her feet. Nora's cheeks burned.

Allison's eyes were penetrating as she spoke. 'You're here to see Gabriel?'

Nora almost laughed at the absurdity of it, as if he were holding individual one-on-one meetings and a line was forming. 'I am.'

'I recognize you from the funeral.'

Nora felt as if she would cry at any moment if the wrong thing or word or person prodded her. 'Yes. I was there. Nora. You're his sister?'

'I take it you modeled for Gabriel?'

'Ye –'

'I see.'

'Yes,' Nora repeated hesitantly. 'I knew Gabriel.'

There was an awkward silence. Nora began to wring her hands.

So She Had Been Having Sex with an Artist

Allison's eyes looked past Nora. 'Did you know . . .' she trailed off.

'Sorry?' Nora asked, disconcerted.

'Did you know, Nora, that when we were in high school, and he was doing his life-painting classes,' she laughed faintly, shrugging, 'he used to try to get the prettiest girls to come back to our apartment, to paint them? At least that's what he said to get them there. He tried to get the entire cheerleading squad, and there was one dimpled girl, one he was always after. What was her name? Selma,' she said quietly, 'or something.'

'OK,' Nora said, laughing awkwardly, feigning comprehension. As if this dimpled girl was an old friend of hers. She didn't understand why Allison was telling her this. The thought of Gabriel with another girl made Nora's left hand squeeze into a fist as it hung at her side, her sharply manicured nails digging into her palm.

'Anyway,' Allison shook her head rapidly, as if returning to consciousness. 'Gabe always had girls around him.'

Nora's throat tightened. 'Yes. He's painted me a few times.'

'I figured that.'

Nora touched the nape of her neck. 'Actually, I work with Karla.' Nora walked forward a few steps but stopped as Allison turned her back to her to redirect her gaze at the headstone. 'That's how I knew Gabriel.'

'Ah, the old friend of a friend.' Allison smiled maniacally, her sunken cheeks expanding. A wave of nausea washed over Nora. 'Nora, did you know Gabriel? I mean did he ever talk while he was painting you?'

'I spoke with hi –'

'Did you know?' Allison began her crazed laughter. 'Did you know,' still laughing, 'I was just twelve when my dad left – "went away" was the paltry euphemism that mom used – and Gabe was there. Always.'

'So you knew, yes?' Nora asked slowly, walking a foot closer. 'Did you know his condition, how long did you know –'

'What? That he was sick? That he was going to drop dead a few months after he moved into my old place?' She slurred her last few words.

'No. I mean, he was so young, you know – I don't know,' Nora faltered. 'I'm sorry.'

'No,' Allison grumbled, and Nora smelt whiskey. '*I'm* sorry, I get carried away.' She straightened. 'Physically, Gabe had always been weak when it came to his heart.'

Nora swallowed. 'He . . . told most people this?'

'The people that he really cared about knew.'

'Oh.' Nora, unenlightened until the day she had found him lying there in his studio, felt the back of her eyes begin to sting.

'But not many people knew. We didn't think it would actually happen.'

'You mean anything major?'

'Yeah. But,' she opened her mouth and then abruptly closed it, continuing a moment later: 'but I just keep thinking of him there, in my tiny studio, alone, the weeks before he died, hoping that whatever he was doing would be remembered . . .' she trailed off. 'You know, for posterity? Gabe was obsessed with outliving himself.'

Nora's face was solid. He had told her this the first night she had met him, in the bar after Karla had given her his number, as he drank his Dewars on the rocks, his arm bent in his tweed coat with its elbow patches stretching.

Allison nodded. 'He was. Really. He made mobiles too.'

'Really?' Nora avoided Allison's gaze as she spoke. 'I thought he only painted.' She paused. Then she whispered, 'Like when I posed for him.'

'What?'

'Nothing.' Nora tried to smile. 'Gabriel's sculpture was amazing.'

'Yes,' Allison said sheepishly. 'But he did other things too.'

'Oh. Of course.'

'He enjoyed his work. Still, I feel so guilty about being there, about being in Paris I mean. While Gabriel was here. Alone.'

'Alone.'

'So fucking alone.' Allison pulled out a tissue and blew her nose loudly.

'Right.' Nora's eyelids fluttered shut briefly. 'But your mother was here for him.'

'That's not what I mean.'

'Oh. But they were close?'

'Sure they were.'

'Karla had said that.'

'I mean, I just wish someone had been there at the time, taking care of him.'

Nora suppressed a laugh. A laugh for the laughs that Nora and Gabriel had had in the studio in Carroll Gardens, on Sackett Street, the one he had been subletting from his sister. The one next to the Korean grocer and around the corner from a hardware store with the flashing neon key in the window.

'I feel guilty,' Allison went on. 'He shouldn't have been alone. But at least he was able to work.' She sighed. 'At least he still had different people to paint.'

Nora tensed. 'Yeah.'

'So you modeled for him in my old studio then?'

'I did.' Nora fingered the key to the studio that she still had in her coat pocket, where she kept it on a chain, its lines distinct. 'But only once or twice.' She hung her head.

'I'm glad he had such an impact on you. Gabe did that to people, to all the people he encountered.'

'He was sweet,' Nora said. Her voice was calm.

'He would have been a great teacher.'

'You're right.'

'You should have gotten to know him better.'

'I should have.' Nora squeezed her hand into a fist again, making half-moon shapes into her palm.

Allison kept closing her eyes. They were red and watery and Nora thought they looked like two almond-shaped pieces of plastic that had been pulled out of shape: distorted, translucent. 'Anyway,' Allison's voice was steadier than it had been before. She wiped the corner of her left eye with a tissue. 'It was very kind of you to think of coming back to visit him.'

Nora's eyes blurred as she watched Allison turn to blow her nose a second time. 'Of course,' Nora said, her voice wavering as she placed her hand on the stone. It was freezing, and she shuddered. 'Gabriel hated the cold.'

Allison looked up at her, her eyes glassy and her eyeliner

smudged above her circles. 'He *did.*'

Nora looked up. 'Yes – yes. He . . . told me he used to regulate the thermostat in his studio so that it would never get too chilly.'

Allison nodded vaguely and hiccupped again in response.

Nora kept her hand on the stone, remembering the light in the studio on that day. How Gabriel's hair was caught in a soft patch of sun that entered through a round window in the center of the room, making it look especially red; how he had dropped his paintbrush next to his hand. Some burnt umber was evident caked under his middle fingernail: he had been painting flesh tones. The easel was pressed under him, against his back, the easel that he had apparently knocked over when he fell. His eyes were looking upwards, and were strikingly blue-green next to the tube of aquamarine blue near his head. She remembered how she had knelt down, her hand gripping the cushion of the couch, the only couch that Allison had left for him in the studio, and covered her face, seeing shadows.

She remembered how she kept thinking about shadows, about how Gabriel used to instruct her to paint him in this seemingly staged position, at this time of day, near dusk.

Lifting a Man My Age
Jasmine Swaney Hewitt

It's so sweltering in this garbage truck that I'm caught off guard when he says: I have something for you, Abby. I'm mumbling idiot-phrases to describe the stench we're sitting in: rancidrinds, curdledcrotch, maggotmeat, diaperdump, and so when Pat Keany says again, I have something for you, I say, Gee, I hope it's an air-freshener because we smell like a couple of poopfish.

He grins at me from the driver's seat and mops his neck with a bandana. We're idling in Sunrise Park – our last park of the day – looking beyond the beach to where a denim-blue Lake Michigan spills into the horizon.

It's *better* than poopfish, he says, then digs through a Meijer grocery sack. I try not to breathe through my nose and wonder what could possibly be better than an air freshener; we stink to the highest heavens. Outside, mothers let us know we're contaminating their air – they herd children through the parking lot, watching with faces pinched in pity and disgust. You smelly, pathetic girl, I hear them thinking, and it burns me up. I want to thump their heads with garbage barrels and tell them it's just my summer job. I want to point out *their* kids' loaded diapers in public trashcans, when Pat clears his throat and places the gift before me.

Matching belts: a his and a hers.

Our belts, he says happily.

Belts? I say.

Belts, he says.

Belts, I repeat, and feel my diaphragm collapse.

Pat's looking at me with an expression that's hope edging on

91

Jasmine Swaney Hewitt

desperation. They're a pair, he says, and then he puts one of his garbage-juiced hands next to mine. I try to be hopeful, like this is purely routine in the Parks Department – that it's my one-thousandth-bag-of-trash-as-a-part-timer award.

I try to be funny. Wow, for when my pants are *really* sagging huh, I joke.

No, for *us*, Pat says floating a smile at me. No, you silly goose, I hear him thinking, they're a pair, don't you see? Pat's gripping the steering wheel so tight I'm afraid he might rip it off the dash. I want to rip *something* off the dash – the smudged Styrofoam cups, the loose trash bags, the upholstery, just to change the subject and rid myself of guilt.

The belts lie between us on the black vinyl seat. The 'his' belt is thicker, more substantial than its partner. The 'her' belt is slender and coy; it says, I was made in 'his' image but I'm the sexier and brainier of the two of us. Both belts are interlaced with Petoskey stones, shellacked to a gaudy shine.

I found them at a craft show, Pat says. It was an outdoor art fair.

I try to picture him trawling through handmade jewellery, asking highly-strung women about the Ben Franklin bead supply, the malleability of copper sculpture, mauve undertones in oil on canvas. I see the women nursing bucket-sized Big Gulps, colluding in pastel tank tops with their dimpled triceps flapping.

I hear them twitter, Gee-whiz, we don't get many grass-stained guys coming here. We don't get many garbage men pawing through our floral afghans and carved malamutes. And I see him traipsing in his steel-toed boots saying: No, no, I don't need a wooden dog. I need something matching, something special, for my . . .

For my *what*, I suddenly want to know.

Wow, I say, but it sounds more like whoa! or ow! or wait-a-fucking-minute-mister-you-could-be-my-father. Pat remembers things my father remembers: Nixon's Watergate speech, Cleveland Cliffs coal freighters, live Simon and Garfunkel concerts. And *I* know Nixon from a textbook, and coal as a Christmas threat, and Simon and Garfunkel from a bargain-basement CD sale.

The belts were hand woven by a local Native American gal, Pat says, then passes me the 'her' belt. It's a snake in my hands – long, leathery, hissing in perfect Ojibwa: You asked for this Mojeet. He wants your Zaghidiwin. He wants to feel your Ahmik.

Pat massages his belt, exhibiting the quality. He fingers it, sniffs it, holds it up. He points out the Petoskey stones and then rubs the buckle up and down his arm.

Definitely not nickel, he says. That makes some people itch.

I avoid his gaze in case I'm expected to rub the buckle up and down *my* arm. In case he's waiting for an affirmative thigh squeeze or a sexy wink and giggle. I convince myself that college girls working summer jobs shouldn't *have* to worry about Nixon-era men.

Wow, I say again, noticing my own steel-toed boots, my own garbage-juiced jeans, my hands perspiring in protective latex gloves. We're in the least attractive place in the world. It's like flirting in a cesspool or kissing amidst a nice, smelly popcorn fart.

You know, Pat says, the Indian lady told me the belts have a history. They are lovers because they share the same stones. I was thinking, he says, that we share the same stones.

Let's not get carried away, I say. I put the 'her' belt on the seat.

Oh, he says softly, you don't like them?

I'm not sure what to say. I'm betting he didn't tell the craft lady that I'm only twenty. I'm *certain* he didn't tell her about his wife; someone he only speaks of in the most casual of ways, like she's a tomato plant or a washing machine.

Pat laughs nervously, Gee, I'm sorry, but I'm in a burning house, you know?

I nod. At the beginning of the summer, when I asked for his story, he sighed in the most noncommittal way: I'm in a burning house, you know? My wife's a flame, my job's a flame, I've got some goddamned thing going on with my knees. I'm going up in fucking smoke; I'll be a crispy sonofabitch soon enough.

I know what he means: He thinks I'm his fireman with a ladder, that I'm the one to haul him out and away.

I want to point to a middle-aged woman. She is there on the beach, soaking in vitamin D and a paperback. I can tell she's a woman with history; a woman with renegade pubic hair, insurance policies and Tupperware. There are a few women near her, all lumpy in lycra. I want to say, you see those women? *Those* are the women you want; they're heavy with living. They have Nixon-era pecan pie recipes – they cry out for real lard. They can haul you. They can set you free.

But I don't say it. I sit and and watch a bead of sweat race past his temple and slip down his cheek. And for some reason, that 'her' belt won't shut up. She keeps hissing: Don't think you didn't see this coming. Don't think you didn't like the attention. Don't think you didn't know what a smile and a young pair of legs could do to him.

Pat throws the compactor into gear. I'll just pack this load, he says. And the voice he's using now is the voice my father used to tell me our dog was put down by the vet. Pat slides out of his seat into the thick, humid fold that is August air.

I feel the gentle rumble of the truck. I hear the grinding, squelching garbage. And with the five tons he's squeezing, I wonder if Pat's thrown his heart in with it. Because I've asked for this. I've been a sucker for his heavy male maturity. It's not a sexy feeling, I convince myself, just a feeling of tight, safe weight. It's what it feels like to be buried in wet beach sand – to be packed and protected up to the neck. The grains pressing down on my thighs, chest and abdomen.

I'm guilty of so many things: of noticing the way Pat's torso sits just right on his hips; of feigning stupidity so I could watch him – strong and confident – start my weedwhip; of letting him slide sleek garbage bags out of my back pocket. Why didn't I slap him, tell him to go piss up a rope? When his finger got 'caught' in my belt loop, why did I let it linger there, hooked to me, for that one, long moment? Why did I hope for the whole of his hand to gently cup my hip?

But a burning house? Even if I *wanted* to I could never do it. Even if he is going up in smoke, with a tomato plant of a wife and a job he despises and arthritic knees, I could never carry him out of it. *I* could never climb the ladder and say, OK! Climb on, Pat! I can hardly lift a man my *own* age – a man without weight or a history or a recipe for pecan pie. I was just being friendly, I think. I am a friendly person. I am just *a friend*.

Pat hoists himself back into the truck and regards the 'his' belt silently. Then he strokes it once with his fingers and slides it through his belt loops. When it's buckled he looks at me with a plaintive gaze.

Well, what do you think, he asks.

Nice, I say finally, looking out over the beach. It looks like . . . you.

And what about yours, Abby? He says. Does it look like you?

So I slide the 'her' belt through my loops and cinch it tight around my hips. He's got you now, she whispers to me.

Wow, Pat says. It *does* look like you.

And I can't look at him. My eyes follow the tossing, tremulous waves of Lake Michigan. All I can think is a resounding: No. No, it doesn't look like me, Pat. It looks like a long, leathery snake with Petoskey stones for eyes. It has a crushing, pulsing squeeze that's dragging me towards your burning house.

Softporn
Tim Hayton

I love Robert, but it wasn't all plain sailing. He was such a wanker in the beginning.

He had a Super 8 projector in his dad's train room and a box full of cartoon bits. Never the whole thing though, three minutes maximum and the screen would go white and the flapping would start. Except no screen either, just the back of the door. But it worked. And I didn't mind, all I really wanted was in there with him, on our own, in love.

(George and Doreen wouldn't let us in the bedroom. They're the kind that think you can't have sex on the living room carpet. As it happens, they were right, Robert wouldn't do anything like that. Not in the beginning. It was hard enough just getting his trousers down without worrying him with the living room carpet. So the train room, watching the Super 8s, holding hands, Doreen with the tea and biscuits. – Your friendly usherette, lovebirds. Robert letting go of me, like suddenly I'm a red hot poker or something, jumping out of his seat. I hated that, it really broke the spell.)

One day, though, it was funny. All the Super 8s were in a box under George's workbench, and Robert was down choosing, me flat out on him, like digging his shoulder with my chin. And I spotted something different, hidden away at the bottom.

– Robert, I haven't seen that.

– Yes you have, I'm bloody sick of it.

Robert is a useless liar. Always. The serious voice. He tries it on with the coppers and they never believe him, and neither do I.

– You are lying, Robert McLeod.

He did his best, pushing the box back under, standing up and me still hanging onto him. I loved that, whisked in the air, screaming out, delighted. I jumped off, and he grabbed me, and kissed me on my neck, which I can tell you is something Robert would never do in the train room, far too risky.

– If you don't let me see, I said, – I'll tell Doreen.

He let me go, and I pulled the film out. It was a rudey one, and I made him put it on, and patted the chair next to me. – Hold my hand properly, I said, – OR ELSE.

It was a stupid film really. But I quite liked it. This girl's car broke down in the dead of night in the middle of nowhere, so she got out and went and knocked at a big spooky house to get help. There was no answer, so she pushed open the door and went inside and started calling out, is there anybody there? I mean, would you do that? I wouldn't. I'd run a mile. Or call out the RAC. There was no sound on the film, but you could tell what she was saying the way her lips moved. I mean, it was pretty obvious. She got to the bottom of the stairs, took off her raincoat and hung it on the banister, and then all of a sudden her blouse just got pulled off and she was standing there in her bra. She looked round all surprised, but there was nobody there. The house was haunted, it was ghosts that had whipped her blouse! And then, well, off came her skirt, and she was going, oh, oh, oh, trying to cover herself up.

I was looking out for how it was done, there were jumps in the film, and you could see wires or something, fastened on her clothes. Next thing, off comes her bra, and she was standing there in just the little black knicks. And, surprise, surprise, she didn't bother trying to cover herself up any more. Although, to be fair, I don't think I'd have bothered either if I had a pair like hers. Not all that big, but nice round, bouncy ones.

Then it took ages and ages, but in the end, zip, the knicks are gone. You couldn't see anything down there really, just her fluff. But I've got to say, she had a lovely, curvy body. She was good-looking as well, with her hair in a nice bob. It was quite a sexy film really. It made me feel sexy. And the girl must've had a laugh doing it, probably saying to the cameraman, listen, goggle eyes, no looking when my undies come off.

Anyway, next thing, the door to the train room opened on us, and in walked Doreen. Heart attack. Even I got a big fright. Robert nearly crushed my fingers. She stood there trying to shade her eyes.

– Listen, lovebirds, she said. – A choice. Home-made jam sponge, or the Battenburg.

Total silence.

– What's the matter lovebirds, cat got your tongues?

She couldn't see anything. She'd have had to close the door. God, it was funny. The rudey-nudey girl was all jumbled up on Doreen's woolly cardigan, the ghosts tickling her bum by now, wriggling it about all over the place, all over Doreen's cardy.

– Jam sponge for me please, Doreen, I said. – Don't be so rude, Robert, keeping your mum waiting. Give him a slice of Battenburg, Doreen, you're really kind, you are.

Doreen went straight out again, and Robert shot out of the chair, scrambling for the light switch, beads of sweat on his forehead, crashing over the Super 8. – Oh, bloody hell, oh, bloody hell.

I could see, though, he was trying not to laugh. He was loving it.

– Bloody hell, Suzie, he said. – I hate you.

– No, you don't, I said.

And after that, we got on fine. – My bum's just as good as that girl's, Robert, I said.

Like The Toad, Ugly and Venomous
Andrea Mason

I have arrived in this town called Milton Keynes. It is a good town. A new town. Several of us have been called, specialists from all over. There is great excitement, on account of a new discovery: some rare footage of a film called *Sodom*. Apparently it was made by a small movement of marginalized artists and film makers who lived on the fringes of San Francisco in the late sixties.

My belly is full of gas.

It is not a good time for this. I am due to attend a meeting at the University Film Archive Centre. We will be poring over individual film cells, squashed together in the tiny storage room, bent over a light box. I will have to do my best to hold in the gas – glorious triumph of mastication and digestion though it may well be. And the odour! Oh no, dear me, the odour. I know it too well already: slightly rank, almost sweet, gaseous, making all who smell it, surely, bilious? I am getting cramps as I walk. The best plan would be to let as much of the evil air as I can persuade to go, escape now.

I continue on, the venomous air blowing out. The insides of my bum cheeks become moist as I force it, like pressing all the air out of a pair of bellows. I see a blackbird peck a worm from the wet grass. Crocuses are in full bloom. Trees have begun to bud. Beauty and nature surround me as I walk, cloaked now by a fug of odious vapour.

At the Film Archive Centre, Professor Krakovksy, a visiting archive specialist from Moscow, greets me.

Andrea Mason

– Dr Kulotta. (I too am an exotic being.) You are looking very smart.

I try to keep a straight face.

– And this is Professor Kantansky, my esteemed and trusted colleague.

From this point on the leakage must be contained.

We examine the strips of film, trying to determine whether it's in a decent enough condition to withstand a screening. A chain gang of male torsos, engaged in the act which names the film, stretches for what seems like miles. Shot from the front, faces bob up and down and from side to side behind the first, the second, the third man, and so on. The scene is then viewed from above, and the whole thing moves and shakes and shivers like a giant caterpillar. Occasionally, the line breaks as one or other of the men comes, interrupting the otherwise pliant fluidity of the muscular conga.

Men appear to be in the act of bestial pursuits. A variety of animals, it seems, are employed. Several men have come together and climbed, one on top of the other, to provide the framework for a tall, graceful giraffe, whose head disappears from view. It is stroked and hung upon. Men delight in bouncing each other up by cupped hands onto the supposed animal's back. The scenes are comic, vaudeville. One man is dressed as a donkey wearing a starched white collar and black bow tie. He rears up onto his hind-legs – just as a large, ape-like fellow arrives to grapple with his behind – and delivers a jet of steaming piss onto a ball of indecipherable arms, legs, backs and heads.

– The film is greatly scratched.

I observe the movements of Professor Krakovsky's lips. The ring of lines extending from their pursed extrusion, surrounded by the neatly clipped thatch of his beard, and the warm puff of air blown out across my cheeks as he turns his face towards me, only serve to enhance the scene now at my fingertips of a full backal (as opposed to frontal).

A man's bent-over cheeks are being pulled apart by what appear to be the paws of a monkey, though closer inspection reveals the clumsy plasticity of fake hands inhabited by a man. A glistening crop of curly black pubic hair surrounds the pink and brown anal orifice. This man might want to speak to Professor Krakovsky and learn the technique and merits of keeping one's extraneous hair in check.

The wind in my bowels is bubbling up again. I lean over further to give the impression of intently inspecting the film, all the time squeezing tight my sphincter muscles. Eager as I am to see the next filmic entry unfold before me, I turn nevertheless to catch the oral droplets falling from the mouth of Professor Kantansky.

– One must handle the thing with care.

Standing to my left, he is one stage behind me as we feed the film from right to left. We both, now, bend over the light-box, observing what appears to be a zebra, adorned with hula-hula garlands, being lovingly fellated by what appears to be a tiny monkey in a busboy's suit. I feel an inadvertent dig in my ribs as Professor Kantansky bends his elbow to scratch his crotch. This forces a sharp intake of my breath as I squeeze and squeeze again to prevent unwanted anal emissions.

We really are cramped together.

Professor Kantansky's lips pull back to reveal a set of yellowed gnashers as he turns to look at me, if not apologetically, then at least bashfully; his fingers are stained nicotine brown, I note, as he brings them up to his nose to sniff.

– The edges, too, are frayed.

He strokes his top lip with the fingers of his right hand, takes hold of his chin, bending closer in to the footage and sniffs his fingers once more. There are flakes of dandruff on the back collar of his tweed jacket; frail, white wafers, little more than the size of a pinhead.

– I suggest we transfer it to another medium.

– But this would be to lose the quality of the film.

Professor Krakovsky turns his head in my direction, being as I am, in the middle.

– No doubt, but we cannot risk, for instance, that it burn up.

– Then there must be one exclusive showing. It will be a great event. Dr Kulotta, we would like to hear from you.

Both men's heads are aimed now in my direction. I feel as if my cheeks are full of air. To speak now would be to let forth a

Andrea Mason

burst of frothing spit and bubbles. I turn to face Professor
Kantansky on my left, pull my eyebrows down and nod,
conveying, I believe, that I share his concerns. I turn then to my
right, to face Professor Krakovsky, pulling my eyebrows back up
into my forehead and smile and nod, expressing, I am sure, my
level of enthusiasm for his proposal. I turn my attention once
more to the film, wondering how much more my stomach can
take. I have shooting pains of heartburn for not giving in to the
building bag of gas.

There are men performing yoga tricks, their legs wrapped
around their heads as they gobble on their own penises. Little
birdies come and settle on the pulled back thighs and begin to
peck and nibble at the exposed hairy balls. This was no doubt an
unforeseen coup. One man is held aloft in a perfect forward bend,
paschimothanasana, his head on his knees, watched by a short,
stocky man chomping on a peeled banana.

I can't hold on any longer. Shooting pains and uncontrollable
mirth attack me equally. I am forced to relinquish the controlling
grip of my lower abdomen and sphincter muscles. There is a noise
like the hiss of steam escaping from a boiler as the offensive
vapour snakes around the room.

Dr Krakovsky is the first to go. His face clouds as he succumbs
to the effects of the hideous gas. I see surprise and
disappointment in the turns and creases of his face as he slides
down, pulling his end of the filmstrip with him. As his legs
buckle, his head falls with quite a crack onto the floor. Jerome,
the archive technician hits the deck next. He was, at that
moment, about to leave the room, and would no doubt have
dissipated the worst of the rank-smelling odour were he allowed
to go, but the smell is too strong and takes him out suddenly,
turning his face a sickly green. He falls with his arm outstretched,
eyes wide open and staring. Professor Kantansky holds on longer,
until I am forced to push out a further pop of air to relieve the
cramp inside my stomach. He lets out a startled – oh, slithers and
creases down, his head and upper body folding first, revealing a
shiny bald crown as he goes.

I allow myself to gorge on the images before me. I am forced
to take hold of Dr Krakovsky's hands and open them out, so that

he relinquishes his grip upon the end of the roll. I slide the film along to view these last parts. I am enthralled: the filmmaking is of such a quality that I cannot deny it delights and entertains me. The shadows thrown out by the acts being committed perform their own ballet. The yoga feats of the men are indeed amazing; their poise and dexterity, the suppleness of their joints are surely to be admired.

I give way, finally, to a wave of uncontrollable laughter, which, in my letting go is accompanied by a tremendous rasping blow of the final breaths from my bum. Were my companions to come round, they would be slain afresh by this final wave of desecrating stink. I can no longer look at the images of the film, and let it slip from my fingers as I crease up and fall to the floor, doubling up with laughter, tears making my vision a blur.

Ark
Sam Byers

I

The girl on the other side of the counter was battered and frayed at the edges, as if over-handled.

'Just tell me how much,' she said, pushing a curl of hair out of her eyes.

The shopkeeper smiled at her from his stool.

'How much?' she said again.

He rubbed the figures gently, savouring their subtle, hand crafted asymmetry. It was the seventh pair she'd offered him in as many weeks.

'I'm not sure,' he said slowly, 'that I want them any more.'

Panic shadowed the little girl's face. 'But . . .'

'I mean, I want them, but . . . There are other things to consider now. Ach, I don't know.'

The little girl's bottom lip began to tremble. The shopkeeper's smile faded.

'I'm not a rich man,' he said.

'But you keep the others behind the counter, in that glass thingy. I'm not stupid. It means they're special.'

He looked behind him. There, lined up on a shelf in the display cabinet, were the other six pairs: giraffes, camels, elephants, horses, monkeys and snakes. The snakes were the ones she'd brought in first, the ones that had fired his interest. The long discontinued shade of green across their flanks, the familiarity of the carving.

'It means they're not for sale,' he said.

He looked down at the seventh set, a pair of doves carved from smooth, light wood, knuckle-sized, tinged with varying depths of grey. He rubbed his chin and sniffed.

'I tell you what,' he said. 'I'll give you ten, to give to your father. But you can keep the birds. If there are others, bring them here and I'll think about it.'

She scuffed her feet against the floor and, after a moment's hesitation, nodded. As the shopkeeper handed her the money, she touched the back of his hand and frowned.

'What's that?'

'Telephone number,' he said. 'I have a terrible memory.'

The little girl shrugged and turned away. The shopkeeper watched her as she left, saw her pass the money to the man waiting outside. Then he opened the glass cabinet and took down one of the snakes from its shelf.

He sat behind the counter, rubbing the little wooden figure gently between his fingers.

II

It was a clear, bright day. The little girl held the old man's hand as they walked round the park.

'So,' he said. 'How was school?'

'OK,' she said.

'What did you do? Anything fun?'

She pushed a finger into the corner of her mouth and hummed, looking skyward for an answer.

'Finger painting,' she said. 'Mrs Montgomery gave us all little dishes full of paint, all different colours. We dipped our fingers in the paint and then made pictures.'

'Well that sounds nice.'

'I got in trouble for finger painting Amy Parker's new dress.'

'Oh dear.'

'She started it. She's nasty.'

They came to the pond. People stood around the edge, throwing bread to the ducks, pushing pushchairs. Children ran across the grass, giggling and squealing, spinning in circles until they fell. A man in a black leather jacket checked his watch and looked about him before stepping behind a bush. A dog strained at its leash, snapping at a nearby mallard.

The old man pulled a brown paper bag from his pocket.

'Would you like to feed the ducks?' he said.

'Yes please.'

'Yes please what?'

'Yes please, daddy.'

'Good girl. There you go.'

The bag contained a stale crust of bread, hard and hollow. She knocked her knuckle against it before tearing off little pieces and throwing them into the water. The bread bobbed on the surface, attracting the attention of a family of ducks. They paddled their way over, following the food-trail, and began to make their way up the bank towards the little girl and the old man. She grabbed his hand.

'It's all right,' said the old man. 'Ducks can't hurt you.'

She gave the bread back to him and shooed the ducks away, flapping her hands and stamping her feet. They ignored her, pecking at the ground in search of more bread.

'I don't want to feed them any more,' she said.

'What would you like to do instead?'

She looked quickly over her shoulder, then back at the old man.

'Ice cream!'

The old man gave her enough money for one ice cream and sent her over to the stand, watching her all the way. The ice cream seller smiled at her.

'Back again little lady?'

She took the ice cream, a large cone, thanked him, and walked back over to the old man, who put his hand on her head.

'Why don't we sit on that bench over there?' he said.

They sat down. From his pocket, the old man took out a scuffed plastic thermos and poured himself a cup of acrid black tea.

'How comes you don't have milk?'

'You don't have milk with this kind of tea.'

He looked at her ice cream.

'So what sort is that?' he asked.

'Strawberry. You want some?'

She passed him the cone. He licked the top gingerly.

'Uck,' he said. 'Too sweet for me, and too cold. It makes my teeth jingle.'

He passed it back. The little girl touched the back of his hand and cocked her head to one side.

'What's that?'

'A scar.'

'It looks like sums.' She paused. 'Or a telephone number.'

She licked her finger and rubbed it across his hand, then shrugged and turned back to her ice cream.

They fell silent. The little girl pushed the final tip of the cone into her mouth and used the front of her dress to wipe her lips. The old man took a handkerchief from his pocket, licked it, and dabbed at the little girl's face. A man in a black leather jacket stepped out from behind a bush and stood a little way down the path. The old man screwed the top back on his thermos, pulled an envelope from the top pocket of his shirt, and passed it to the girl.

'It's all there,' he said.

'Thank you.'

She stood up to go. The old man touched her arm gently.

'Wait,' he said. 'These are for you.'

He pressed two little wooden figures into her hands, a pair of pale grey doves. She slipped them into her pocket quickly.

'Thank you, daddy,' she said again, and ran off towards the man in the black leather jacket. His hands shook as he took the envelope from her.

'Good girl,' he said. 'Very good.'

The little girl looked at her shoes. He lifted her chin with his finger.

'What did he talk about?'

'School. Just like always. He asks what I did at school and I make something up. He's not like the other ones, though. He's nicer.'

'Did he give you any more?'

'No.'

'Don't lie.'

'He didn't.'

The man looked around him quickly before pulling her behind a bush, where he slapped her face once, hard. Snuffling, she pulled the figures from the pocket of her dress and handed them to the man.

'That's my girl. Now let's go.'

She dragged her feet as he led her away.

III

'It's cancer,' said Albert between sips of black tea. He leant back in his worn brown armchair and nodded to himself, avoiding the eyes of his old friend.

Ivan took a deep breath and placed his cup gently on the table.

'Well,' he said after a moment. 'It's a good job I beat you at chess today then isn't it?'

'I was distracted,' said Albert. 'Next time will be a different story.'

They were quiet. Ivan stared around the small living room, his eyes roaming over the jumble of objects: paintings, vases, wooden toys, crammed into each available corner and strewn across every surface. Albert looked unusually lost amongst it all, as if the dusty clutter was now leeching the life out of him.

'How long have you known?' said Ivan.

'Seven weeks.'

'I thought as much.' After a pause, he added, 'It's a good time. They've waited long enough for you.'

'They'll be there, you think?'

'Yes my friend. I am certain.'

'All these years,' said Albert slowly. 'I have hated myself.'

Ivan leant back in his chair and rubbed the back of his hand. 'It was God's choice. Not ours.'

Albert chuckled briefly. 'Just don't let them cremate me, no?'

Ivan smiled. 'Not a chance,' he said. 'I swear it.'

He scanned the room again, nodding to himself. He breathed deeply, spoke carefully. 'You know, I would have kept it for you.'

'Kept what?'

'The ark. I would have looked after it.'

Seeing the frown spreading across Albert's face, Ivan added, 'I noticed it was gone, that's all.'

'I'm giving it away,' Albert said. 'I can't take it with me. And besides, I wanted a child to have it. I made it for . . .'

Ivan touched his friend's leg and nodded. 'Ach. We all lost so much.'

'Anyway, you'd only have sold it.' Albert winked at Ivan.

'I wouldn't,' said Ivan. 'I would never have done that.'

Albert drained the last of his tea and placed the empty cup on the table, beside Ivan's.

'You didn't drink your tea, Ivan.'

'No.'

Albert checked his watch and stood up. 'Where does the time go, eh? I have an appointment.'

'And I must get back to the shop, Klara has the afternoon off. Next week?'

'Perhaps I'll let you win again.'

'Ah,' said Ivan, shrugging into his jacket and standing by the door. 'Maybe I won't miss you so much after all.'

They embraced. Albert closed the door and walked back through to the living room, stopping in front of a dusty cupboard. Bending stiffly, he took out a cotton-wrapped object.

It was a wooden ark, lovingly crafted, the grain of the wood deepened with a variety of brown inks. There were five pairs of animals left inside, along with a bearded man and a smiling woman. Albert took out a pair of doves and dropped them into his pocket, then re-wrapped the ark.

He checked his watch, patted the envelope in his shirt pocket, and slipped on his coat.

Pieces of You
Charlie Thurlow

You were beautiful. I think that was what caused the problem.

Your name makes me shiver when I hiss the final syllable. I used to say it aloud when I was alone in the flat and keep myself company with its sibilance. I say other words now, our favourite phrases, to conjure the feeling of you whispering in my ear before we went to sleep. If I close my eyes I can almost feel your breath. I miss your warmth and the way your legs move while you dream, desperate to be awake.

I loved to watch you in the morning, in front of the mirror: moisturising, making-up. Defining your details with a practised hand. Pastel hues around your blue eyes: blue, like the glass pelican you placed on my empty window sill to catch the light. Palest pink lipstick, subdued brown tones in the hollows of your cheeks: your look.

I wonder why you never spent more time staring, how you managed to resist wallowing in your reflection. Perhaps you were afraid you'd be hypnotised.

I loved to watch, but could never understand why you needed the mask. Do you remember the time we almost argued? When I tried to change your routine? Why do you cover such skin, I said, hide yourself behind the layers? You didn't think I was serious, but I pushed and pushed. You were annoyed, thought the question pointless, said you felt naked and I made some kind of joke to hide behind.

I took my first piece that morning. It was an earring: an amethyst set in a silver teardrop that shone when it nestled against your lobe. You let the pair fall carelessly to the dressing table. I watched one drop onto the exposed floorboards, where the carpet struggled to meet the wall. The clasp prevented it falling through and it hung over a crack.

I lifted the boards for you, looked long and hard into the dust between the pipes. But we couldn't find it. A mouse probably moved it, I said, and you shivered at the thought.

I didn't mean to frighten you, the time you woke to find me inches from your face. I was only looking, committing every pore to memory, every fragile hair, every mole and curious blemish. It helped me during slow days; recalling your features when you were too busy to answer the phone or call back if I'd left a message. I'm sorry that I rang so often, if I distracted you from your work. I needed to hear your voice in the claustrophobic gloom of the lounge: a silver bell to mask the muffled tick of the clock.

I know you were faithful, now. Do you remember the day I put my fist through the window pane in the front door, and you fainted in the hallway when you saw blood fountain from my arm? I had to fit a makeshift tourniquet while you lay insensible on the floor. You were out cold for a long time; I revived you with my good arm once I'd stemmed the flow. You were sorry, but I didn't mind.

And I'm sorry for not trusting you the night you went for a drink or two. I was stupid, angry. I cut a piece from the lining of your favourite coat, inside the sleeve, where you'd never notice. It calmed me: meant I was able to say sorry for being so childish when you came home late, drunk. I sewed the frayed edges together, hid the damage.

I love the fabric. I don't know what it's called, but it changes colour – purple, red, green – when you move it in the light. You loved that coat. Is it still with you?

So many different smells to miss: your skin in the morning – fresh bread, soft suggestion of coconut, the sour trace of toxins purged by sleep; your mouth as I kiss you staggering home – tobacco musk, warm wine, smudged lipstick; your body wet from the shower – tea-tree, toothpaste, oats from the face-wash you preferred.

But I captured the one scent that can evoke you for me, the one fragrance that is bound to you in my memory. Your perfume – dew-soaked grass, lemon, the fizz from a gin and tonic, held together by something heavier, like sweet tea or rosewood. French, a name I could never pronounce. You teased my attempts. I siphoned the bottle the weekend you went to Colchester with the firm: team-building in some god-awful field, you said. I had a little brown vial with a pipette, half-full of eye-drops; left over from the time I had conjunctivitis. I poured out the evil-smelling liquid, replaced it with you.

I found the lashes that weekend, too. Three of them, trapped in the cotton of a pad you'd used for removing make-up. I freed them with tweezers, studied their curve, the minute particle of mascara that clung to one of the hairs. They were so fair, almost transparent at the roots that sat like microscopic pearls on my fingertip. I tried to imagine the microbes that fed on them, wished I could be that much a part of you, envied the symbiosis.

I remember trying to explain that to you, my wanting to be part of you, an essential element. You clicked your tongue, turned the paper noisily, folded the subject under World News. I knew you didn't like it when I spoke like that, but I had to tell you. You had to know.

I loved the sounds you made: the tick-tick-tick of your heels; the thrum of your impatient fingers; the way your gentle accent slipped around words; even the clicking of your tongue. When you yawned you always squeaked before you exhaled. Did you know that?

You were snoring, softly, when I took your hair. And your hand lay on the pillow in front of your face; the silver ring I gave you, with the oval amber, twisted halfway round your little finger. I used your nail scissors and snipped a lock from close to your nape, so no one would notice the loss. I tied it with a piece of thread retrieved from the waste-paper basket: you'd cut it from the skirt you'd bought that day. It was the perfect length, the thread: it formed a tiny bow around the curling lock; pinched one end into a delicate brush, like an artist would use.

Those same scissors harvested another piece for me: a carefully cut crescent of nail. It's from your forefinger, off-white

Charlie Thurlow

and textured on the underside, a millimetre thick, two or three wide. The upper surface reflects like mother-of-pearl when I turn it in the light. I think that must be the varnish you used. You cut it so perfectly, no snags or chips. I found it on the corner of the bath. You must have missed it when you cleaned.

I remember when we used to rush to bed and I would spend hours exploring your marvellous contours: nuzzling the crook of your neck; licking the blue vein that crept into your right nipple, marking four o'clock on the areola; nibbling the puckered skin around your belly button; biting your soft swathes of flesh, sucking, stroking, squeezing. Back then, you said that was what you loved about me: the attention I gave you, the care I took to make love to every fragment.

All truly beautiful things are flawed, aren't they? Isn't that what sets them apart? The dimple above your left knee that didn't match the right; the discoloured smudge of the birthmark on your shoulder blade; the patch of cellulite on your left thigh. It was your imperfections, you see, they're what made me love you.

You'd had a hard day. You looked so weary I almost didn't go through with it; but I'd been waiting, building to that moment, knew it had to be then. You evaded my questions, erected the wall to which I'd grown accustomed. I offered to cook dinner. No, you said, you'll ruin it; I'll do it. You kicked away your shoes and peeled off the tights I knew would have been itching all day. At least let me prepare the vegetables, I said, and you agreed. So I took the board, the broccoli, onions and peppers, and the heavy wooden-handled knife, and we stood side by side in the cramped kitchen, me in my boots and you with bare feet. I chopped, and you marinated the meat. It's funny how I can't remember what kind it was: pork, or chicken; I'm fairly certain it wasn't lamb or beef. I threw the dark mess into the bin when we returned from the hospital.

I spilled a glass of red wine, to distract you. Then I dropped the knife. I'd practised, knew how to make it land a certain way, hoped the weight would be enough.

The wound started at the big toe of your right foot and ran across the digits, deepening, slicing the tendon of the middle, and the next, nicking the bone, as the heavy end severed your little toe. Blood spread quickly into a puddle on the lino. You cracked your elbow on the table as you fainted. I'm sorry that had to happen. It hasn't affected your handwriting, has it? You had such a wonderful looping scrawl, almost indecipherable, like you were writing in code.

I had a jar prepared: it used to contain anchovy paste, but it's the perfect size. The toe remained attached by a flap of skin. I had expected this, or a similar complication. I took a tea towel – the one from the Lake District – and held it to the wound, removing the jar from my pocket as I did so. I sliced the remaining skin with the knife, and placed the toe gently into the ethanol. By the time you came round I had the wound compressed, and the jar safely stowed.

The surgeon did a good job, managed to save the middle toe at least, but you were still quiet when we finally arrived home.

Where is it? You said, unwilling to enter the kitchen to look. I said a mouse must have taken it. You dropped your crutches and started hitting my chest; but when I closed my arms around your back, you fell limp and sobbed into my collarbone. I tried to console you, to breathe in the salty fug of tears, but it was too late, I knew. I stayed in the kitchen as you packed.

The blue pelican's gone from my empty window sill. But I still have you. You sit in this box – finest silk-lined walnut, a month's wages – mine forever. The earring; the fabric; the vial, two-thirds full; the lashes; the lock; the carefully cut crescent of nail; the toe suspended in the clear liquid, a speck of dirt or fluff trapped at the corner of the nail – a tiny imperfection. You.

But I do miss your eyes.

Apples on Fire
Andrew Mackenzie

Nurse Christina has left the door unlocked. It's now or never. He tiptoes along the corridor to the hospital's reception desk, says a cheery 'good afternoon' to Patsy, the receptionist – who responds with a quizzical look at his shorts and trainers – and dashes through the hospital's front door. Phase one accomplished. The sun, slipping down the cobalt sky, has lodged itself between two white clouds, absurd cotton wool caricatures of themselves. He feels conspicuous. The still air, treacly with pollen, tickles the back of his throat. He can't afford a sneezing fit. Not now. He bites his tongue. And hurts himself.

From their windows, a hundred lunatic eyes are sticking into his back. He peers over both shoulders, on the lookout for more immediate danger, as he crunches down the gravel drive, past the enemy ranks of red and white peonies and garish orange tulips. Then the road turns its head and bolts into a dark wood of monster chestnuts, where dryads peep at him from behind gnarled tree trunks and the sun drips on to his bare thighs through holes in the foliage.

Emerging from the shade a hundred yards later he stops to let his eyes adjust to the sunlight's glare. And then he stares. On the other side of the clearing is a wrought iron gate, almost as high as the ten-foot wall either side of it. The gate is closed. Coming out of a kiosk next to it, and marching towards him, is a uniformed security guard.

What did he expect?

Nicholas lied to him about going home. Bastard shrink! This is Auschwitz. Treblinka even. They need him for their grisly experiments. He's been locked up for good.

His eyes trace the top of the wall right, then left. He must escape now! But how? Bribery? He has no money. Will the man accept an IOU? What if he were to strike up conversation with the guard, lull him into a false sense of security, boot him in the balls and vault over the gate? But the guard might see him coming. He's lost so much strength and his opponent looks a burly sort. What if he can't clamber up quick enough? What if he can't scale the gate at all? It might be electrified. And God knows what's on the other side. Suppose he does manage to climb over, won't the police chase him? Radio news flash: 'Escaping lunatic kills security officer – "nice man," say his neighbours, "devoted father of six" – do not approach under any circumstances.' Surely there must be an easier way to escape.

He watches the guard's hand reach behind his back for his revolver. The hand reappears a second later clutching a white handkerchief, with which the man then blows his nose.

Why on earth does he want to escape anyway? Aren't they trying to help him here?

'Good afternoon, sir,' the guard says brightly, without a trace of suspicion in his voice. It's a ploy. He's a fine actor. But not quite good enough. Closing in, the man looks him in the eyes and then glances down, as Patsy did, at his shorts and Nikes.

He senses the window of opportunity closing fast. It's now or never. 'G . . . g . . . good afternoon. I thought I m . . . m . . . might go for a run,' he says improbably, rediscovering his stammer.

'Lovely day for it too. What name is it, sir?'

He is flabbergasted. 'G . . . G . . . Golder. Richard Golder.'

'Date of birth?' asks the guard, wheeling round, returning to the kiosk.

'I beg your pardon?' The back of the man's head cries out to be struck.

'Just a precaution, sir.'

'Yes of course,' he says, writhing in the coils of his cowardice. He gives his date of birth and waits by the gate, pretending to stretch his ossified hamstrings, as the guard closes the glass door of his box and picks up a telephone.

They won't let him through. He is certain. As certain as he

was, aged eleven, that he'd flop that first somersault from the high diving board. As certain as he was, aged thirteen, that 'jumbo tits' Cathy next door would refuse to go out with him. He is sure the guard will detain him until Christina and the muscular Rico arrive with a straitjacket to escort him back to his room. Why didn't he jump the man when he had the chance?

And then he watches in amazement as the gate glides silently open. As smoothly as all doors have opened for him before. Why on earth does he have no self-confidence? In spite of a lifetime of success. It's high time the mystery was resolved. And where better than here at Beadale Hall?

'Have a good run sir,' the guard calls after him.

He sprints two hundred yards or so, out of sight of the security man, turning one corner and then another. And then he stops and bends double, struggling to catch his breath, exhilarated by his flight to liberty, close to tears. Running is painful and he wonders if, with the drugs in his system, he should be doing it at all. Finally he stops panting, straightens up and dries his eyes with the bottom of his tee shirt. He looks about him at a sea of semi-detached red brick houses, oppressively symmetrical, with pocket-size, perfectly tended front gardens. So this is the Winnersh he found on the map in the hospital library. Probably no more than an hour's drive up the M4 to London. Home. To Melanie.

Breathing easier now, he continues on, but walking this time.

A woman with two young children is approaching him on the footpath. Sane, normal people at last. The mother, tall and skinny, wears a wan put-upon expression and a white dress printed with weary pale blue flowers. She has passed down her angular chin and hooked nose to a stocky boy of eight or nine who trudges glumly at her side. A hungry tyrannosaurus glares from the front of his black tee shirt. Lagging a couple of yards behind, as if asserting a newly acquired independence, is a small girl of four or five, with curly red hair and rubicund cheeks, in denim dungarees.

But as the trio come closer still, they are not just bigger. They are brighter. And their luminosity continues to intensify until, just five or six yards in front of him, they have lit up like

Andrew Mackenzie

Christmas trees. At a standstill now, and a little frightened, he watches the mother's face glow, the boy's eyes burn, the girl's hair smoulder. As they arrive he examines them from head to toe: the perfect form of their burning features, every minute detail of their blazing chests, their fingers . . . their dazzling clothes! Each garment has switched on some inner light of its own: the flickering blue flowers on the woman's dress, the lucent lime green eyes of the dinosaur on the boy's shirt, the lambent pink of the girl's baseball boots. Where have these bright angels come from? By what strange sorcery have they set themselves on fire?

The mother throws him an anxious glance on her way past. The boy seems vaguely interested by his attention and slips him a shy half-smile. A few steps later the woman turns round to see if he's still staring. Well what does she expect? She stops for a moment to let the girl catch up and, taking her by the hand, hurries away, with the boy behind now, surfing on the wake of her stardust.

He watches the glowing family until they disappear. And then he turns to face the houses to his right. They aren't ugly any more; their bricks are now an exquisite confection of plum, violet and rich burgundy, of burnt orange and cherry, of russet, chestnut and toffee. Their every sill, roof tile and chimneypot part of some exquisite pattern, these houses look good enough to eat. His eyes pan down to the garden wall at his feet, and he falls to his knees as if before an altar rail, compelled to wonder at its bricks with their multiform cracks and crevices, at its cement, home to a million minuscule quartz crystals sparkling in the sunlight. Closing his eyes, he brushes his fingertips against the wall's surface, caressing it, feeling the coarse graininess of the bricks, licking the satin smoothness of the cement. Delicious!

Light-headed with pleasure, he turns away and sinks down on to the pavement with his back against the wall. He stares at the apple tree in the garden across the road. It has transformed into a fizzing kaleidoscope, its bark and leaves a finely woven tapestry of cinnamon and avocado, caramel and olive, auburn and emerald. Some surfaces absorb the sunlight, secreting it away, while others – like prisms – transform the sun's dancing rays into a thousand brand new colours. Giddy before this neon rainbow, he blinks the tears from his eyes, and then, worried he might lose consciousness, he closes them.

Suddenly fear runs screaming through his head as his breaths come fast and shallow.

But why be alarmed by such radiance, such beauty? Because it reminds him of regaining consciousness a month ago? Because he fears regressing? Because he hates to lose control? Or is there a more arcane, medical explanation? He has no idea. He just knows he's had his fill of illuminations for one day. But how can he escape this psychedelic stupor? For even now a multicoloured laser show is rehearsing on his eyelids. Perhaps he should try subjugating the sensory world to the conscious one. If his breakdown has taught him anything it's that thoughtful people cannot see. Perhaps he should start to think.

Screwing his eyes shut even tighter and insulating them with his palms, he begins to consider the details of a recent deal at work. A dazzling deal at work. Would Eurotelco reap all the savings he promised them by merging their acquisition? The duplicate central office costs? Certainly. The sales and marketing costs? Probably. The operations costs? Hard to say. If he is honest – and he'd like to be – he hasn't a clue about the operations costs. So much will depend on the unions. If he is honest – and he'd like to be – he no longer cares about the operations costs. Or the union. Or Eurotelco.

Several thinking moments later he opens one eye surreptitiously to see if the spell has been broken. Opening both eyes wide, he finds that, sure enough, he has lost his appetite for the monotone square houses. And the plain green apple tree in front of them. Ignoring the knot of nostalgia in his belly, he pushes himself up from the pavement and ambles back to the hospital, past the security guard and up the drive. He walks round the main building and flops down on the grass in the shade of an elm on the other side of the lake, exhausted, still thinking, thinking, thinking.

dead cat bounce
Aifric Campbell

London, Wednesday 16 January 1991
06:54: Allied troops poised to invade Kuwait – **Reuters**

I put the cappuccino into Al's hand as he stands admiring his life-size cut-out of Norman Schwarzkopf on the wall.

'You never said if you saw it last night, Geri.'

'What?'

'Stormin' Norman's interview with that guy from *On the Edge*.'

'Like watching a snuff movie,' says Rob from the other side of the desk and Al swivels around tetchily, the way he does whenever Rob cruises into his US political airspace.

'You don't know what you're talking about. As per usual,' says Al, chucking a tight paper ball in the bin behind Rob's head.

'Oh and you do, right mate?' says Rob.

'Whatever,' sighs Al, sliding into his chair.

'You mean you've actually seen one Al? I ask, speed-dialling the dog walker's number while he raises his head face up to the ceiling, arms behind his head.

'Maybe.'

I kill the outgoing.

'I don't believe it.'

'He has? You HAVE?' Rob shoots out of his chair and, in a second, is crouched between the pair of us, doing a quick headscan of the floor.

'Come on mate, spill.'

Al taps a shiny right shoe under the desk.

125

'Come ON Al,' I plead. 'You can't just say that and not follow it up?'

'I reckon he was too busy being top of the class,' adds Rob.

Al lowers his arms and adjusts his cuffs.

'It was in my Freshman year. That's first year at University to you, dickhead,' he grins down at Rob.

'I don't believe it,' I say, leaning closer.

'Hey, I'm not proud, you know it was like my roomie's friend of a friend . . .'

'That's flat mate to you Rob,' I say.

'Shut the fuck up Geri. OK, OK. So? Al?'

'He paid like 300 bucks or something for this video, a really shitty copy. And we were wasted one night, so he puts this thing on and there's just the four of us . . .'

Al bends forward in the chair, elbows on knees, considering his spreadeagled hands.

'Yeah?'

'So we watched it. Or some of it. I can't remember.'

'And what happened?'

'And then I fell asleep.'

'In the film I mean.'

'A girl . . . a Mexican girl . . . that's where they, uh, get them. Y'know, smuggle them in or something, or do it there I guess. It was pretty hard core stuff, I mean gang bang and she was a kid really. And then they did it.'

'What?

'You know, held her down and beat the fuck out of her.' Al stares straight ahead like he sees something on his Reuters screen.

'Did she die?' I venture.

'What the fuck d'you think Geri? It was a snuff movie not *Sleeping Beauty*.'

'Jesus CHRIST Al,' I hiss. 'And you watched this?'

'Hey it's not like I wanted to, or paid any money or anything. You gotta remember we'd been tequila slamming since lunchtime after this ball game, I can hardly even remember. Like I said it was one of those things.'

'I can't believe you even admit to it.'

'You asked. And hey I don't want to hear this coming back.'

'Alright mate, alright. Be cool,' says Rob.

'So what about the guy who owned the tape?'

'Never saw him again. He was a fucking asshole anyways.'

The tannoy cuts across the floor: Morning meeting begins in ONE minute.

Rob stands up, stripping his eyes away from Al for the first time, shaking his head and smiling.

'Gotta say mate I'm impressed. And there's me thinking you were just a swot.'

I join the warm herd of bodies bottlenecking at the entrance to the conference room, remembering the morning after the markets crashed, three years and three months ago almost to the day, when the Grope assembled the whole floor to say this would be something to tell our grandchildren about, *If you can keep your head when all about you are losing theirs*. The smell of money in the morning: laundered shirts and exclusive cologne and all of us shuffling to attention, none of the usual pushing and shoving at the back, the guys up front lip-chewing with folded arms and quite a few of us nodding at things the Grope said. Like we knew what was happening. Like we understood.

Trooping back to the trading floor to man our posts, waiting for the FTSE to limp out of the box and drip blood all over the Topic screen. Tim's mum actually managed to get through to him to ask about her ICI shares and he snapped, *Yeah well mum first you go to University and do an Economics degree, then you come and work in a big bank for a few years and then maybe I'll explain*.

The greenback flipped and bounced as the East Coast yawned its way into a fury and we sat breathless in front of the flickering screens, watching the Dow struggle to even reach an opening, shuddering through a spiral as the programs puked all over it. This new little nerve in the Grope's temple that kept twitching as he stalked the floor, like he was in a hospital visiting casualties. *There is always a price at which we do business and the trading phones will always be answered. Not like some British banks I could mention.*

The spreads opening up like earthquake crevices, the little gap that was Rob's mouth just after buying some BBB+ bonds at 60 that he could only knock out five minutes later at 45. *This market is disappearing up its own asshole.* So they flew in some fire-fighters from New York to show us how to behave in a crisis and they sat around with little American footballs on their desks, mispronouncing the names of European companies and going *yeah yeah uh huh*, putting in practice risk containment strategies they learnt at Harvard. Schlepping home in the October evening to watch the TV action replay of our day, where other people in other banks sat staring at screens, everyone looking to everyone else for an answer.

Day 2, the Dow off 22%, someone whispered 'buying opportunity' in the morning meeting and the Grope looked like he was going to machine gun the whole room. Rumours of people jumping off buildings, chickens coming home to get axed, the day that God left the storm-ravaged City and everything got out of control. *When the dust settles, someone is going to pay for this*, said Rob. Then the Red Adair hand-holders showed up at the office in their travel suits and shook our hands, *Good luck you guys*, like we'd been in the trenches together, took their little leather footballs and jumped in a cab to get the Concorde back to their guaranteed promotions, leaving us with collapsed premiums on all their hedge positions and Rob swearing down the phone for months.

It all ended in a universal fight about who had predicted this, who understood it and who knew what to do, a big scramble to lay the blame. Saying things like, *The markets have a life of their own*, which really just means that nobody has an overview, nobody is in control. Talk about how the index shouldn't be able to fall like that: blame it on the futures and those smartasses in Chicago, blame it on the champagne, blame it on the arbitrageurs, and then suddenly everything that was good before became bad. Strolling through the debris, picking up the pieces, reconstructing the business, putting toes back in the water and getting philosophical over margaritas about the excesses and how every cloud has a silver lining. Turn disaster into opportunity, seize the chance to get rid of the walking wounded who shouldn't have had jobs in the first place, get lean and mean down the gym, run a red pen through the expense accounts, cut out the dead wood.

Only the fit will survive. Just like Bruce says, *A lot of guys went and a lot of guys never came back.*

But a year later we were liberated by the release of *Wall Street* and the confirmation that greed is good and lunch is for wimps. The boys were flying in truckloads of Brooks Brothers' button-downs, dragging their girlfriends along to see how cool their jobs looked on a big screen, some even gekkoed their hair but couldn't carry it off like Michael Douglas. And the book stores were swamped with block orders when *Bonfire of the Vanities* came out: the trading floor elevated to an art form, 400 pages longer than anything most traders have ever read, but there it was in black and white: we were Masters of the Universe.

So today even as we wait, this hardcore platoon of Crash survivors, traders unzipping the stinking body bags of their long positions, sales people fingering their blood-spattered rolodex, we know it's just the same old thing of damage limitation: watching your ass and living to tell the tale. Just like before, there is traffic on the streets and people going to work, the western world flexing a collective muscle while deadlines expire all around us.

'There's four hundred thousand US troops out there just itching to barbecue Saddam's ass,' said the Grope when he called me in to his office last Thursday, an hour before I left for Hong Kong. 'And you're happy about travelling?'

'Sure,' I said.

Like there was an option.

'You'll see. This war will be wrapped up in a week,' he said snapping the briefcase case shut.

'But if it escalates?'

The Grope leaned forward in his non-swivel and placed both hands on the desktop.

'Take it from me, this stuff your newspapers write over here, Bush the wimp? They're wide of the mark. When I was a kid at Andover –'

'Andover?'

'Philips Academy, Andover,' he waved a dismissive hand. 'It's what you'd call the American Eton. I was ten years behind George Bush, but my tutor often told the story about Stimson's address and how it set him on the road to greatness.'

I inclined my head. The Grope exhaled, sliding his hands apart.

'Stimson. Secretary of War in Roosevelt's cabinet. Visited Philips in the summer of 1940. Delivered a vision of America's destiny. Subject? World leadership, the great battle between liberty and the enemies of liberty.'

He paused, turned his head towards the door and then suddenly swung back.

'You know he flew 58 combat missions, got shot down, spent thirty-four minutes in the Pacific before he was rescued by a destroyer.'

'Stimson.'

He slapped a hand against the desk wood.

'BUSH.'

'Oh right.'

'Does that sound like a wimp? Does that sound like the kind of guy who walks away from a tough job? Does that sound like the kind of guy who pulls a deal?'

'No, absolutely not.' I sat upright in my chair and uncrossed my legs.

A crease formed around the outer edges of his mouth.

'This deal is going to happen, just like this war is going to be won. There's 10 million dollars of fees riding on this, Geraldine, I don't have to tell you that. You're at the frontline. You go out to Hong Kong and do your stuff. You've got Jeremy in for 20% of the deal, it's the lead order and we all know the rest of the clients will follow suit. I'm counting on you. Hold his hand and tell him everything's going to be fine.'

'Sure. Great.' I said, rising from the chair.

Snowgirls
Diana Evans

Two weeks before Christmas, the Neasden branch of Woolies gleamed red, gold and holly green in the gathering dusk. Its hazy sweet-wrapped windows blinked like Georgia's secret eyes. Scented crayon, glittered pencil cases, rainbow umbrellas. Chocolate honeycomb, sherbet sachets, pick 'n' mix galore. On weekdays, herds of schoolchildren, catapulted by the 3.30 bell from dreary classrooms to the rolling freedom of after-school hollered and loitered in the precinct outside. The boys from Watley Boys' High ogled and asked out the girls from Watley Girls' High. Older brothers and little sisters were reunited. Ties were stuffed into satchels. Crushes were confidentially disclosed.

Amongst them were the twins, Georgia and Bessi; Forehead 2 and Forehead 1, Georgia's backwards and upwards, Bessi's upwards and backwards. They were working hard towards their future flapjack empire and developing a professional attitude. While Georgia blinked at the blackboard and raised her hand in 2G to answer 'Why did Boudicca lead the revolt against the Romans?' with 'because the Roman army killed her husband and attacked her people,' Bessi raised her hand in 2B to answer 'Where in Australia did Captain Cook first hoist the British flag?' with 'Botany Bay.'

They were flanked by their best friends Anna and Reena. Anna was also known as Pigeon-Shit Nose because a pigeon had once swooped overhead up Waifer Avenue and opened its bowels onto the end of her long sharp nose. Bessi's best friend was Reena, a grinning, four-foot-eight Pakistani tomboy who wiped snot on the insides of double-decker bus windows to declare her hardness. They were actually token best friends, less best than Georgia and Bessi were to each other. This was unspoken and accepted, because for the twins, walking towards each other across the playground from their different-classroom lives at lunchtime was the same as walking towards themselves.

The four of them wore identical, roomy white corduroy coats with explosive cream cuffs from Wembley Market. At the school gates, in the playground, in the precinct, the foaming four arrived always as a waddling, frothing arctic vision; a vision that was reluctantly discarded at the end of each winter, and washed, wardrobed and yearned for until the next.

Woolies glistened. It beckoned. The security guard peered out at the after-school with a mixture of dread and good will. Georgia, Bessi, Anna and Reena approached the double doors. Snowgirls risen from the ground. He bowed as they entered, setting off four scruffy giggles. He watched them scuttle away, past the gurgling prams and nattering mothers towards the stationery section, where the girls, top teeth holding bottom lips, fiddled with pencils of fresh, aromatic lead and sharpeners whose blades flashed under the lemony neon lighting, and smudged their pencil fingerprints onto the latest selection of rubbers. He watched them, rocking on his feet and clasping his hands behind his back. More schoolchildren sauntered in and his darting eyes tried to keep track of all ten bouncing lallygaggers. It was not easy. He did not see the foaming four journeying towards the sweet aisle, where the Twixs beamed in their silken caramel wrappers and nudged the bubble-light Maltesers and the pick 'n' mix twinkled with sugar-coated stars – the undisputed crown jewels of Woolies Wonderland. They huddled together, rustling for change.

'28p,' Anna held out the coins in her palm.

'13p,' said Bessi.

'What about your paper-round money? I've got 50p left from mine,' said Georgia.

'I spent it at lunchtime,' Bessi said.

They all looked at Reena. As usual, she was penniless. Without warning, she picked a lime-wrapped mint toffee from one of the pick 'n' mix trays and shoved it in her pocket. Their eyes lit up.

They swerved around to see if anyone had seen.

'*Reeeena!*' Bessi hissed. 'That's *naughty!*'

'Oh, don't be so goody goody. ''S only a sweet.' Reena lifted a white chocolate milk bottle from another tray and popped it into her mouth.

Anna giggled.

'It's *stealing!*' Georgia and Bessi said.

''S not stealing. My brother said anything under £1's not stealing. It's the law.'

They thought about this. It sounded feasible. They would ask Bel when they got home.

Fizzy cola bottles twinkled next to rainbow vermicelli. As Reena sucked on her milky prize she arranged her face in a skyward, orgasmic grimace. The other three watched her jealously. Milk-livered. Scaredy-cat. Chicken. Reena reigned supreme in the ranks of hardness.

'Dare you,' she sucked.

Pigeon-Shit Nose sidled up to the pick 'n' mix. She looked around with beady eyes. She caressed jelly baby bellies with sweaty fingertips. Deep breath. Hand opened like an impatient flower. Gather. Seize. Remove fisted hand. Look around. Raise hand. Five jelly babies. Open mouth. The babies jumped in. Yippeeeee. Tee-hee. A chomping mouth stuffed with candy babies. Anna's eyes flashed. Reena the pioneer punched her shoulder in revolutionary fashion. They doubled over raucously, cavorting, laughter wrestling with jelly in Anna's triumphant mouth.

'My girl's *bad*, you knoooow!' said Reena.

'You *knooooow* say!' Anna agreed.

The twins bit scaredy-cat lips with chicken teeth. They touched eyes. Shrinking. Georgia nudged Bessi. 'Let's go,' she said. But Bessi didn't move.

'Goody goody twinnie twins!' said Reena.

'*Shaaame!*' said Anna.

Two aisles away, the security guard, sufficiently assured that the other lallygaggers were up to no more mischief than replacing unaffordable goods incorrectly, heard the hooting of the forgotten four. He walked to the end of the confectionery aisle.

He peeped down it, seeing nothing but the loitering snowgirls, two guffawing, two silent and shuffling their feet. No hands pocketing sweets. Not then.

He watched.

Bessi knew what they had to do. 'Come on Georgia,' she said. 'We've got to.'

In a hasty telepathy of embarrassment, they decided that something sugared, something superior to jelly babies or milk bottles, yet something worth less than £1 had to be *taken*.

Woolies didn't sell flapjacks so they chose a Twix. Not one, but two. A twin bar each for the soon-to-be *bad* girls.

Georgia and Bessi sidled up to their biscuit-centred prey. Facing one another, they checked for sweet-police, sliding their eyes nervously. It was safe. A clammy left hand and a clammy right hand wiped white corduroy. One last, terrified check. One sudden image of their parents. Butterflies tickled their intestines with frenetic wings. Deep breath, one each. Place hand on Twix. Open flower. Softly lift. Seize. Remove fist. Check for police. Fill pocket, one each. Touch eyes, gleeful, guilty. *'S not stealing.*

Then why was the security guard charging towards them without his smile? And why were their best friends slinking away from them? Why did their hearts rattle and reel? Terror snowballed. They whirled round and saw the sweet-policeman, kind eyes replaced by ice, the mouth now pursed and lined with punishment.

'Right girls, come with me.'

No buts. No *'s not stealings*. Just hold hands and follow him to a very tall sweet-policewoman with disgusted, mercury eyes and a Woolies Manager badge – Mrs E.F. Winters. Two Twixs are retrieved. Two twelve-year-olds quake. Anna and Reena slink away, out the doors to freedom.

Georgia and Bessi's sentence was worse than imprisonment. The most perplexing, most frightening, most intimate kind of exposure.

Mrs E.F. Winters ordered: 'I want you to go home now and tell your parents what you have done.'

Tell their *parents*? Aubrey's wrath. Ida's disappointment. To Anna and Reena, for example, this would have been a lucky sentence. A let-off. *They* would have promised to inform their parents, strolled away, and 'forgotten' to keep the promise. But for Georgia and Bessi, whose quivering memories dipped back to three years ago, when Bel had stolen socks from C&A and Ida had chased her around the dining room table, over and over, and then sat on her when she had flopped onto the sofa, surrendering – *sat* on her – and Aubrey had made her stand in the cupboard under the stairs for a whole afternoon with no dinner afterwards, the punishment was devastating.

Their stammers staccatoed in time with each other.

'I p-promise.'

'I-I promise.'

And together now. 'We p-ro-miss.'

Mrs E.F. Winters watched the two brown snowgirls waddle away, hands interlocked, heads earthbound, and out the double doors.

White corduroy returned to the falling snow.

On the way home, through the dusk that had become night, the twins shed tears. Georgia's arm looped through Bessi's, they assessed their choices. They walked back up the steep narrow alley. There were cracks in the ground and when it rained it looked like silver veins. In the mornings, when they were the first to tread it with their papers, fat orange slugs still slept there wetly, making them dodge. Tonight, the alley was snowing. Everything is white, thought Georgia through her anguish. When the white is over, the cracks will show.

They slipped once or twice on sketches of ice.

'What shall we tell them?' Bessi said.

Georgia thought of the most obvious thing. 'Let's say there's a cockroach in our room. Then we can tell them upstairs.'

'You don't get cockroaches here.'

Yes you do, thought Georgia. She looked at Bessi sideways.

'A spider,' Bessi said.

Georgia nodded.

They would keep their promise. They would tell. But not Aubrey and Ida. They would tell Bel, which was almost telling their parents, except that Bel did not have the authority or the

Diana Evans

bulk to sit on them.

They walked in through the back door of home. Kemy was drawing a woman in a red dress at the kitchen table. She looked up when they came in.

'Where've *you* been? Mummy's annoyed.'

Bessi was the first. 'Only at the library with Anna and Reena.'

Georgia followed. 'We were *working*.'

'*I'm* working.'

'No you're not,' Bessi said. 'You're crayoning. That's not working.'

'I *yam*! It's homework. I'm going to be a dressmaker!'

'Where's Bel?' asked Georgia.

'In the sitting room watching telly. Daddy's home early.'

The twins shuddered. Kemy carried on drawing with added sobriety, determined to prove to Bessi that she too had important things to do.

They hung their coats in the hallway and crept into the sitting room. Aubrey's eyes were attached to the TV. Snooker highlights. The kiss and crack of red and yellow balls and a white one colliding. Bursts of applause. Bel was sitting on the sofa with her legs tucked beneath her. She looked bored. Safer than Aubrey. The twins touched eyes. Deep breath. Hello.

'*There* you are. Where were you?' asked Bel, not quite angry.

'Library.'

'Working.'

Aubrey did not adjust his vision. 'You should've phoned,' he said. 'Your Mummy's been worried . . . why didn't you phone?'

'Forgot.'

'Sorry.'

Aubrey glazed back wearily into snooker land. Bessi dived in.

'Bel . . . Can you come upstairs for a minute? There's a spider in our room.'

'Yeah. A *really big* one,' Georgia confirmed.

Bel looked them over. 'You just came in. How do you know?'

'We went upstairs first. It's still there. It was there this morning as well. It's got hairy legs,' said Bessi.

'Hairy? I don't think so, I hate spiders. Why don't you ask Dad?'

'Nooo! We want *you* to come.'

Bel huffed. 'It's probably gone now anyway. I have to help Mum with dinner.'

The twins looked at one another and squirmed. They could not insist. It would arouse suspicion. But they had to tell.

And then it occurred to Bessi: perhaps they didn't have to tell. Perhaps this was their chance at being *bad*.

'Oh, it doesn't matter then. We'll sort it out,' she said.

Georgia was confused. She opened her mouth to speak but Bessi pulled at her hand as she walked out of the room, her eyes aglitter like the sweets in Woolies. 'That's it!' she hissed as they climbed the stairs to the loft. 'We did it!'

They marched to school the next morning. Bessi told Anna and Reena they'd got away with it, shrugging as if she hadn't been terrified. 'It was nothing,' she said. 'They couldn't touch us.'

Anna and Reena were impressed. 'Bad girls,' said Reena.

For a time, the cool grey eyes of Mrs E.F. Winters haunted them in the stillness of night. But the snow melted. The cracks in the ground showed through. Another summer blushed and the eyes faded away.

'Bessi,' said Georgia, as they lay in the dark the night of Woolies, without a spider in their room.

'Yeah.' Bessi waited.

Georgia wanted to tell her about the cockroaches, about what happened. But she felt them crawling towards her, up the bedspread.

'What?' said Bessi.

'My eyes don't work properly,' said Georgia.

Bessi was silent.

'I think I need glasses.'

'Me too,' said Bessi.

Skating in the Cremator Room
Jo Wroe

Some thought it was strange to live in the grounds of a crematorium. My mother had no patience with those who voiced surprise, like the man we met in the waiting room of the dentist the day I had my braces fitted. She was still cross on the way home, driving too quickly through the wrought iron entrance gates and lunging the car up our driveway, which sat on the top of a short but steep hill. She stopped abruptly in front of the garage. From my usual position directly behind her, I saw the St Christopher she wore had inched around her neck. It seemed in keeping with her mood, off kilter, snagged.

'Does he *really* think no one's made that joke before?'

'Which one?' I said as I climbed out and felt the warmth of the afternoon sun slink around my bare legs. 'Bet there's not much life around there? Or, bet you don't get any trouble from the neighbours?'

'Both!' she snapped from inside the car, arms drilling into her handbag for the front door key.

I knew then, at ten, that my mother's tolerance for men who weren't funny or clever was unjustly low. I knew when they weren't funny or clever too, but I also saw something that my mother didn't. For such men, telling old jokes was the only way to be friendly to a beautiful woman who held herself so aloof. When she glowered at the man waiting for his root canal work, I recognised a helpless look hidden in his bright eyes and I curved my mouth in a non-committal half smile, so he wouldn't think I despised him too.

Mum preferred to be alone and loved the seclusion of the

Jo Wroe

crematorium. If anyone ever had managed to make a truly funny
and original joke about living there, I doubt that she would have
laughed.

My father was the crematorium's first Superintendent and got
to live on the job. He helped to plan the landscaping, requesting
hills, ornamental fountains, an enormous lake, trickling streams,
and paths that wound and swooped, instead of simply getting you
from one place to the next. The grounds were set amongst wheat
fields, and once you were inside them, the only buildings you
could see were the simple chapel and our bungalow. It was an
innovative piece of crematorium design. My father was very
proud of it.

'You don't know you're born,' Mum would say to my older
sister Julie, who struggled with living amongst the ashen dead,
and frequently begged our parents to move somewhere with
neighbours and no cremators. Mum had a point; at six o'clock,
the gates were padlocked and the entire place was handed over to
us: two young girls and a Boxer-Alsatian cross called Bill. During
daylight hours, we could go wherever we wanted, down paths, up
steps, over bridges, through arches and up and all over the low-
limbed climbing trees.

On the day of the brace fitting it was half-term. I cried
because I was hungry and couldn't eat a chocolate digestive with
metal wires in my mouth. Mum had given me her cup of coffee to
soften the biscuit in. Being cross and kind at the same time was
never a problem for her.

My father appeared at the back door, breathless. I knew it was
important, because he talked to my mother without
acknowledging me.

'Put Caroline in a black dress. *Now*. Mr Fleming hasn't turned
up.'

Mr Fleming was my organ teacher. Dad wanted me to learn to
play the piano. He'd given up any educational aspirations for my
sister. She was so determined to be interested only in horses that
she'd convinced my father it wasn't even worth asking her to
attempt anything else. We didn't have a piano, so I learned on the
chapel organ instead. My father recruited Mr Fleming, the
crematorium organist, who had bunches of wiry black hair

sprouting from his ears and nostrils but none on his head, to teach me. His nicotine-yellow fingers and wheezy breathing made him more like a set of creaky bellows than a human being.

Mr Fleming was ill at ease sitting on the organ bench next to a ten-year-old girl who was ill at ease with him. They were very awkward half hours. I wasn't a good student and my father didn't keep track of my progress. He merely popped his head through the chapel door every now and then, slipping Mr Fleming two pounds at the end. When I was meant to be practising on my own, I was distracted by all the pure white organ stops: *flute, oboe, swell, trumpet, mute, tremolo*. They were curved at the end like the wooden sticks the doctor presses on your tongue and I liked to slap each one down as quickly as I could and then flick them all up again, running my finger along their undersides. I loved their *tickticktick* against my fingernail. There was also the giant keyboard down below to play with my feet. Julie laughed when I stomped out chopsticks with my short skinny legs. If I was thoroughly bored, I stood up and ran back and forth on the wooden keys.

'Ask her how she got on at the dentist,' said my mum, without looking up from the sink.

'Miriam, the funeral should have started! Put the girl in a black dress.'

'I haven't got one.' I said, noticing how my 't's sounded strange with the brace and already worrying about the waiting mourners.

Mum pushed her glasses up on her forehead, and walked out of the room, scattering words over her shoulder. 'Her sister's got one, but it'll be too big.'

I didn't come clean until I was walking down to the chapel, pushing the dress back on my shoulders every two steps.

'Dad.'

He took my hand so I would walk faster down the path towards the chapel.

'Yes love?'

'I can only play one proper tune.'

He didn't miss a beat. 'Well play that one, properly, *slowly*, over and over. The most important thing Caroline,' he stopped walking and bent down so his face was level with mine, emphasising each of the four words, 'is not to smile.'

'Because of my brace?'

'No you daft bat!' He marched us on, ruffling my hair. 'Because a funeral is a serious business.'

So I did as I was told and played my tune over and over again, slowly, poker-faced. I got £3 from Birmingham City Council as though it was no big deal, but I know I would have asked some questions if someone I loved was seen off by a ten year old in a baggy black dress to *Home on the Range*.

That evening Julie and I took our bikes down to the car park.

We wrapped skipping ropes around their handle bars for reins and used the enclosed circle of tarmac as a horse-riding arena. We could gallop in, down the slope and canter all the way round without pedalling if we held our nerve and didn't put the brakes on at the beginning. After half an hour we left the bikes and walked down to the lake.

When we weren't riding, we mostly hung out by the lake, with the moorhens, giant goldfish, bulrushes, lilies and, in the spring, frogs in swarms of biblical proportions. The lake sat in a little valley. You could walk down a path from the right, or steps from the left, and where they met at the bottom, was a delicate footbridge that crossed the water. One icy January afternoon, Dad threw Bill onto the frozen lake so we could see him skate. We laughed at his sprawled legs, unsure of whether to swim or run, but it made me anxious because the kinder thing would have been not to throw him on.

We had at least an hour to play before it got dark, but pin-pricks of rain made circles on the water, so we started to walk back towards home. My head was down, counting the steps it would take me to get back. Julie said,

'Dad's coming.'

Striding down our drive towards us, he had a pair of roller-skates in each hand, their weight made his arms swing higher than usual.

'Come on,' he said, 'I'll take you inside.'

Dad had to be somewhere in the building if we played inside the crematorium. We usually went on a Sunday afternoon when he had office work to catch up on, but it was half-term, and my mum would have had enough of us for one day without us being under her feet all evening as well. We knew that's what was going on.

The crematorium had a front of stage and a backstage. The contrast between the two, and my ability to cross freely from one to the other put a wriggle of excitement in my stomach. Front of stage was the chapel, ripe with the clean smells of quality and care. The pale wood was polished so heavily that you could run your fingernail through the gloss. The thick carpet smelt like new car upholstery, absorbing any noise your footfall might make, as if to say, 'Sshh! Show some respect.' The fragrance of fresh flowers thickened the air further and their colour splashed against the beige wood and blue carpet. Pine beams vaulted the ceiling and one whole side of the chapel was glass, overlooking a small, enclosed garden. The window was kept so clean that it reflected the garden too well, and I lost count of the small birds that died smashing their skulls against the glass. Julie and I tried to cremate a thrush once. We kneeled over it on the cold concrete, striking forbidden matches we'd found in the toilets, holding them to the bird's tail feathers. It was too windy so we had to give up.

Backstage was the cremator room and the groundsmen's workshop. When we saw the red leather straps and white laces of our skates swinging from Dad's fists, we knew that we were going to the cremator room. The noisy *clackclackroll* of our novice skating was amplified by the tiled floor, tiled walls and twenty foot high ceiling. When we fell, the tiles were cold and hard, but when we were doing well, we could go a long way, quickly. It was a great place to learn.

To the left of the door, embedded in the wall, were three steel hatches, perfect squares. Next to each was a metal lever, topped with a red spherical knob. The vast room was completely empty except for one thing. In the far right-hand corner, there was a platform with rollers on top. It was joined to the wall and sat flush with another giant serving hatch. When it opened, you could see right through to the chapel, where there was an identical platform.

At the end of a funeral, the organ played just loud enough to cover the electronic whiz and burr, the curtains closed around the coffin, the hatch came up and the coffin was rolled through, leaving the soft, muted chapel, entering the cremator room. No more respectful undertakers' suits, ties and cufflinks. The tattooed arms of men wearing overalls and chewing gum pulled the coffin through to wheel it across the wide expanse of floor, to one of the three hatches on the other side.

Every day I saw hearses roll past my kitchen window, I ran over soil that was grey with freshly scattered ashes and heard the roar of the cremators in full steam. But it was this alone that snapped my imagination into a dance of terror with the idea of death; the thought of that journey from one side of the cremator room to the other, because it was across those tiles that you stopped being a daughter, a sister, a friend. You became a thing, which had to be burned. What if, just what if, you somehow recognised that moment when it came, and you knew your family weren't coming after you, that you had been handed over to strangers with only one intention?

When Julie and I heaved on one of the long cold levers, we could open the cremator itself and look inside. But more often, we just grabbed them to stop ourselves hurtling into the wall. We were never very good skaters.

July
Colin Carters

Fr Antonio   **Barcelona, July 18th**

Fr Antonio sat back in the ragged comfort of his chair and allowed his nape to crease around the leather sweep of cushion. His horn-rimmed glasses rose up onto his ruddy forehead in an act of submission as he thumbed the electrified circumference around his eyeballs. Allowing the book a final exhale, he closed it over and laid it upon his lap. It was late.

Reading was impossible these days; Antonio's mind attacked every word and paragraph. Images from his day crammed into the purgatory of white space between the printed text, and before a sentence was pointed, he was wandering. The story was nothing more than a catalyst to memory, each phrase being said by the countless people he had spoken with, seen, or scurried guiltily away from that day and other days like it. He sat in silence fighting the temptation to nod off and let his head sink down towards the yellow mark upon his shirt, which recalled the grains of rice that had fallen there hours earlier, over lunch.

After eating, everyone had gone back to waiting. Some of the men played cards to pass the time, others wore their shoes around the room and others re-read the letters they carried with them; the delicate paper creased like moth wings, and the fading words fluttered off the page. Soon they would be unreadable, the paper would fray and holes would appear in places where beautiful sentences about love once ran. Barely had a letter been rested in the darkness of a stale scented pocket, than it was called upon again to relieve the boredom.

Sometime after lunch, a distracting squint of sunlight coming through an opened door, ironed the pervasive silence and brought any conscious movement to a halt. A brown face had appeared around the doorframe and ushered in three more. The four men, with their string-tied beds held tight under their arms, resisted entering the unknown enormity of the church. One of them held a recognisable white card in his hand. Antonio went over slowly, and smiled.

'Hola,' he said, 'habla Español?' The men didn't move. 'Français?' One of the men, whose grey jacket was frayed along the lapel, raised his hand and surrendered the card. 'English?' said Antonio, at which the man nodded with vague recognition of the word. 'My name is Fr Antonio.' It made little impression. Antonio gestured them to follow, as he led them through a small wooden door at the back of the church. 'Are you hungry?'

The four strangers seated themselves silently around the table. Antonio left them at ease while he prepared food; their eyes hovered around the room. At the sound of a woman's voice in the corridor, all eyes lit expectantly on the door. She was young. Her brown hair was pulled back off her face, emphasising a smear of red on her face, which by the look on the four men's faces, they'd clearly interpreted as blood. Antonio laughed, swished the spatula like a sword and said 'paint', hoping that his smile would convey the word's meaning. The men tilted their frowning foreheads towards each other and went back to watching the postered walls.

'You're over doing it,' she said. 'All we need is for you to have a heart attack.'

'I'm fine. Anyway, someone has to feed them.' He slapped his heart with his hand 'Bo-boom, bo-boom, bo-boom.'

'Don't test fate. Antonio, it doesn't *always* have to be you.'

'Aghhh. I'm not in my grave yet, and I've tasted your food.'

'And you wear it too I see.' As she walked from the kitchen her hand caught the frame and she pulled back for a moment, 'go home and rest Father, we can manage. OK?' She paused. 'OK.'

Antonio sat with the men as they ate, and listened as they told him their story about being in the wrong country. How magnificent their aspirations made England sound and how suspended these aspirations now were. Hours later, a gentle tap on the arm instructed him to go home and rest a while. He went without complaint, shuffling out the door to the comfort of the armchair he now slumped in.

Antonio lifted his head from the solidity of the book and realised that the stained window, which drew light into the small study, had lost its colour; he hadn't noticed the darkness fall. He tried to remember how long he'd been sitting, or if he'd slept. The clock on the wall tickled the room like an irritated housefly whose inability to understand glass, forces it to tap tap tap against the transparency of a world that's all of a sudden flattened and defined. Irritated, and hopeful of a cool draught of air, the fly continues; tap tap tap tap.

Antonio adjusted his weight in the chair and switched on the small lamp on the table. He filled his lungs and prised open the book again. Music from the street filtered into the small panelled room and took its place on the page. He caught the smell of frankincense and made a mental note that he needed to order more. He began to read, *There lived in Westphalia, at the country seat of Baron Thunder-ten-tronckh, a young lad blessed by nature with the most agreeable manners. You could read his character in his face. He combined sound judgement with unaffected simplicity; and that, I suppose, was why he was . . .* a conversation in the street brushed against the window and brought Antonio back into the smallness of the book-walled room. Where was Westphalia, he wondered? He considered looking it up in the atlas, then realised he was having problems enough focusing on one book; what chaos would two throw up? But an atlas was different, was it not? He closed the book and considered ringing the church, just to check, but restrained himself with a glance to the bookshelf. He'd lost count of the number of times he'd rung that poor girl in her studio yesterday; would she collect blankets on her way over, could she help serve lunch, what about . . . it was enough to buckle the intentions of a saint.

He looked at the clock, heaved himself out of the chair and brought himself over to the mirror. The bulb's bare light made him look as diaphanous as he felt. He pulled on his cheeks with

Colin Carters

his fingers in a vain attempt to restore the vigour and youthfulness he had hoped to perceive in the man he saw there. The stranger's grey hair was speckled with only a few remaining black threads and the creased skin that dressed his face, was worn like a suit that was bought with good will from the wardrobe of a widow. He lit a cigarette and watched the line of smoke cut vertically across his face as he inhaled, and then purposely, pulled the dog collar free from around his throat and crumpled it into a tight little ball before letting it fall onto the dark wooden floor. There was no room for such a statement anymore, he thought, all the while fixing his glare in the eyes of the old man who searched back. Wrinkles and blotched skin had somehow concealed the ideals of youth and no amount of prodding could reveal anything other than the grey old man he now was. He pushed a breath from his chest and gripped the smooth wooden edge of the dresser. So much change, he thought. Only those close to death search for any hope or clarity in the emptiness they call faith; the rest reliant on the god of illumination, who appears in their living room and can be altered with the flick of a polished rubber button. The church shelters believers and unbelievers alike; Christian, Muslim, Hindu, Jew, Jain, Agnostic, Atheist, Desperate and Despised; their skin is white and cream and brown and pink and black and yellow and none of them can understand a word the other is saying, nor cares. They all have a story, each more weary and defeated than the other, yet barely strong enough to be told. Countless disappearing homelands replaced by sleepless worlds with faceless people who are unable to see anymore; their bodies decorated with the curved scars of another's invention, their downcast eyes unable to lift with the weight of expectation. And, it is not just those in the church; there are men in other disgruntled creases in far off places, unfit to hide the hollow echo that resonates in their eyes, with their noses pressed against the glass like urchins in a Dickens tale, unable to make sense of the world just beyond; houses ringing with laughter, flowers without smell, and inherited beds that are warmed by cold memories.

Antonio took the cigarette from his lips and set it on the

148

mantle with the extension of ash hanging over the fall. The clock ticked. He pulled on his black jacket and prepared to go back to the church, then stopped, his hand resting on the brass door handle. He went over to the bookcase and pulled out the small atlas his sister had given him when he joined the seminary and flicked to the index at the back. Westphalia, Westphalia, Westphalia; but it wasn't there and he found it impossible to furnish the word with people or landscape. He closed the book and forced it back into place. Perhaps, I need a better atlas, he thought, as he made his way from the room.

The heavy wooden doors creaked behind him as he stood facing the shuffle of people who perambulated along the street. Young lovers walked with a firm grasp on each other's intentions, elderly couples held a porcelain grip on their loved one's hand and smiled at the people who were about to step into the gap their progression along the street created. A little girl pulled at the sleeve of her mother's jumper, eager to dislodge and play with a kitten that would not be hers 'til she got home. A policeman walked by and tossed an insincere smile to Antonio, before twisting his owlish head away. Antonio recognised him, as he did everyone else, but he could not recall if they'd spoken. A camera clicked off to his right, and he realised that he too wanted this silent vision to last; that he could remain here, and have all these people continue round and around, like glittering funfair horses galloping a million miles away, forever, or until the gradual unwind of the ride restores you to the task of stepping down and moving on.

He looked left, then right, then left again, then right again. He couldn't decide which way to go, yet knew, no matter what decision was taken, he'd end up in the same place. He became conscious of standing too long on the steps, and even though the collar was removed and his presence was no more significant than anyone else's, he felt uneasy on such an exposed pulpit. An old woman stepped a foot onto the lower step as she hurried past. Her eyes were the colour of wet cement, and her silver skin looked as though it was woven from hundred-year-old cobwebs. She went like a ghost, barely noticed by anyone. It took Antonio a few moments to recognise and remember her, and in the time he took to commit to chase, she was taken by another street.

Antonio looked at his watch. Pulling his jacket close, he stepped down the three uneven steps and lost himself in the throng of people.

Gunella's Grievance
Anna Sayn-Wittgenstein

On a night of merciless cold, I once saved Hermann Göring's life. It was during the winter of 1925, a few weeks after Hanukkah, that time of year when the sun complacently ignores Swedish soil. A wave of pneumonia was rolling through Stockholm's playrooms, and I was often called in the early morning to help the little ones fight their fever.

I dare say I was widely known to have saved a few children's lives. But only that one time, twenty years ago, did I save a man. Yet nobody was to learn of it, except for Gunella, the gentle and gracious. It was her house I was heading towards. That night there was no sick child, no nervous father rushing me on. That night there was only Gunella waiting to welcome me. A few stolen hours from my sound-asleep home. I delighted at the thought of her as I walked the lonely streets, every step diminishing the distance between us. Fresh snow crackled under my boots. Icicles tinkled in the branches. The day's storm had come to rest. Now the sky was clear and the stars winked as if to say that they were in on my secret.

The sea breeze pulled at my scarf as I crossed Liljeholms Bridge. It was well below minus twenty degrees, but I enjoyed the taste of the frozen air, forcing into my lungs over and over. I tucked the scarf back under my coat collar. I exhaled into it and felt the warm breath on my face. The scarf had been a present, to be worn on these nightly travels, and this was the first time she'd see me wearing it. I tried to imagine what she would say. *It looks beautiful on you*; or rather, *I knew it would look beautiful on you*. Probably the latter; Gunella always knew.

Anna Sayn-Wittgenstein

I was smiling at that thought when suddenly I heard a rustle. Or did I hear it? A breeze lifted over the bridge and carried new snow across. A moan? I slowed. I've learned not to trust sound in winter. Thick layers of snow can fool your ears. You may think you're hearing a wild beast roaming nearby, when really it's just the pulse in your own ears. Or the sound of your fingers scratching the insides of your gloves. Maybe I was just hearing my own thoughts: the creaking of the door as Gunella opened it. I walked more briskly, then heard another moan. I stopped. There could be no doubt now. Somebody was nearby. A splash. I climbed over the snow piled up on the side of the bridge. Maybe a drunk, I thought instinctively. Once in a while one heard of drunks who had drowned when crossing the ice. I peered down, but all I could see were two big holes, the ones fishermen drilled to reach their prey, clearly marked by tall flags.

I climbed back down the snow pile, walked on and had almost reached the shore when I heard a cry. It was not a word, more like a loud gasp. It echoed in my ears as I hurried around the railing and down the embankment. Through the knee-high snow I headed for the holes I'd seen from the bridge. They were empty. But I could see footprints clearly stamped into the snow. Under the bridge, I saw an arm reaching out of a third opening that hadn't been visible from above. Those drunks, I thought. With an angry sigh I pulled off my scarf and coat, throwing both aside as I ran for the arm.

Most people break through the ice in the spring when the thick layers begin their slow melt. But that night in mid-winter the ice was still thick. This hadn't been an accident, and that thought made me even angrier.

I grabbed hold of the arm and pulled at it. It was blue and fleshy and kept slipping out of my hands. When I finally got a grip and pulled again, a thin-haired head emerged. Its face surfaced like the moon: white, big and round. The mouth hung open and the eyes were closed in a sick grimace. I slapped the face several times, harder, until there was a faint movement. It was a tired face, as if the man had already resigned himself to going. It was then that I recognized him. The doctor in me remembered the man's desperate drug addiction, which had ruined him. As his head disappeared under the surface, he seemed to pull back his arm.

'Come on!' I shouted, for now I was furious. If he was going to ruin my night, then he was at least going to live. 'Get up!' He didn't react. I reached down, gripping him under the armpits. 'Come on now, push!' It may be hard to save a man from drowning, but it is even harder when that man is heavy as hell. 'Bastard,' I shouted, moving closer to the hole to get a steadier stance, 'it's easy to die when you're on it. Try again when you're sober.' A rope would have been good, I thought; one is supposed to have ropes to rescue people. I pulled once more, trying to heave my own weight against his, when my left foot lost grip and slid into the water. I fell, hurting my back on one of the warning flags. The body I held disappeared under the surface. 'Hell!' I shouted, the freezing water trying to swallow my leg.

After a few seconds I didn't feel my limb anymore, and decided it could just as well stay where it was. I put my foot against the opposite edge of the hole. Now seated, I got a better grip around the man's chest and managed to heave him up. His arms lay stretched out on the ice and his head sunk into the snow. 'Kick now,' I screamed at him. 'Kick, for God's sake!'

'Nein,' the man said. Never has a word sounded so quiet and yet so adamant.

'You, devil, you're pushing your damned luck!' I shouted at him, 'And you *will* kick now!' I grabbed his belt under the surface and pulled at it with all the strength I could summon. My back ached, my leg was cold and my night was ruined. With a sputter the water set him free. He lay on the ice like a stranded whale, his face buried in snow. I shifted him over on to one side, and he began to cough, water seeping back out of his body.

'Damn.' I sat down in the snow, rubbing my wet leg. Disgust rose in my throat as I remembered the night I'd met this war hero of the losing side. Once quite popular in Swedish society, he had been handed around in his later wife's aristocratic circles as something of an exotic novelty, a thing that Stockholm is chronically short of. That night, he'd sat opposite me at a dinner party. The beautiful Carin was at his side, although still married to Nils von Kantzow. The German was young, quite slim and looked stately.

'Do you think you will move back to Germany?' I asked.

'Oh yes,' he answered, then searched for words, 'of course.' It was only later that he gave us a taste of himself. He was not an accustomed drinker, we soon understood, but his assertions did not seem to spring from his mood. On the contrary, they came straight from the heart. The host felt compelled to counter his views slightly, probably just for my sake. But this merely egged the German on. He finished with an excited proclamation, speaking in a voice that was far too loud for the little town house salon.

'The rich and the Jews have brought this upon Germany, we all know that,' he said, then added with emphasis: 'But my martyred country will persevere through the terrible and shabby burden of Versailles.' His German accent was much stronger now. It made his words heavy. 'I guarantee you.' He was slurring. He paused to look around the room, staring past the eyes that were fixed on him. 'Germany will get its revenge.' He laughed. 'And that revenge will be . . . unlike anything you have ever seen.' Carin pulled at his arm softly and whispered something in his ear. The host seized the chance to distract us by offering more wine. I was relieved to see the German and Carin leave the party, and a few months later I heard that they had moved to Munich.

Three years later little Thomas von Kantzow caught an ear infection on the West Coast, which would not heal. His father called me one night when Thomas lay in pain. After I had attended to Thomas, his father asked whether he could offer me something. We sat in their spacious reception hall, sipping sherry.

'It is a strange infection that should keep him ill for so long,' I said.

Herr von Kantzow looked at me, then leaned forwards and said quietly, 'The boy is worried, you know? His mother is trying to get custody of him.'

I nodded. The news of the von Kantzow divorce had already spread.

'But the lawyer thinks we have a good chance of keeping the boy. Her new husband, that German Göring, is a wreck, you know. Exiled for treason, and a drug addict at that. He's been interned as a loony in Långbro twice. I think it's the morphine that drives him crazy. Spends all the money on the drugs and forgets himself. Gets into these rages.'

'Doesn't seem fit to be a father anyway,' I said, and Herr von Kantzow lifted his eyebrows in agreement.

The whale had stopped coughing and seemed to be falling asleep. Freezing to death is supposed to be the most peaceful way to go. There were clusters of ice on my wet trousers. I stood up and jumped to wake my legs, then went to fetch my coat. I wiped the snow off it and wrapped the scarf around my neck, looking at the motionless body.

'Let's go,' I said, and I kicked against his legs. I dragged him to his feet: 'Freezing to death after I've rescued you from drowning, you'd like that, wouldn't you!'

I told Gunella, the good and gorgeous, later that night.

'He would never have saved you, had he been in your spot. He'd have left you to die with a big grin on his face.'

That thought, above all, caused her anger, and that I didn't feel any myself made it worse. It was my duty to swallow her fury. Later, when we knew it all, she went further.

'You should have left him to die then and there!'

Still, many years later, she remembered it at the first glimpse of winter. Lying in my arm, tugging at my fingers, she liked to say that these hands had saved her, but also Hermann Göring.

'A Jew rescuing Göring – how macabre does life get?'

I tried to be funny, 'I just did it once, Gunella. Only once did I save a Nazi's life.'

White Space
Carol Baxendale

E ven now, her Norwegian fluent, she finds her grandfather hard to understand.

'What?' Celia twists away from the log fire, and sits cross-legged before the coffee table. Her face and arms cool as her back begins to warm.

He repeats, slowly: 'This other student, the one who came with you from England . . .'

'He didn't come with me,' she cuts in.

'Javel.' He rolls tobacco, looks up at Siri, her grandmother, and winks. 'We know he didn't literally come with you.'

'Don't worry, Celia.' Her grandmother stands over the table, about to pour brandy, and stops to squeeze her arm. 'He's not pairing you up if that's what you think.' When she takes her hand away Celia can still feel its warmth through her shirt. The last time her grandmother touched her was at Fornebu Airport – a gentle hug, and brief. Celia smiles up at her, but she is already pouring drinks.

'I was going to ask where he lives,' says her grandfather.

'He exchanged with another student, in the flats over there,' she waves her hand at a corner of the room. Her words sound awkward, the emphasis in all the wrong places. The first few days always make her edgy.

'Invite him for dinner,' he says. 'Make him feel welcome. He is a friend? You do know him?'

'I know him. The art school's small, like the academy in Oslo. I wouldn't say he's my best friend exactly. He's OK. A bit strange. But he's OK. You'll have to speak English.' She laughs. 'So I guess

Carol Baxendale

you and Steve won't be saying much, will you?'

'Ha!' A puff of smoke erupts from her grandfather's mouth.

'Celia.' Her grandmother sits down on the other side of the long pine table. Celia is now looking at both of them. 'Come now. Come now, be polite.'

'Siri, she doesn't mean any harm in what she says.'

Her grandfather has blue eyes; they are like her father's, but older; they are laughing eyes, always – even when he is sad, which can be confusing. He nods a great deal, as though willing Celia, or himself, to understand – a habit formed in her childhood when neither spoke the other's language.

Her grandmother sighs heavily. 'Maybe I'm getting old. I don't know when people are being nice and when they are being horrible.'

Celia changes position and leans one arm on the table. Now she can see both the fire and her grandparents. Her feet are almost too hot in thick wool socks; pulled over a thinner pair when she came in from the art school, her feet aching with cold. She likes the feel of them, padding under her feet. When she moves through the house, over its smooth wooden floors, it's with the familiar shuffle of skiing on impacted snow.

She suddenly wants them to go, so that she can look at the family album alone. It lies at the end of the table where she left it last night, and the night before. She gives it a sidelong glance. Please go, she thinks, because she knows three nights in a row is obsessive.

'Do you remember,' her grandmother begins, 'when you were eleven Celia, and you spent Christmas here?'

'Yes.' She casts her eyes over the long tablemat; she has never really looked at it before, its fringed white linen embroidered with candles, stiffly flamed; reindeer bounding after each other, forever in the same place, identical. Their legs arch away from their bodies, looking for ground to land on. Should be on rockers, thinks Celia. That's what's missing, rockers. They'd look more natural . . .

'Well,' continues her grandmother, 'it's funny to think of the battle that went on between you and your father because you didn't want to move here.'

There is a wooden bowl with oranges and monkey nuts; Celia

would like to throw them in the air and juggle furiously, faster and faster, just to stop her grandmother's talk.

'And here you are, after all that.' Her grandmother laughs, incredulous. 'Here you are. Funny how life turns out.'

Celia hears something – the hiss and pop of damp, burnt wood. She pulls out a single orange, and tries to puncture the skin with her thumbnail. It is bitten down – a habit forgotten since she was twelve, coming back.

'It's temporary,' she says, pressing the skin, making it sweat; she digs until her thumbnail shines; the smell of it floats out – the orange smell of Christmas. 'I'm only here until the summer, maybe. That's different.'

After a long silence her grandmother says, 'I'm going up, it's getting late.' She juts her chin up at the dark window, at the falling snow, as though she could read the time there. As she heaves herself up she says: 'Yes, do invite Steve for dinner. We must think of others.'

She places her glass on the table with a wooden clink. The old nylon of Celia's shirt prickles under the arms, a drop of sweat runs all the way down to her waist.

'Oh yes,' she says loudly, hoping to drown out her grandmother's words, 'we must invite him for dinner . . . sooner the better,' and she thinks: I do think of others. I do!

When they are gone Celia opens her own photographs, kept in a child's cardboard case that she bought from Oxfam. There are details she hasn't noticed before. In the photograph her grandmother took, her mother is resting her hand on her neck; that's what she always thought. But, having developed so many photos over the last few years, she now knows it for what it is – a splash of movement. Instead, her mother is flicking her dark hair over her shoulder, and it's possible that her hand is about to move forward again. Maybe she'll lift her cup of coffee, or pick up the fork on her plate, caught by the flash. Her mother must have said something – perhaps a comment to her father, since her mouth is open; not a smile as she thought before, but tensed as she forms a word. Celia can't remember what it was she said because she was only listening to her grandfather, and it was such a long time ago. She sees now that her mother is glancing at her father's

Carol Baxendale

newspaper, and he is looking past her, at Grandpa. She sees now that her mother and father only appear to look at each other.

There is a blurring in her father's features, but rather than disguise, it emphasizes them. Astonishing how similar they are, she thinks; was it these similarities that attracted him to her mother, and he couldn't see it, knowing that he was drawn to someone whose colouring was opposite to his. Was that what he saw first – her mother's darkness?

The candle holder, which she had drawn towards her to make the scene look cosy, reminds her of the Norwegian objects in the house back in London. There is a brass candle-stick holder back there, its small handle welded to a wide and dented base. It sits on the window-sill in the hallway. It's something she doesn't see any more, since it has always been there. For a while, when she was little, it stood on her bedside table, holding a lit candle, while her father told her stories about Norway.

She looks at another photograph, given to her by her grandmother. It is a family portrait, taken in front of a wooden house. Her great-grandmother stands at the edge of the group. It's either spring or summer. The patterns on her smock could be the shadows of leaves shading her from the sun, or they could be marks on the surface of the paper; as there is no colour it's hard to tell. Like the photo of her mother and father, she sees something different each time she looks. Her great grandmother's light hair, tied back, has come loose and falls on one side of her face; it's hard to see at first. It could be the sun bouncing off the house behind, or a mark on the surface of the photograph. She's not smiling, because in those days you had to keep absolutely still.

Celia has pasted recent photographs of her own into a sketchbook, along with her old layered images. Maybe, she thinks, I'll remove the old ones. All of them. Try them out on the wall. She has wondered recently if the space between them might turn out to be as important as the images themselves; it was something her tutor discussed with her back in England. Stubborn, she had shaken her head. But now the idea begins to appeal. She looks back from her little case to the family album. Not sure, she thinks, but I'm willing to try it out. It's just an idea.

The Sun Roars In Circles
Michael Gleeson

1

Dead summer.

The appointment is for noon. Adam sits on the steps of the apartment building with his eyes closed. A million voices speak a language, the easy slap of a million tongues beat out the words, the every word, messages bouncing over the streets and against the walls, he sees walls, escaping out of kitchen windows, from underneath bed clothes, the corner of mouths, he hears scratching from within them, the tenement buildings and the Georgian houses, casual asides and the radio broadcasts letting it slip, a word here, a word there, rolling over the hot pavements and into the gutter, kicked along by the bodies chasing past.

To his right he sees the estate agent approach and recognises something in the figure. Tall and young and in a suit too big for him, his body moving freely within the shell of navy pinstripe, hair gelled and cut short.

Adam stands up and they touch hands. The estate agent speaks, a short sentence, and Adam nods having only caught the final word; his last name.

They enter the building.

2

The estate agent extends an arm and says, 'this is it.'

A two-bedroom basement apartment on Mountjoy Square.

'Seven windows,' he says pushing open the door into the front room, 'in total. A major plus because you're below street level and need all the light you can get.' He brings his hands together. 'Okay what else?' he says, looking around. 'We've got walls, yellow, a table and some chairs, only three at the mo but we're working on a fourth. A couch and two armchairs, I suppose you could call it a suite. A lot of dirt.'

They move into the kitchen

'Right,' he says, 'I know the lino on the floor here is a bit . . . rotty?' He stops to ask if rotty is a word and then shrugs, 'whatever, it's not good. We've got a fridge, a cooker, some other stuff, a sink, cupboards, another window.'

They walk back into the front room. Four televisions sit stacked on top of each other by one of the windows. 'All broken,' the estate agent says, watching Adam drum his fingers against one of the screens. 'Shall we take a look at the bedrooms?'

In the bedrooms the mattresses are wrapped in plastic.

'Wrapped in plastic,' he says, 'means they're new, another plus.' The estate agent grins. 'Basically,' he says, 'a shithole.'

Adam shrugs and the estate agent nods. 'Eight fifty a month,' he says. 'Our office at four for signing.'

In the hallway on the way out the estate agent is sure they've met before. 'Don't think so man,' Adam says, looking into the bedroom on his left.

'Definitely know you,' the estate agent says, trying to catch his eye.

'Maybe you could have cleaned the place.'

'I know you,' the estate agent says.

'Some of my friends, my girlfriend, Rachel Donovan?'

'Nope. It's you I know. From a long time ago. You're from Galway aren't you?'

'No.'

'Yeah you are.' He lights a cigarette. 'I remember you now, we hung around together in primary school.'

'I don't think that's right.'

'Course it is. I remember getting conkers with you from the nun's field on Taylors Hill and your dad got transferred to Dublin by the bank.' He pauses and smiles, 'it's funny how people's faces don't change.'

Adam focuses on the alarm, smashed and hanging limply from the wall. He squints at the wires, letting his eyes travel up and down the length of exposed copper.

'This is the tenth time I've shown this space,' the estate agent explains exhaling, 'Z priority. No one wants it.' He leans against the wall. 'And I don't care anymore. I definitely know you.'

Adam can feel his head shaking.

'We sat beside each other.'

Adam keeps shaking.

'In third class.'

Shake. Shake.

'I'm Robert Wynn.'

'That was a long time ago,' Adam says.

'I think we were best friends.'

Adam opens the door and tells the estate agent that he doesn't remember. He tells him it was a long time ago. He tells the estate agent that he's very sorry and he walks into the hallway pressing the elevator call button but thinks better of it and takes the stairs instead.

3

He is in the bath when Rachel calls. He's been drinking and isn't sure whether he can make it to the phone, let alone stand. The telephone rings out and Adam watches the door and begins to count. At six it starts up again.

'Adam.'

'Rachel.'

'Is that you Adam?'

'It's me.'

'Why didn't you pick up?'

'I was in the bath.'

'I could have been ringing all night.'

'I'm sorry.'

'Unacceptable. I mean I've been ringing for ages. What am I supposed to think? You haven't called in two days and my car is full of your stuff.' She pauses to take a breath. 'And I don't even know where you *live* for God's sake and your parents have no idea

Michael Gleeson

where you are. Where the hell have you been? Your father wants
you in his office tomorrow. *Bigtime*. Where are you? We're all
waiting for you.'

'I was in the bath.'

Rachel hangs up.

Gazes at the room, at the televisions, at the three chairs.

By the curtain he sees a footprint halfway up the wall and he
thinks of his father handing him the cheque, the man's face and
the man's voice explaining that the money was not only a birthday
gift but also an instrument of trust.

'I'm trusting you Adam, and you in turn have to trust it, and
yourself. You must trust your investments.' His father smiled.
'There are some stocks I've been keeping an eye on. Maybe this
evening before you go out we can go to my study and have a chat
about what you're thinking of doing.' He smiled again, 'I know
you're busy but I'll be away for the big day and it would be good
thing to do,' the man paused before adding, 'only if you want to of
course, hang around with an old person that is.' His father laughed.

Adam told his father he wasn't old and put the cheque into his
pocket.

That afternoon he instructed the estate agents and that night
under a dull and edgeless sky Rachel piled his things into her car.
He waited for morning behind his bedroom window, looking into
the trees, listening, the nervous stirring of the animals in the
undergrowth, their click, click, click, their way in the summer
and he reached his arms out to them.

4

Protesters are gathering. They hold signs and wear Halloween
masks. Adam counts eleven protesters in total. One of them beats
a drum and a girl with blonde dreadlocks hands out flyers. He
gets as far as 'No Space' but can't continue; the injustices are too
remote and he hasn't heard of some of the countries.

'It's your duty,' the girl with dreadlocks says watching him, 'to
be outraged . . .' but she stops when she sees him trying to hand
it back to her.

Their eyes meet.

'Today's my birthday,' Adam says.

'You will need this,' the girl says, pushing it into his chest.

Whiteness. Buildings bleached and superimposed against the sky. Black windows. A police car stalls outside a restaurant with black windows. People, their limbs and their heads, shadows in the black glass, a memory of a nightmare.

'Yeah, yeah, yeah,' the girl says, moving away.

Everywhere there is noise.

Adam looks around.

5

'What scares me the most isn't the height of these buildings, it is not about vertigo or being the Financial Centre, a legitimate target, I emphasise the word *centre*, no it's not terrorism or fear of weather; earthquakes, tornados, whatnot. It's that my reflection is out there and I can't see it.' He touches the glass. 'When I am standing at this wall, on this floor, this umpteenth floor and I'm staring out, I know that my face is out there, somewhere, saying what I'm saying and bouncing off glass. Reaching out in a terrible way.'

'What are we talking about here Dad?'

'Crossing t's and dotting i's.'

'I came because you asked me.'

'Adam,' he says sitting down.

The telephone rings. They both look at it and wait for it to finish.

'I'm going.'

'I know. And you know it's not about the money. Something happened to me in the bathroom this morning. I was in there and I caught a glimpse of myself. Do you know how rare that is? To catch yourself unawares, like a photograph you don't remember having been taken. Anyway, what struck me was that I don't amount to much.'

'Jesus, Dad. Can I at least get a drink or something?'

'My secretary is off. She keeps the bottles in a cupboard somewhere. I'm just breaking the ice. I hear things.'

'What, like voices?

'It occurred to me that I don't make a dent in the space.' He smiles.

Adam stares across the office, out the glass wall. 'I don't think this concerns me,' he says, eyes on the bay and mountains, the city outside. 'And I'm still wondering why I'm here.'

'I'm telling you Adam, forget about the money. Besides I'm writing you off on the P&L as a Charitable Subscription, same as your mother, so don't worry.' He brings his hands together making an arch with his fingers. 'I hear about your activities.'

'Activities.'

A breeze moves through the room.

Adam glances at the ceiling.

The man makes a noise.

'This is what I hear,' he says, closing his eyes.

'Dad?'

'I remember being twenty-one; in fact that's the reason odd socks make me nervous. There was a girl you see and she always wore odd socks.' His eyes open.

'We were twenty-one and the more she visited and stayed over the odder my socks became until not a match existed. When we broke up this was the first thing I noticed. I'll be fifty soon and I'm talking about physical presence.' The arch collapses. 'But either way you should be careful of the space. This denting.'

For the first time Adam realises that there is nothing on the desk but the phone, and he hears his father say, 'it might be hereditary.'

'Do you even do any work any more?'

'On no.' He shakes his head. 'When you get to my position there is a whole industry dedicated to making sure that this is the case. I have knowledge, experience, a track record. I sign documents, my name carries a resonance. I have a full head of grey hair, which inspires confidence in the business pages. I keep my eyes open and I talk. That's what I really do, I talk.'

Adam opens his mouth.

Below them is the city. Buildings and streets. A river. The lazy hum of a June evening, its final hours, reflections and orange skies crawling everywhere and all over the bay, the mountains on fire, turning the water red.

Nearly Sealed
Sarah Raymont

J ohn moves through the house with his power drill, making sure the screws are in as far as they will go. John is getting a degree but he says he wishes he were just a carpenter and nothing more. Like Jesus, says Mona. Like Jesus, says John, and he grabs her round the waist and pulls her down. He always wins when they play at anything.

John stays in his workroom typing away and making drawings of furniture. He is very meticulous. The last thing he made was their dining room table. He's made many perfect surfaces and places to put things, but Mona suspects the furniture isn't on her side, that nowhere, hidden in back in corners of drawers, can any secret of hers be found. But if John ever dies, Mona imagines herself wandering around the house, sniffing the pillow for dried breath and the smell of his head. Repolishing the table and palming handfuls of sawdust and getting down to read all those typewritten pages with a cup of tea and a box of Kleenex, as if he's doing it all so that she can find it later. Mona sees herself weeping. She sees herself moving forward in her life without John's shadow stuck to her skin.

The first time John had Mona on her back she nestled her head deep into the pillow and noted the time on the bedside clock and the color of the sky: 5 a.m. blue. He went to work, unzipping, moving aside garments without a care as to what they looked like, the fabric, the feel or the design. Sticking his thumb into her he exhaled like a bull and her pubic hair exploded out from its safe home beneath her underwear into an Afro in his face. Mona lay there, kindling for the fire. As her eyes rolled back to the window, she consoled herself with the thought that she was merely dropping a coin in God's collection bucket.

Mona knew Elliott from well back, when Mona was still waiting for something spiritual to happen to her. She had hoped it would happen with him so she played hard at prophet, that person who could be called on to say what was lurking behind the obvious shape of gestures. She tried all different kinds of feelings out onto Elliott, ones that she knows John would laugh away, letting herself sound depressed on days when she was actually happy.

Elliott never writes back the way she wants him to. But still, she tingles when he comes up, over email or through the phone. He never offers much sympathy for the woe, but he doesn't throw anything back to her in pristine condition either. He turns Mona's words into anagrams, he writes things about his lawn or his lunch or tells her about the yoga class where the man in front of him let his balls flap out of their shorts in his face each time he turned up into a Downward Facing Dog, or, a Lesson In Control. They drag their lives through the stink and hold them dripping for the other to see.

Mona's sympathy for Elliott is great. She thinks it is fine that he doesn't vote. He has never been interested in politics, and there is a beauty about him that forfeits that kind of costume. But when he told her about the summer accident when he bit off his tongue, it was real. He even fished out the ball from his mouth and pinched it between two fingers like a rose petal for Mona to see.

It is autumn now and terrible weather is predicted, the kind they save the muscle words for: gale-force, squalls, and tornado. Boats in the harbor tip over and point into one another. The sky is sunny one minute and the next it's a black mess. Everyone is made late and a tree falls over in town and breaks onto a baby in a baby carriage. John holds Mona and they stand braced in front of the bending trees in the window. She is afraid, but John understands that the elements can be pernicious. He pats her shoulders and kisses her face and puts his hands down her pants because he likes sex best when she's vulnerable, when she's scared or crying.

Little storms follow and leave more trunks and leaves to mope atop lawns and sidewalks. Nobody bothers to clear them away. To Mona, the world seems as if she herself has been let loose in it, running from tree to tree and pulling on the limbs as the little people sway and get wet from the all raindrops. John tells Mona that the best one can do is to build from it all and he plans a trip to make use of the treasure. He says that the wood is at least two hundred years old and it's just rotting back into the ground. He says that he'll build a table for the porch and maybe even a rocking chair. Mona says she would love a rocking chair, that she had one next to her dollhouse when she was a little girl. John does his impression of Mona as a little girl and then kisses her head goodbye. After he leaves, Mona wanders around the house, ordering cosmetics and refolding clothes. Everything of theirs gets so messy all the time.

Elliott and Mona rarely talk on the phone and she is taken off guard by the sound of her heart as she dials his number, it is beating so loud that she can feel it in the handset, as if she is dialing herself. When Elliott answers, Mona tells him to come over and see the house, that John is out, dealing with the weather in his own way.

Elliott's tongue is limp, jelly in a bag, going left and right and all around. Mona can feel the groove of it with her own tongue, but it's good enough. Mona tries to assert herself the way John has taught her and puts her hand around Elliott's head like it's an outboard motor. But there is nothing alive that quivers in his mouth. And Mona, without any flourish, crosses the line of pining and dusty dreams for this sloppy kiss, wet on her face. This broken-mouthed kiss Mona isn't even strong enough to pilot.

Her thoughts Ferris wheel about her head. Elliott looks so out of place in the house. Despite the fact that John is gone, Mona fears for Elliott's safety. He is fragile and John could break him. Elliott whispers, 'Mona, Mo-na,' but her name sounds so ridiculous and wrong. She opens her mouth to swallow the sound of it, she takes it like cough medicine and there it is: a flavor of sadness looking for some haven. Elliott etches away. He bites her bottom lip and runs down the flesh as if she were an artichoke leaf. His hands hold onto the sides of her face and then his fingers come alive, tracing her skin and raising the bumps, making holes through her hair to find her ears. His fingers go in like birthday candles and Mona's mind is let off its leash: she can no longer hear. Not even the sound of their lips popping against one another like a whale family feeding together beneath the sea. She is nearly sealed and it is a beautiful sound.

Tightrope
Nina Cullinane

The steps downstairs were littered with people, pounding bass increasing with each descent. White strobe hit randomly, lighting up heads and arms, bodies out of time with each other. A sea of people too dense to penetrate; too vague to make out. If they weren't here then they must be outside on the roof terrace having a sneaky joint.

She had to pass Nuno's office to get to the upper staircase. Through a frosted window, his silhouette at the desk, arm raised to ear, voice booming out. She hadn't seen him since she'd refused his offer of coke and didn't want to bump into him now, and so stepped lightly.

Full moon shone against a star-speckled sky. She turned each corner, searching. The roof terrace was vast: grey concrete and low gritted walls, beyond which the motorway; the crumbling houses of Alfama to the left; the bridge to Oeiras on the right; the docks with their cranes in front of her. She kept turning. The boys were nowhere to be seen – only places left to hide would be the toilets downstairs or on the balcony deck below.

She bent over the side.

Down to her left: a group of people, a blond head and several darker ones, but there – right at the bottom of the deck, almost out of view – two Marty and Jared-like shapes and Jared's laugh, loud, reckless. Marty had come all this way, she thought, and now his attention was being swallowed; she should have known she'd have to compete with Jared for the attention of her own ex-boyfriend. Even if she shouted they wouldn't hear, none of Lisbon would either. Her voice would have been blunted by space and

Nina Cullinane

the steely waters of the Tagus docks. What would be the point? They were obviously having fun without her.

'You like to be alone up here?' The voice was close. She turned.

'I was looking for my brother and his friend.'

'Ah, his friend. Is your English boyfriend, namorado não é?'

'Who told you that?'

'No one tells me Dami, I see your face at the bar with him. It's her boyfriend I say to myself.' Nuno's voice slow, relaxed. Smiling, he went to the ledge and sat.

'He's not my boyfriend.' She looked at the narrow ledge and the distance to the balcony below. 'I don't know how you can sit there.'

'When I was a kid I want to work in the circus, I practise all the time, swinging in the trees. I wanted to do the, como se diz, trapeze?'

'You're crazy. So what happened?' She smiled at the image of Nuno in a leotard on a tightrope and looked at his youngish face, skin smooth despite laughter lines around his eyes.

'I grow up and get sensible. You will too one day.'

'What, when I realise that life's not all about clubbing and dancing and drinking, you mean?'

He frowned. 'Dami, you are too serious. To grow up doesn't mean you have to give up a good time. You know that I am an entertainer, like a musician, comedian, actor. This is the most essential industry for the happiness of the Portuguese people and that's what I do. It's not a crime to dream of this, to want to make people happy. Inside my club you forget everything, you have a drink, smoke a cigar, whatever gets you off.'

She noticed that the more fluent he became, the more American his accent. She wanted to tell him that she was only joking, excuse it all as a spontaneous slip, but it occurred to her that he was right: people couldn't live without fun.

'Can you dance Dami?'

'I think so, what do you mean?' Hand on hip, she screwed her eyes up at him.

'I get some champagne and I show you.' He walked towards the stairs.

She turned, hesitating, and glanced down at the figures on the balcony below. She could hear laughter and loud voices. She walked along the wall, the figures becoming clearer, until she was almost directly above. But Nuno had returned, his voice coming towards her. She turned back to him.

He held up two glasses and a bottle, before letting the cork fly over the edge with a bang. She shrank back as heads turned upwards. They stood for a while, drinking.

'Let me show you how to dance salsa.' Taking her hand, leading her backwards through the basic moves, he shouted instructions:

'Left foot forward, move hips, right foot back, move side, foot forward . . .'

She mirrored his movements, body and limbs loosening, feeling her hips rotate in time to an imaginary rhythm. His pelvis dipping towards hers, the warm brush of his leg forcing hers back, bodies jigsawed then pushed apart by the force of his two arms. Together, apart, together, apart . . .

'Very good.' He pulled her in, hot breath touching her neck, skin prickling with sensation. She unfurled outwards, hips dipping away until pulled back in, thighs entwined, groins touching. Snaking in and out, in out. His voice louder, ecstatic, 'Tens ritmo menina. Muito bom, muito bom! Now we waltz. Follow okay?'

His arm found its place at the curve of her back, hands held rigid at the side. His chest on hers, leading forwards and back.

'Easy easy, smooth, we glide. Don't be tense, relax, always relaxed.'

She rested her cheek on his shoulder, smiling.

'You sleep?' He whispered close to her ear.

'No.' The taste of lemon and musk on his skin.

Five minutes passed, her feet becoming used to the pattern of steps. Gliding, lulled into synchronisation by the gentle rhythm of his body, she pulled her head up, cheek almost touching his.

'One thing I would like to change in my club is the couples should dance together sometimes, like this. Why always so separate?'

'Nuno, you're showing your age mate.'

'Fode se! Thirty-eight and you think I'm out of date. Let me tell you I know as much about the techno, house, the hip hop as you little girl. But one thing should never change; people always need the touch. In New York I go to a club where the men and women dance close. Is amazing.' He did a small whistle. 'Not like your modern dancing, all this –' he pulled away, jerking up and down from the waist, arms waving frantically. She exploded with laughter, struggling to breathe.

'We drink some more wine.' He put his arms on her shoulders and directed her to the wall. They sat on the floor, resting against the ledge as he re-filled the glasses. Out of breath, he ran his fingers through his hair and bent forward, shaking his head, letting black hair fall over his face and as he took off his jacket leaving a crisp white shirt – just the top two buttons undone – she noticed the emerald green of his suit reflect the light.

'Ai,' his voice gasped, 'Is amazing up here, don't you think? Of course you do' – he breathed out a long satisfied sigh – 'you are not so stupid as some Portuguese girls who never been anywhere, never travel.' His eyes rolled a little. 'But we must see the river, the river!' He propped himself up and got to his feet, pulling her with him. They turned and rested against the edge, looking out over the Tejo. She glanced down to her right where the shapes still sat, voices ringing out and quickly turned back again. Nuno inhaled, leaning further forward as if he might touch the night itself if he leaned far enough. Dami followed his movements as he asked her why she had refused his drugs; if she had a reason for abstaining.

'I just don't want to take them any more.'

'Never again?'

'Maybe.' Her breath rose and fell sharply. She took a long swig of champagne.

'Smoke?' He took out a cigarette packet. She agreed, taking one. 'I love it here, I never want to leave my Lisboa.'

They leaned for a while in silence, watching freight ships and passenger ferries pass over petrol water shot through with slithers of moonlight. He asked her about her future plans. She told him that she didn't have any, at which he laughed and said that a girl of her age always has a plan. Alright, she told him, so I might go back to live on the Island, try and make a go of it. He laughed,

'Your island,' eyes twinkling, then, 'But what do you *really* want to do?' And she told him that she never wanted to get a real job, at which he laughed louder, 'So, working here is not a real job?' And she tried to think of what else she could do for a living but the thought faded as he poured another drink.

'You are funny Dami, I like you.' Turning to her, smile widening. 'I should kick that boy's arse for ignoring you. Always the same these cabrónes.'

'What do you want to do when you grow up?' Eyes glinting.

'Me? I want to live every day on the beach at Peniche, maybe take up surf, eat seafood and sleep a lot every night. Read some books, Hemingway you know? Have a quiet life.'

'So you'd leave all of this behind?' Looking back at the docks, her arms resting on the ledge.

'One day, ainda não, my body is still young.'

She raised her eyebrows at him and rolled her neck, head feeling suddenly light, vision swimming and feeling the urge to vomit. She groaned as the muscles in her neck gave way and she had to struggle to keep her head up.

'Come, come we go downstairs.' Nuno helped her to her feet and walked her to the steps leading down to the doorway.

'I need to sit, let me sit here.' Holding onto the railing, she plunked herself down on the steps and sat with knees bent, head in hands, breathing deeply.

Nuno stroked her hair back from her face. 'You are white like a sheet.'

'Thanks.'

'I don't tell anybody.'

'Cheers Nuno, that really makes me feel better.'

'Fode se, you are so hard to please, what can I do?' His eyes enlarged as he turned to look at her, brought his hand up to her cheek, letting it linger over her skin.

She rolled her eyes, but his hand was clasping her chin, pulling her round, face to face. Lips soft and warm on hers. Tongue, wet and champagne bitter, locked deeper in. Her body relaxing as his hand brushed the hair from her face and rested on her thigh. She leaned in towards him.

'Wait, one minute.' Standing, he went to the door below. She heard the cold clank of the key as the lock tightened, and he was back at her side.

She looked up at the sky as he kissed her neck and edged her trousers down. Lay back as he pushed into her, thinking about a condom but it was too late now, arms around the curve of his back. Felt the tip of his shoulder blade jut forward and thought she could hear Marty's laughter in the distance, but her mind probably just playing tricks, so looked hard at the sky; blue black clouds layered upon denser blue and wondered how far it went back before you came out of the darkness and into light. She closed her eyes, feeling the top of her back rub against cold concrete, hearing Nuno's breath become louder and more frequent, thinking of Keely's laughter as she tried to explain tonight's events on the phone.

The Windmill
Angharad Hill

Tripney-on-Sea is built on a vast brown marsh beside the mouth of the River Gracie. The river is hemmed in on either side by steep, clay-seamed banks: when viewed from above, it appears as a dark fissure in the yellow sweep of the marsh reeds. Bleached, makeshift jetties are evenly spaced along the water's edge, held together against the wind by ropes. All the wooden wharves display their torn shipping flags on creaking poles.

Three bridges cross the river, tethering the town to the marsh: The Scurf, The Tinker, and The Weathercock. The Weathercock is a rail bridge, buckled around its mossy middle on account of years spent bearing the Tripney train across the wet, while the Tinker and the Scurf serve as little more than flimsy gangplanks for ramblers and wandering marsh dogs. Beyond the river, a tangle of raised clay paths form an intricate cat's cradle over the reeds and silt pools. In between these walkways, hidden by rushes, scores of wading fen birds croon, bob and paddle on the muddy wash.

There is only one building on the broad marsh. It is a black windmill, long abandoned: a dark tower with no roof and no sails. There is just one doorway. Briars and brambles form a low moat around its base. Nobody has been inside the windmill for a hundred years, although, at night, noisy pink-legged bean geese roost on its old beams.

From overhead, the windmill is like a bullet hole shot through the muddy landscape. It is like a full stop on brown and yellow paper, printed next to the long dark margin of the river.

Local children call it The Eye of the Marsh.

*

Angharad Hill

Edward wanted to show his new friends an abandoned windmill on the Tripney marshes. It was fine and bright, but a low mist still hung over the reeds. Tom and Catherine followed Edward out of town, across the common and along the path of the railway. The children passed a bag of hazelnuts and chewy pecans between them as they trampled over the damp, springy grass. Tom remembered one of their old city songs and sang it to his sister in time with the thump of her footsteps.

> *In my hands I brought the mud*
> *In my ear I brought a pebble*
> *In my mouth I brought the devil*
> *Downtothecellar, downtothecellar . . .*

The grass became thinner and more yellow as the town receded. Soon, the children were marching across the rail bridge and towards the marshes along thin tracks of baked summer mud. Edward interrupted Tom's song with a story. 'I know something horrible,' he said, and pointed at the distant beach.

'See where the sand and shingle stop? Where the sea begins? Once, a very long time ago, that border place – that line between dry land and the ocean – it would have been *over a mile further out.*'

'That's not very horrible,' said Catherine. She reached into her wellington boot and scratched her ankle. They all stopped walking while Tom shared out the fig rolls. As they munched, the children turned and looked back at the far-off town gleaming on the skyline. It was small and strange, as though they were peering at it through the wrong end of a telescope. It wobbled, mirage-like, in the high sun.

Catherine was imagining the town as an island outpost, moored between the marsh, the river and the awful sea. I am afloat, thought Catherine. She wondered whether she might be sick.

Tom was imagining an alabaster ice floe, drifting on the polar deep.

Edward was still talking.

'But listen,' he said. 'Here's what I mean. Everything you can see,' Edward swept his hand through the air, 'I mean *everything –*

my town, the marshes, the common – they would all have been one mile inland.'

'So?' said Tom.

'So . . . it means places that were once built inland are now buried at the bottom of the ocean. There might be a village out there, beneath that buoy. There might be a school below that cormorant.'

Tom and Catherine thought about their own Cottingley Street home underwater. It was satisfying to envisage kelp forests on the stairs and shoals of herring in the kitchen. They both cheered up and paid attention to Edward.

'Last year, the tides were low all through the spring,' he said. 'The sand stretched out for miles and new rocks sprang up from it, rocks from the bottom of the sea: secret blue boulders that hadn't been seen for centuries. One day, some children from the Tripney Boys' School walked out across the beach with their teacher. They had a project. They wanted to make rubbings of fossils from the new rocks – from the new old rocks. They chose the biggest blackest crag and trekked towards it. The beach was enormous and empty. At last they got there, and all the boys clambered over the rock with their pencils and brown paper. What do you think they found?'

'Smuggler's loot?' suggested Catherine.

'A slimy selkie?' ventured Tom.

'Wrong!' cried Edward. 'They found a human skull embedded in the rock!' He paused, and then added, 'It was yellow and had no teeth and the eye sockets had worms crawling out of them.'

'Was the person murdered?'

Edward shook his head, triumphant. 'That's the thing. It was an ordinary man, who died an ordinary death and was buried in a normal grave. But the ocean ate the graveyard, and the soil that he was buried in became compressed by the weight of the sea.'

'And now the crag is his coffin,' said Catherine. She munched a hazelnut and pondered this. Tom began his song again.

> *In my shoe there is lizard*
> *In my pocket is a blizzard . . .*

Angharad Hill

The train tracks fell away into the flat distance, curving over the rushes, mimicking the bend of the coastline. The children abandoned the railway, tramping into marsh country along dust paths in a neat procession. Soon the smell of boggy silt filled their noses. They left boot prints on the damp ground. Tall reeds rose up around their heads.

They were still half a mile from the windmill when Tom's singing was interrupted by a scream. It was high and wretched, like a stone splitting. Everybody stopped walking. The terrible cry was followed by series of smaller shrieks and some commotion in the rushes, a sort of hissing and wild flapping. A bright white shape rose out of the reeds and floated above the children for a moment before swooping away.

Catherine was convinced that the ground below her was about to split and buckle as some long-submerged spire rose again on the marshes. Tom's head was full of yellow skeletons. He looked at his sister. *Ghost*, they thought.

Edward was hopping about from one foot to another. 'A barn owl! A barn owl in broad daylight!' he cried. 'I can't believe it. It must be nesting around here – maybe even in the windmill. Perhaps that's where it's going right now . . .' Edward began to trot and skip into the reed bank. 'If we run it might even be awake when we arrive!'

Catherine also started running.

'Why is the owl awake? Why isn't he roosting?' she called.

Tom watched his sister. He stood very still as the pecans and fig rolls swelled up in his throat. He knew that it was bad luck to see a night bird before dusk.

He remembered all the superstitions he had ever noted in his tatty pigskin journal.

> *Arrange your shoes with the toes pointing away from the bed at night.*
> *Hang a stone with a hole through it on a piece of string outside your bedroom.*
> *An old toad in the cellar means good luck.*
> *Control bewitched horses with a rowan whip.*
> *Never gaze directly at a barn owl in the sunshine.*

The old mud tracks were confusing now, hardly paths at all. It became impossible to see between the stems or over the tall reed tops as the children scurried through the marshes. At one point, they turned a corner and surprised a skulking bittern. It leapt up, terrified, and flapped in a circle before disappearing amongst the stalks.

Nobody saw the windmill until it was barely ten feet in front of them: a sudden cylinder, dark and lopsided, like a crooked finger pointing skywards. 'We're here!' said Edward in surprise.

A ring of trampled mud surrounded the tight mesh of brambles at the base of the mill. The brambles were taller than both Tom and Edward. The old doorway, long-collapsed, was in any case completely veiled by thorns.

'But how do we get in?' said Catherine.

The children edged forward, gingerly poking at the needles and spikes on those barbed branches. Tom lay down flat on his stomach and tried to peer under the briars. Edward made three exploratory trips around the windmill. The tower seemed impassable; impossible. He said, 'I don't know if we can.'

But Tom cried, 'Look!'

By the time Catherine and Edward had run to the front of the windmill, Tom's legs alone were visible; the rest of his body was obscured beneath the thorns. He was wriggling forward on his belly. After a moment, only the soles of his boots remained. He had found a crawling space under the brambles, hollowed out by something fox-sized or dog-like. 'I think the old doorway has collapsed,' Tom called. 'There are bricks everywhere.'

'Is there any way of scrambling into the mill?' asked Edward. He looked sidelong at Catherine, who was the smallest.

'There's no room at all,' called Tom, 'all the bricks are sort of piled up here.'

Catherine dropped to her knees and crawled into the thorns. She scratched her hands and forehead on the prickles. Her left arm was pressed up against a nettle patch. She knocked her head against Tom's boot, wriggled backwards, then pushed into the space beside him.

She found her brother moving his open hand along the mound of bricks. 'There are cracks in it,' he said. He poked his finger into one hole and found it clogged with a channel of dust. He blew. 'I've seen inside. It's awful. Look.'

Catherine pushed her face up against the chink. The windmill smelt of obnoxious rotting things: she smothered her nose with the sleeve of her jumper and looked again. She saw that the secret interior was thick with thorns and fen creepers. Brown marsh water had crept up through the foundations, forming puddles on the swamped flags. The crumpled sail of the old mill lay angled across the tower with its split ribs poking upwards.

Hardly any sunlight filtered in through the lattice of beams overhead. In the gloom, it was a moment or two before Catherine realised what she was looking at.

There was something wriggling; some weak thing aflutter in the dim turret.

'Is it the barn owl?' called Edward.

Tom could not describe the scene. He backed out of the crawlspace on his belly, making room so that Edward might see for himself. Meanwhile, through her chink in the mill bricks, Catherine kept on looking at the wine-coloured blot on the flags; at the terrible white spikes of bone; at the glossy, slimy redness. She glimpsed the sheen of blue sunlight on grey plumage. But there was a dark wetness on the grey.

She had a vision of her parents with their teeth bared, yellow and bloated in the underwater house on Cottingley Street.

'It's something injured,' Catherine said.

Look Then
Yannick Hill

I t was the day after Martin's fortieth birthday and seven days since his father's death.

In the evening, Martin thought up a pop-up book, wanted and decided to make one. There and then, in his garden, he knew the dimensions of the thing, the colours that would make it up, the materials he needed.

The pop-up book would describe a childhood holiday, a place he remembered where people flew dark kites and popped up from behind dunes in stolen costumes. The book would be about bricks and sand and sea, about creatures who lived under and above the water. There would be humans, and a horror aspect.

He was near his favourite tree when he had the idea. Then he was ready to build a prototype. The garden was caught in a chorus of crickets. A bird flew from the tree and landed on his wrist and pecked his hand. Martin screamed and forgot his pop-up book idea for some minutes.

It came back to him in colours, the idea, then as a memory of the holiday, a time and a place he could picture in three dimensions, made of folded card and red thread. One colour thread. Red.

Martin's father, a quiet absurdist, a folder of cardboard, a pioneer of pop-up, had made and successfully published his first pop-up book in his early twenties. He had become a hero. Hundreds of children loved his book.

They wrote him letters about his pop-up sea, the ingeniously folded autumnal forest with tiny golden and red leaves that really fell, his folded underworld of moles, badgers and rabbits, his pop-

Yannick Hill

up hill with a trick view of a cardboard town made up of houses with roofs and chimneys, and a sun that rose over the landscape on a concealed lever. Everything that could possibly pop up from the surface of the world popped as you turned the glossy pages of *Here, Look*, Martin's father's famous book.

Martin's father was called Peter. Peter's book was world to one hundred creatures. The idea was for children to find all the creatures, some hidden, some not even. Most of the creatures were real, but some of them were invented by Peter to make up the numbers.

The thing was, Peter did not know one hundred animals. He knew animals from books and had never left town, except for one holiday with his family. But Peter could imagine animals. He thought up creatures in the bath, before he went to sleep, and when he was eating vegetables. When he ate carrots, he imagined creatures with particular eyes for seeing in the dark. When he ate fish he imagined animals that could breath water and think about things.

It was something else, this book. Is. Out of print now. The seven-year-olds who wrote Peter letters said they weren't so keen on the animals that their parents could identify.

*

Martin waited for the next morning to begin making his book.

Martin had nearly drowned on that holiday with his father and mother. But it wasn't nearly drowning that accounted for the feeling that always accompanied Martin's memory of that holiday, that time, that week, that end.

Martin did not have his father's problem of not wanting to leave the house. Martin's mother, Alice, had had to go to the shops herself to buy all the materials for her husband's new project.

Now Martin still lived in his parents' house, the house he grew up in. His mother was staying with her brother. Martin prepared himself to go to the shops. He would take hours to prepare. He estimated he would be putting his coat on sometime in the early afternoon.

Martin prepared some vegetables before going out. He peeled

and diced and sliced and opened vegetables of all shapes and sizes and colours. The vegetables were his birthday presents. He had asked for vegetables and his cousins and friends had obliged.

After doing that he folded all his clothes. After that he had to feed his one hundred animals. Almost all of his pets respected him in their different ways. Martin did not know whether or not his spider respected him, but then the spider was always busy weaving webs in the corners of his rooms.

There was only one pair amongst the animals. Two ravens, a husband and wife. Martin respected his ravens more than the other creatures who lived in and around his house. The birds advised him on his every thought and move and utterance. They circled over his bed at night to send him to sleep, not that Martin needed that much sleep. They didn't respect Martin at all, but he suspected nothing.

Martin fed the ravens last. He stood in his garden and made uncanny raven sounds, until the two, his advisors, alighted simultaneously on his scarred wrists. He fed his ravens charmed worms. The birds told him it was time to go, time to leave the garden and the house, to find materials for his pop-up book. Martin told them what he intended to call the book.

*

He found town by two o'clock in the afternoon. One of his ravens had followed overhead, was circling the town centre now. The town was busy with people not buying materials for pop-up books. Martin thought everybody looked ridiculous not purchasing coloured cardboard and a needle and thread.

The stationery shop and the haberdashery were next to one another on a dead-end street overshadowed by two chestnut trees. The shops had their respective shop fronts (the stationery shop on the left was called *Look* and the haberdashery on the right was called *Here*), but once inside, Martin saw that the dividing wall had been knocked through. He could see where the wall had been because one half of the big space was taken up by paper and cardboard, and the other half was occupied with needles and miles of coloured thread. Martin looked down the

Yannick Hill

middle of the room, at a confused frontier of folded and sewn together cardboard and bent and snapped needles.

Materials, Martin thought, *for my book.*

At first, he didn't know if he was coming or going, so many blinking things, but soon he got talking to one shop owner, then the other, and then both at once.

The keepers sat on chairs at either side of the shop space, finishing one another's sentences. They spoke laconically about the materials surrounding them, the things they had to sell. They apologised in advance about the prices of things, explained that they needed to feed their children and each other's godchildren vegetables every night. Then Martin and the keepers got talking about vegetables, about how they cooked them: caramelised, fried, grilled, roasted, boiled, smoked, sun-dried and blushed. They talked for an hour about cooking before returning to the subject of Martin's project.

Martin had to look at every kind of needle, shade of red thread, size and type and colour of cardboard available in the shop. He didn't make any decisions until everything was registered at the back of his head.

Finally, at six in the evening, sometime after the closing hours of the shops, Martin made his decisions and presented the shopkeepers, in turn, with the materials he had selected and wanted to buy. The two men stayed seated, always and throughout.

Martin spent money on needles, card, red thread, a ruler and a sharp pair of scissors. One of the men reminded him of his father because he had his shirt buttoned up to the top and his dark mouth belonged to the head of his dead dad.

The men wouldn't let Martin leave the shop before he had joined them for a double whisky. Martin had to prepare the whiskies. It took him ages, and the two men were not patient, least of all the one that reminded Martin of his father.

Martin walked out into the afternoon sun warm with the whisky and with the idea of the pop-up book stinging him all over like summer bees. The shopkeepers hadn't said goodbye. Actually, Martin was quite sure the pair of them had cursed him as he left the shop.

May your book be haunted by that holiday, that costume horror, they had said together. Martin did not turn round and react. He closed the door behind him and the sun and the whisky made him forget everything but his book. He had the materials.

By the time Martin got home, the sun was setting and everything was edged and stained in red and gold. Martin thought the reds of his threads were the best colours in the world, after the red of his blood.

*

His house smelt of one hundred animals.

Time to feed them all, make some dinner and then go to bed to think about my book, which I will start constructing tomorrow, he thought.

At seven o'clock, the ravens arrived at his kitchen window and urged him to draw up a list of everything that was going to be and happen in his pop-up book: the light, weather systems (bad and bad), waters (troubled and not), sand, soil, trees, buildings, people, words and events, plot and an ending. And cardboard mechanisms, cut and turning to a dream, a pop-up logic.

A rising and setting sun, rain, heavy at first, a wind, south westerly, a sea and a harbour town and a beach and dunes and woods; characters, his family, himself at seven, events, drowning, a disappearance, an appearance.

Martin got halfway through his list and then went to sleep with some of his new materials under his pillow.

*

He slept badly. He dreamt about that holiday by the sea, by the dunes and the woods, and in a small hotel. He remembered the kite he had been given for his seventh birthday, intended for use on their first and only family holiday. A dark blue diamond kite, and a coil of strong red string attached.

He remembered flying the kite, and being frightened of letting go of the string and drowning in the sea. He didn't remember how flying the kite and drowning were related, but they were. Their relationship was the second most difficult aspect of Martin's memory of the holiday.

Yannick Hill

There was weather in his dream, and things happening, but not always things that had really happened. Sometimes his dream took bad turns, and he would be on holiday with ravens for parents, telling him what to do, deceiving him, and his hands and face would be too big, and he could not talk, could not tell his squawking parents to shut up, especially not father bird.

*

Mother and father loved costumes. Especially bird costumes, with wings. When they were on holiday, they played in the dunes and pretended to fly and meanwhile Martin made holes in the beach.

*

Martin was woken the following morning by his ravens telling him to get started on the pop-up book. They were human-sized now, standing either side of his bed, looming over him, their wings spread.

Start folding, young man, they said.

The Shearer
Tegan Zimmerman

I am just nine years old when my father tells me about sheep. We live, like sheep, all keeping close to my mother and the house. Our house, like the other ranchers' and farmers' houses, sits comfortably on our land, plunked down ever so gently and shifting ever so slightly. I run through the trodden wheat, where the beasts get up in the middle of the night, to go tell my father he is wanted on the telephone. When I meet my father, he is busy. He is not laid back; he is not jovial. He is my father, serious without a fault and I can't understand it because my mother, she is the exact opposite.

– Dad, I tell him. You're wanted on the phone. No, it's not the bank with a foreclosure, it's nothing, nothing really at all. It's probably Gillis whose cow is having trouble with her birth. Dad will do that. Dad will bend down and grab a calf still half inside the womb and turn it right around. It's magical, like our house, that sits, surrounded by sheaves of wheat. My father says nothing. He turns to go inside, Willie at his heels. His loose stride could never be confined to a city.

My mother hands him the telephone. Her face is not as red as my father's, but she is more annoyed. She knows this is the time of year when my father must shear the sheep. He never relies on the hands to do it for him; this is his. He is something of an icon in our village - strong backed, strong willed. All of us, all the boys my age want to be him. I talk about my father to my friends like he is in the Bible, like I could open it and say here, this is where they talk about my father, now where is yours? Where is your father?

– Are you going to be here for supper?
– I don't know. I still have sheep to shear.
– Was that Gillis?
– Yes.
– What did he want?
– He wanted to go for a drink.
My mother wipes her hands unconsciously on her pants. She goes to the fridge and takes out the milk pitcher. She moves around the kitchen quickly, doing three things at once. I wait for her to ask my father another question but she doesn't. She just keeps moving back and forth, table to counter, counter to stove, stove to cupboard. Her hands are never empty. I can't tell if her actions are deliberate or not. Her obliviousness to me and my father seems to get to us. My father, without being prompted, finally speaks.
– I've still got too many sheep.
An answer to the question my mother never asked. It must be the right answer. My mother stops. She looks up, and with her breath blows her bangs away from her forehead. She smiles and goes to my father. With her wet fingers she tousles his hair.
– Why don't you take Abe with you?
I watch my father's face. His lip quivers. His head hangs down as he looks at the tiles on the floor. He looks at the tiles like they tell him everything he needs to know. All I can see are the muddy paw prints of our border collie, Willie.
– All right, come on boy.
I want to kiss these rough tiles, these over-read pages, these mills where the wheat is ground. The tiles speak to him and now I am going with him. He does not wait for me to pull on my jacket. He walks out of the kitchen and back outdoors. I struggle with my coat, tugging at the zipper. I am frantic.
– Wait for me Dad!
Father was out of earshot and out of sight. I shoved on my boots, fumbling fingers trying to tie the laces.
– You better hurry up! You don't want to make your father wait.
I look at my mother. She holds her wooden spoon in her hand instinctively stirring the mashed potatoes. Chops for supper. I

see the red on her hands. I will not have to set the table tonight. She smiles at me. I nod and run out of the house, following my father's muddy footsteps.

The path to the barn is dimly lit. Late spring. The sun sticks its tongue through tired branches – lanterns on a string. I run as fast as I can towards the lit windows of the barn, hurling myself over rotting fence poles and slick tree roots. I don't have time for caution. My head thumps with the push of my legs and awkward arms at my sides. I hit the wall of the barn with a thump. The green chipboard digs into my palm. I pause for breath. I can hear my father moving around inside, the sheep bahhing, my own breath pounding in my ears. I am too excited to stop. This is it, it is really happening.

When I go inside the barn, I am surprised by its darkness and coldness. Nothing seems familiar. I can't see the stalls where hay bales are piled in a pyramid. Slowly, I move around the corner. My father is there with a sheep pinned down beneath him. I see his strong legs firmly planted, his hat pulled down over his eyes. He is poised. I am afraid to speak. I am afraid to do anything. I stand silent in the middle of the hall, my eyes never leaving that great man, my father.

– I want the fleece in one piece.

I don't know how to answer. He is revealing his ritual, teaching me his life, but I can't respond. His face is lined, like the kitchen tiles, and he is trying to tell me something but all I hear are his words. He breaks his art down for me with concrete instructions. He stands on a tarp over the cement floor. The lamb is giving him trouble. He won't stay flipped. He keeps bobbing up and down. My father needs to stay with him.

– Pass me the rope.

Pass me the butter, pass me the potatoes, pass me that bottle, that was how he said it. Without thinking I walk over and grab the rope. It rubs against my fingers but I refuse to show any emotion. Mom will rub cream on the redness later. I want my father to see that I see how it is supposed to be. I hand him the rope. Quickly, he ties the lamb's back legs together. The lamb still stands up. My father sits down on the lamb with determination. He ties the front legs together. The lamb's black eye floats like a

Tegan Zimmerman

man lost at sea. The coat is all black and the skin too, it is as if there is no eye or starting point at all, just darkness. My father keeps his clippers in his right hand the entire time. They are an extension of himself, filled with finesse and experience. The lamb is exhausted. My father stands triumphantly over him ready to shear.

Now I shear. Stationed in Georgia, just as another war has begun, I am a civilian in the army. $5.75 is the charge. I have perfected the art of the electric clippers. The young private in my chair talks incessantly. I listen. He is a farm boy and for this reason I take to him. He has a common shy grin and a handsome face. He has dark eyes and dark brows. It's hard to tell just how old he is, because his voice is very deep, and almost lulling.

    – I want to be an officer.

    – Everyone wants to be an officer.

    – I know that, but I mean it. The other boys talk about stuff like girls, and cars, they talk about things that are behind them. Things that don't matter. All they talk about is the past. The future's murky for them. Not me though, I have nothing in the past I want to hold onto.

    – What about your parents?

    – My brother's going to take over the farm. We've all known for a long time. It was never meant to be my responsibility. And he'll be good at it too, much better than I could ever be.

    Mechanically, I swish the hair from the back of his neck, moving around the chair from side to side, like summer wheat on a windy day. I go for my shears. The young man waits while I retrieve a push broom from the tiny closet at the back of the shop. I begin to sweep up around the chrome plated Belmont barber chairs, and under the long Formica counter. I stare at the tiles. The young man waits for me to shear the last, the final hair that is left. I hold the shears in my right hand. Always the right hand.

    The counter extends the length of one wall beneath an expanse of mirror. I cross to the antiquated cash register near the front door and punch the cash key; the register chimes and the drawer rolls out with a clatter. The young man leaves bumping his shoulder against the door. I step out from behind the register lowering myself into one of the functional chairs that line the back wall of the shop. This is where generations have had to sit to await their turn in the barber chair. This is my kingdom, though I can't help but remember when I was nine years old and the way my father's hands never shook that night or any night while he held the shears.

Hemingway Heard
It In The Rain
W. David Hall

This episode starts like every other one this season: It's minutes before dawn on a Tuesday. I am counting the shells exploding near Panmunjom – 39, 40, 41 – when the sirens go off and generators hum. The company clerk's tinny voice screams 'incoming wounded', 'incoming wounded' over the loudspeakers. The opening credits are rolling. Hawkeye kicks my bunk. BJ throws pillows. 'Time to rise and shine, Watermelon Man,' Hawkeye says. 'The work of the war waits for no one.'

Three transports, school busses in their civilian life, rush into our perimeters and choppers fill the night, bringing in the wounded. I don my scrubs. A nurse ties my mask. I take my place on the white 'X' used to mark actors' positions.

Lights. Camera. Action.

The parade begins.

By 'work of the war' Hawkeye means the meatball hack and stitch jobs that pass for surgery in the OR. Operating Room. Oscillating Realities. I do what I have been trained to do, remove shrapnel from forearms and thighs, sew up perforated bowels, plug punctured stomachs, make Raggedy Andy soldiers fit enough to return to active. BJ and I work methodically and in silence. Hawkeye, however, works in comedy. 'Look at all these bodies,' he says. 'Who told them Sinatra was playing tonight?' He usually offers a single one-liner per patient. This morning, he hasn't stopped with the jokes. He's scared he's going to lose someone in the onslaught and I tell him to hold it together. In 28 minutes (with two 30-second commercial breaks, one where I discuss the merits of a new life insurance plan and the other where I sing the jingle for Ovaltine), it will all be over. Between patients, I time it. 29 minutes later, he asks me how I knew and I say it's my system. Happens this way once a week every week. As I pull off my gloves, I see a piece of paper under the table. I pick it up.

```
WATERMELON  hesitates.   SHIPMANN
twists,  contorts,  and  screams.
Then SHIPMANN dies.
```

'OK,' I say. 'Who's the wise guy?' Nobody confesses.

I take a break to tell the priest what I had found. 'You doctors are elbow-deep in near-death every day,' he says. 'I admire your imagination with these elaborate coping mechanisms.' 'It isn't about coping,' I say, 'it's about the show.' He asks for the page. When I look in my pockets, I find lint. He shakes his head. He makes notes. 'It is good you came to see someone about this hallucination,' he says. 'It was not a hallucination,' I say. 'It was as real as you are.' 'And as real as you, my son. When was the last time you had a decent night's sleep?' 'A week ago, maybe,' I say. 'Not since then?' 'No. That night, I had a sheet dream,' I say. Hemingway heard it in the rain. Infantry say sometimes you can see the bullet. We surgeons have a saying: don't dream about the sheet. I did. In the dream, I was operating with the white sheet covering me. 'I've never known a good surgeon who put any faith in those dreams,' he says. 'But there's more,' I tell him.

Or at least I start to. There's another siren, another 'incoming wounded,' and I'm back in OR. I'm trying to stitch a kid up, but he's a real bleeder. The nurse running the suction is in my line of sight. 'Only way I can get to the wound,' she says. 'Do better,' I say. She twists a bit and I see the soldier's face. 'It's Mark Shipmann,' I say, 'he played Ben Bradley on *City Detective*.' 'Chart says Private Lucas,' she says. 'No, he's Mark Shipmann.' She ignores me. Shipmann or Lucas turns his head to me. 'It's sweeps week,' he whispers. 'Get me an Emmy.' Blood erupts from somewhere inside him. The suction isn't working. The nurse is screaming at me to do something. 'Let's make this death really real, okay,' Shipmann whispers. So I wait. BJ rushes to my table, but I force him back. 'Let me save him,' he says. 'No,' I say. 'It's for the show. Give him a second, just for the camera.' We wrestle, knocking into beds and nurses and IVs while Shipmann or Lucas twists and contorts and moans. I slam BJ against a table and move toward Shipmann. He spasms and two nurses are holding him down. Then he stops moving. I try what should be a simple tuck and fold stitch, but my hands won't cooperate. They only shake. 'He's dead,' the nurse says. 'Just for now,' I tell her.

At mess, I try to work through the 'X', the script, Shipmann. 'What spooked you back there, spook?' Hawkeye asks. 'Just going for the Emmy,' I say. 'Hope I can win me one of those,' Hawkeye says. He humors me, but he wonders about this war, too, asking the same questions with his jokes, trying to find the answers in punch lines. It's cutting comic relief. A role to build a career on. BJ just looks at me. I've told him over and over that this is just a show but he insists on being difficult. I've told him to see his agent about getting a better part, but he won't listen. 'I could have saved him,' he says. 'He'll be fine,' I say. 'It was in the script.' He glances at Hawkeye. We sip our coffee in silence. Nobody eats. Just like on television.

After mess, I'm reassigned to triage with Catherine, a nurse. I examine the wounded, along with the beds, the sheets, the clipboards, the props. Damn near authentic. 'Tell me about your ideas,' she says. 'It's television,' I say, 'what's to tell?' 'I hope I'm played by someone beautiful,' she says, moving towards me. 'Of course you are,' I say. I want her. I want our own episode or even a spin-off. We kiss and everything floats along on the strains of violins. 'Mozart?' I ask. She pulls away. 'What?' she says. The music is gone. She touches me and it returns. 'The incidental music. You know, the kind the music men use for love scenes.' 'Love scenes?' She slaps my face. 'If you think you're gonna get some from me, you're crazy.' She runs from the tent.

BJ relieves me moments later and I'm sent to see the priest. 'Tell me about Shipmann. BJ says he could have been saved. Hawkeye says so, too. They say you were negligent.' 'I wasn't negligent,' I say. 'Shipmann wanted an Emmy. I helped him get it. He's not dead.' 'He's a soldier, not an actor,' he says. 'No, he's an actor, starred on *City Detective*.' The priest pauses. 'Tell me about the dream,' he says. 'I did,' I say. 'I mean the rest,' he says. I feel the cameras pressing against me for a close-up. I nod. The flashback sequence starts.

At the end of the dream, I pulled the sheet off and I see that I'm sewing this kid up, just a routine closing, and I heard someone off-stage yell 'cut, that's a wrap' and the wounded and the nurses in the background became stage hands and they moved parts of the OR tent to a different location on the sound stage. A suit from Story Development pulled me aside and whined an apology. 'Nothing we can do about history, eh,' he said. 'What history,' I said. 'No black surgeons in Korea in the 50s.' And I stopped and the kid I was working on became a dummy and the blood turned to red water and I was thinking about calling my agent but I don't have an agent because I'm a doctor but I couldn't remember how to sew the kid up and I told the suit 'I'm a doctor, not an actor.' 'You method people kill me,' he said. 'But I'm there, now, really,' I said. 'And you were doing a great job,' he said, 'but veterans watch this stuff.' Hawkeye was there but it wasn't Hawkeye, it was Alan. 'Nothing we can do,' he said. 'I tried to fight it, but the network won't listen. Talk to your agent.' But I didn't have an agent. Then I was in a taxi moving through Hollywood and I knew it was Hollywood because I saw the letters on the hill but it looked like Korea and I expected to hear the explosions or see the choppers but the sky was clear and the hill was peaceful then there's a squawk and I expected to hear 'incoming wounded' but it's the cab driver's radio and he told whoever was on the other end that he was taking that guy who plays Dr Watermelon downtown and I interrupted and said 'I'm the real Dr Daniel Wilson. In Korea, my nickname was Watermelon Man.' He laughed. 'This is why I love you people. Think you always have to keep up the act for the little guys.' Before I can protest, I'm at the agency watching another suit pace the floor, then he leaned on his desk. 'Look, network brass is like that,' he said. 'They just write characters in and take them out. I can see about getting you on again, maybe as a mechanic or something.' 'But I'm a surgeon,' I said. 'You *played* a surgeon,' he said. 'Why doesn't anyone believe me,' I said. 'No, it wasn't that. You were convincing. And those commercials you did, the life insurance thing and the Ovaltine spot, grabbed some viewers that way, believe me. But it's research.' 'But I'm telling you, I am research. I was there.' 'I hate to do this,' he said, 'but you need a break. Take some time away. Go travel. Now I've got another appointment, you understand.' I nodded, but I didn't understand. He reached out to shake my hand and when I gave him mine, I saw my hands dissolve – brown skin to pink flesh to red blood capillaries and veins, to bone, to nothing. I was a surgeon without hands, an actor without a job.

The priest writes something down. 'You believe in life after death, right?' I say. The priest nods. 'Follow me back to the OR tent. I'll resurrect Shipmann.' We go back to OR. Shipmann has a sheet over him. I pull it off. 'I bet you've got your Emmy,' I say in his ear. 'Time to rise and shine.' I shake him and he is cold and emotionless. He doesn't move. 'Give me another take, Father,' I say. Just one more would have done it for a new storyline where Dr. Watermelon Wilson saves the kid but Shipmann is cold and unresponsive. 'He told me he wanted the Emmy,' I say.

The priest wraps his arms around me as I cry. 'The colonel okayed a week's leave for you to see a psychiatrist in Seoul,' he tells me. When we go collect my kit, Hawkeye and BJ raise martinis in my honor. 'We'll have a few nurses keep your bunk warm,' Hawkeye says. I snicker as I pack and when I'm done I salute everyone. I step out of the tent and see the words, white against the black backdrop, clean and clear, scrolling in front of me.

The ending credits roll.

The Scripts

Introduction
Val Taylor

The Scriptwriting stream of the MA in Creative Writing at UEA grew out of a module, *Script & Screen*, taught by Malcolm Bradbury on the techniques of screen adaptation. The stream has evolved considerably since those early days, and is now a discrete programme that runs concurrently with the Prose Fiction and Poetry streams. Its distinctive character lies in its interdisciplinary study of writing for four dramatic media: theatre, film, television and radio. Throughout the year, in the UEA workshop teaching format, writers tackle core issues of dramaturgy such as the creation of a believable 'story world', characterisation, plot and story structure, point of view, genres and styles, and explore differing strategies invited, or demanded, by the four performance media.

The workshop group comes from a wide array of writing backgrounds: some are feature film screenwriters, others, stage dramatists; some are already steeped in radio storytelling, whilst others wish to write in series or serial formats for television. All of them sit around the workshop table, taking apart first the case study texts, and then each other's writing, each bringing to bear a different combination of knowledge and expertise. And this is the exciting part: listening to a radio writer attuned to the possibilities of sound suggesting to a screenwriter how *she* might evoke those same pictures, or to two stage and television dramatists haggling over the means at their disposal to give access to a character's secret moments. Sometimes it's almost like watching a cartoon – a light-bulb going on above someone's head as an idea from straight out of left-field strikes, and the next time

Scripts Introduction

the script comes up for discussion, there it is.

Since 1998, when the Scriptwriting stream began in this format, the writers have seized the opportunity to experiment with several of the dramatic media – one even found herself adapting her feature film as a possible 10-part radio drama for *Women's Hour*, whilst simultaneously continuing to rewrite her screenplay for her film producer! Others have found that the experiments of colleagues have served to deepen their own sense of commitment to one particular form. Because the explorations are collective and interactive, everyone gains, in his or her own particular fashion. For me, this is the most valuable element of the MA: writing is a lonely business and often a frustrating one – just being in the same room with a group of one's peers, trading insights (and sometimes, friendly insults) can make all the difference. Everything is generously shared – except, of course, the royalties . . .

– Val Taylor

Full Metal Jackets
Marcus Robinson

FADE IN:

INT. DAIRY CANNING HALL – DAY

Gleaming tin cans rattle along the production lines that twist through the canning hall of a dairy. The whirring blades of a large extractor fan set in the wall chop the natural light that seeps into the room. RUFUS *and* BEN, *two teenage production employees in grubby white overalls, are caught in the strobe effect.*

> CHARLIE (O.S.)
> Your mission is imperative to the continuing success of this operation.

BEN *and* RUFUS *survey a chaotic scene. Two puzzled* ENGINEERS *peer into the innards of a large industrial cooker. Thousands of tins, which bulge unnaturally, are strewn across the floor. A mop-up squad of* OPERATIVES *tentatively gather the fragile tins onto wooden pallets.* CHARLIE, *an imperious shift supervisor in his fifties, watches them from a safe distance. He turns back to* BEN *and* RUFUS, *who jump to attention.*

> CHARLIE
> Situation analysis. Cooker jam at o-seven hundred hours. Four thousand tins of creamed rice pudding. Cooked for three hours. Normal cooking time thirty, that's

three-o, minutes.

> RUFUS

That's bad?

> CHARLIE

It's a question of pressure and volume.

A bang is followed by a yelp from one of the OPERATIVES. He falls to the floor, covered in creamy goo. A tin-shaped welt can be seen on his forehead. CHARLIE sighs and rolls his eyes. BEN and RUFUS swallow.

> CHARLIE
> *(shouting behind)*

Get that man to a medic!

> RUFUS

What's our, er, mission?

> CHARLIE

Special assignment. I want you to take them out.

> BEN

Take them out?

> CHARLIE

Take them out. All of them. Asap. Down to the incinerator. And burn them.

> RUFUS

Burn them?

> BEN

Won't that be –

RUFUS
– dangerous?

CHARLIE
Standard operating procedure. Risk is within acceptable parameters.

BEN
(*under his breath*)
Whose risk?

CHARLIE
Burn them, lads. With extreme prejudice.

CHARLIE *turns and marches away. His wellington boots flap and his white coat trails in his wake.*

EXT. LOADING BAY – DAY

A forklift truck loads the last pallet of over-cooked tins onto the back of a rusting electric milk float. The forklift hurries away, the flashing orange light on its roof blinks madly in warning. RUFUS *and* BEN *clamber into the cabin of the milk float.* RUFUS *carries a pint of milk.*

INT. MILK FLOAT CABIN – DAY

BEN *familiarises himself with the float's archaic controls as* RUFUS *takes a swig from his bottle.*

RUFUS
You driven this pile of junk before?

BEN
Once. With Charlie supervising.

                    RUFUS
        How come he ain't doing this himself?

                    BEN
        Charlie don't drive.

                    RUFUS
        You sure you know what you're doing?

                    BEN
        A doddle. Electric power. One forward,
        one reverse gear.

                    RUFUS
        CD? Aircon?

BEN *points up and sticks his arm through a hole where there used to be a sunroof.*

                    BEN
        Top of the range.

RUFUS *sticks his head through the hole and turns to assess the pallets and loose cans piled high in the back of the float. It looks dangerously over-loaded.*

                    RUFUS
        That's quite a payload we're carrying.
        OK, let's get on with it.

BEN *turns the power key and the float comes to life with a faint electrical humming. He taps a dial on the dashboard.*

                    RUFUS
        What's up?

                    BEN
        Power level dial isn't working.

BEN *engages reverse and eases his foot onto the accelerator pedal. The float lurches backwards.*

RUFUS

Easy does it!

EXT. LOADING BAY – DAY

The float jolts as BEN puts it into forward gear. It turns laboriously and trundles out of the loading bay. The loose cans in the back roll around.

INT. MILK FLOAT CABIN – DAY

As the float makes slow progress past the buildings in the dairy complex, BEN taps the power level dial again. It still points to zero.

RUFUS

Problem?

BEN

Nah, faulty dial more like. This thing is charged every night.

RUFUS

You sure? Says who?

BEN

S.O.P. Standard operating procedure.

RUFUS

Good, then all we've got to do is keep it smooth. And we'll both get home in one piece.

The float shudders and it pitches violently sideways. BEN stops the motor and he and RUFUS step out of the cabin to survey the road ahead.

Marcus Robinson

EXT. TRACK TO THE INCINERATOR – DAY

The moss-covered concrete track leading to the incinerator is cracked and uneven. To BEN'S *vivid imagination every crack look like an abyss. Likewise* RUFUS *sees the potholes as deep caverns.*

> BEN
> Oh hell. We'll never make it.

> RUFUS
> *(shrugging)*
> Ain't nothing for it. Ours not to reason
> why, ours just to –

> BEN
> Do or die?

> RUFUS
> I was going to say 'shift the pie' though
> technically, it's pudding.

BEN *and* RUFUS *climb back into the float and brace themselves.*

INT. MILK FLOAT CABIN – DAY

RUFUS *places his half finished pint of milk onto the dashboard.*

> RUFUS
> Saw this in a film once. All you gotta do
> is focus on the milk. Keep it from
> slopping around and we'll be okay.

> BEN
> Smoothly –

BEN *edges the float forward as gently as he can. The milk bottle immediately falls off the dashboard and shatters in the footwell of the cab.*

There is a clanking sound on the roof. BEN and RUFUS look up as a tin falls through the hole and lands next to them on the seat. It bulges at the seams as burnt cream oozes from it.

> RUFUS
> Incoming!

BEN and RUFUS simultaneously evacuate the cabin from either side.

EXT. TRACK TO THE INCINERATOR – DAY

BEN and RUFUS dive into ditches at the sides of the track. There is a loud pop followed by a squelch. A close view of the float shows the inside of the windscreen covered in coagulated rice.

EXT. INCINERATOR – DAY

The float arrives in a field. BEN peers through a small clean patch in the rice pudding-splattered windscreen. He disembarks, followed by RUFUS. They look as if their nerves are shot. They stare at the incinerator, no more than an open burning pit, in disbelief.

> BEN
> Talk about cutting edge technology.

> RUFUS
> So what now?

> BEN
> I say we reverse up to the pit, tip in everything from the back, then leg it.

> RUFUS
> It'll never work.

> BEN
>
> Got a better idea?

BEN *reverses the float up to the burning pit then joins* RUFUS *in the back. They start shoving pallets and loose tins into the fire.*

> RUFUS
>
> Quick as we can. Then we can get out of here!

The rapidly heating cans start to hiss. The smoke grows thick and black.

> RUFUS
>
> Ben, I don't like the look of this!

> BEN
>
> Chill man, we're nearly there.

> RUFUS
>
> I really don't think putting these tins into heat is such a good –

An exploding tin erupts from the flames, arcs through the air and deposits scalding hot rice over a wide area.

> BEN
>
> Light-my-bloody-fire!

The wooden pallets closest to the incinerator start to burn. Several more tins fly out of the flames. One hurtles towards RUFUS *and explodes.*

> RUFUS
>
> Arggh! I'm hit!

> BEN
>
> Hang on, I'll cover you!

BEN *steadies* RUFUS *who clutches his abdomen. Rice pudding seeps out between his fingers.*

> RUFUS
> Gross. Bought it right in the gut.

BEN *helps* RUFUS *into the cab.*

INT. ELECTRIC MILK FLOAT – DAY

BEN *switches on the motor, engages forward gear and presses the accelerator. The float surges forward six inches, then stops. The humming of the motor fades. There is no power.*

> BEN
> We'll have to bail!

BEN *and* RUFUS *scramble out.*

EXT. TRACK TO THE INCINERATOR – DAY

BEN *and* RUFUS *run away from the float, which is now also on fire.*

> BEN
> Don't you just love the smell of burning
> milk in the morning?

> RUFUS
> Never mind that, Rambo. How are we
> going to explain the collateral damage?

> BEN
> *(sighing to self)*
> Dairy is hell.

Behind them, the fire rages like napalm. The float is ablaze. The air fills with acrid smoke and exploding cans.

FADE OUT.

Dappled Shade

An extract from a one-act play for stage

Margaret Johnson

A leafy garden in summer. Two women sit at opposite ends of a garden seat.

CAROLINE
When we moved to this house the garden was just grass. No borders, no rockery, no arbour.

CARLA
The trees must have been here.

CAROLINE
And out there it was all allotments. Until they bulldozed them to make a school playing field.

CARLA
At night, the floodlights are four full moons shining through the poplars.

CAROLINE
Seven years, it took. Seven hard years of toil and imagination. God only knows how much money. PAUSE. But I couldn't stay just because my garden had come into fruition.

CARLA
I liked to sit in the arbour to listen to the garden.

CAROLINE
I designed the rockery. All the basic layout of the garden, really. A lot of those plants in that big border over there are my cuttings. Most people in this road have plants that started their lives on my windowsills.

CARLA   The shrubs at the front of the house protested through the window at me, clamouring to be pruned.

CAROLINE   Forsythia. Love Lies Bleeding.

CARLA   Yellow. Red and white.

CAROLINE   Was it a competition?

CARLA   It seemed like one.

CAROLINE   Carla gives us sausages and Yorkshire puddings! Carla sold five paintings in an exhibition! Carla says we can have a dog! PAUSE. It was very difficult to give my girls up to a stranger you know, even if it was only for two days a fortnight.

CARLA   And Wednesday nights. Half of the long holidays.

CAROLINE   Without them I rattled around in my rented house.

CARLA   There were such a lot of holidays.

CAROLINE   Sewing party dresses and baking cakes.

CARLA   And one day you made a fairy castle cake for Ellie's birthday with perfect regimented turrets and tall, graceful towers. And she rejected it because it was pink instead of blue.

CAROLINE   You knew that?

CARLA   We laughed about it.

PAUSE.

CAROLINE   You saw what you wanted to see.

CARLA   I was in love.

PAUSE.

CAROLINE   So was I, once. And he with me.

CARLA   I couldn't think about that.

CAROLINE   I don't expect you could.

CARLA   And then one day while he was at work I looked through his drawer to find some envelopes, and I carried on looking after I'd found them. And there were your wedding photos. The honeymoon. Shared kittens. Suzie, new-born at your breast. None of it matching the woman he talked about. The flat, toneless telephone conversations to make arrangements for the girls.

CAROLINE   Ex-wives. Ex-girlfriends.

CARLA   I shoved the photos into the bottom of the drawer and when he came home from work he kissed me passionately as he always did, and I told myself he would never have done that to you. He would have given you a peck on the cheek at the very most and eaten his tea without asking anything about your day.

PAUSE.

CAROLINE   Before we moved here and the babies came, I'd paint all day in the studio he built for me in the garden. Losing myself in composition and form. And he'd come to find me when he got home. Often we made love on an old rag rug on the studio floor with the last light of the day glancing in through the dusty window.

CARLA   And having children changed all that forever.

CAROLINE   But you never had children, did you?

Carla lowers her face to hide her hurt.

CARLA   No. No, we didn't.

PAUSE.

Without looking, Caroline reaches for Carla's hand and squeezes it briefly. They both stare straight ahead into the trees, their faces painted by sunlight and dancing leaf patterns.

Hard Sell

An extract of a screenplay

Rob Kinsman

FADE IN:

INT. MARTIN'S OFFICE – DAY

Documentary 'Talking Head' interview with MARTIN PIGGOT – early 40s. He is being interviewed by JOSH, early 30s.

> MARTIN
> No, I wouldn't say the artwork was bad. I mean, certainly, he would have improved with time. But he had a career change, you know? Ended up pursuing other avenues.

> JOSH
> You think if he'd gone to art college . . .

> MARTIN
> Yeah?

> JOSH
> He would have improved his technique?

> MARTIN
> Of course.

                    JOSH
If we could get back to the protesters.

                    MARTIN
God. Yes?

                    JOSH
I mean, they obviously think this is
wrong. That it's offensive.

                    MARTIN
I can understand that, and I respect
their views. But look, I'm just trying to
make sure everything is presented as
sensitively as possible. Because hey, I
know this guy has had some bad press
over the years. There were some things
he was responsible for . . .

                    JOSH
The Holocaust.

                    MARTIN
Yeah, that's one of them.

                    JOSH
World War Two. The death of 40
million people.

                    MARTIN
Both valid, you know, valid examples.
But maybe this work can help us
understand why. And if we can do that
with this exhibition then, I don't know,
maybe we can make sure it never
happens again.

CREDITS

INT. MARTIN'S OFFICE – DAY

Through the lens of a documentary camera we see a
RECEPTIONIST leading the crew into Martin's office.
MARTIN sits looking thoughtfully out the window. Behind him
are posters for 'Hitler: A Retrospective.'

                    RECEPTIONIST
          Martin, the TV people are . . .

                    MARTIN
          Yeah. Hi guys. Good to meet . . .

He looks up at the crew. He double takes when he sees them.

                    MARTIN
          I didn't know you were going to be . . .
          OK. Welcome one and all. Have a perch.

                    JOSH
          Thanks.

As the crew settle into seats we catch our first glimpse of them.
They all look extremely Jewish.

                    MARTIN
          Very welcome here. All of you. Very, very
          welcome. Thanks Rach.

The RECEPTIONIST leaves.

                    MARTIN
          So, here we are. All friends together.
                    (beat)
          You guys got here OK then?

                    JOSH
          There were some protesters outside.

Rob Kinsman

                    MARTIN
Ah, them. Maybe . . . Can we build to
that? Probably best if we do a bit of
background first. Before we get into that
whole protester can of worms. You
think?

                    JOSH
OK.

                    MARTIN
Yeah, let's just remind people about the
Africa thing. Here.

He pushes some magazines across the desk. On the front covers
are photos of Martin meeting African tribesmen.

                    MARTIN
The whole tribe will be extinct soon.
And what are we doing about it? I mean,
sure, I set up the permanent exhibition;
a lasting tribute to their dying culture.
But it's just not enough, damn it.

                    JOSH
You got mixed reviews for that
exhibition, didn't you?

                    MARTIN
If you call four 'must sees' in leading
national papers mixed, then yeah, I
guess I did.

                    JOSH
I'm thinking of Adrian Bradley.

                    MARTIN
Ah, Adrian Bradley. Well, bless him, he's

not what he used to be. You know.

He mimes drinking from a bottle, then remembers the camera and flicks a guilty look at it with his eyes.

                    JOSH
          I suppose many people were surprised
          you chose this as your next project.

                    MARTIN
          Well, some people see a brick wall and
          try to go around it. Some people go
          through it. Or over it. I'm that kind of
          guy.

                    JOSH
          Which kind?

                    MARTIN
          Through. And over. Kind of the best of
          both really. I don't shirk at a challenge.

                    JOSH
          Have you been surprised by the media
          coverage?

                    MARTIN
          Well, yeah, to be frank. I mean, where
          do these people get their information
          from? They take something done with
          the best intentions and corrupt it.

                    JOSH
          You think they've misunderstood your
          aims?

                    MARTIN
          Absolutely. I mean, that's why we invited

you guys here. We thought it would be
good to have someone close to the nerve
centre. Show people how it really is.

                    JOSH
And how is it, really?

                    MARTIN
Busy, you know? It's a complex
operation. Lots of different strands.

                    JOSH
What's your role?

                    MARTIN
I guess I'm Commander In . . . I'm
overseeing things. Keeping everything in
line. We're trying to appeal to the youth
market. No way anyone's going to be
calling this exhibition elitist, let me tell
you. Unfortunately, making the artwork
available for everyone creates certain
demands.

Someone snorts off camera.

                    MARTIN
Is he all right?

The camera swings round to see where he is looking. SAMUEL,
the elderly sound man, is facing away from MARTIN, the boom
slung casually over his shoulder.

                    JOSH
He's fine.

                    MARTIN
OK.

(beat)

He's not moving.

JOSH

He's fine.

MARTIN

Yeah.
(beat)
Where were we?

JOSH

You were telling us about your role.

MARTIN

Yeah, I'm glad we're talking about this. Because the thing is, the thing people don't seem to understand, is that a lot of the elements were already in place when I got this gig. The board had set up this deal with the Yanks, managed to get hold of some of the rare pieces. Things that are usually kept in military buildings. And the board, they've got an educational remit. Bringing art to the, you know, the people that don't want to see it. They thought this project could have a popular appeal, so they signed the deal and started inserting other elements.

JOSH

Elements?

MARTIN

Yeah. Then they needed someone to tie things together, track down some of the other works. They knew there was a risk

this thing could get out of hand if it
wasn't handled carefully. And who are
they going to find who can do all that?

He points his thumbs at himself.

MARTIN
So here I am, trying my damnedest to
make sure everything's executed
tastefully.

JOSH
You think holding the exhibition in a
mock-up bunker in Romford is tasteful?

MARTIN
That was one of the given elements.

A History of Large Birds Disappearing

An extract from a radio play

Virginia Fenton

FX	*The clacking sound of an old-fashioned typewriter.* *Pause.* *The sound of pages being turned.*
Colin Hollings	In the moa we see the result of laziness and neglect. Life was so easy in New Zealand that the great bird first refrained from flying then lost the power of flight. It is an emblem of stagnation and decay and its fate is a shocking example to all who are inclined to give way to slothful habits. James Drumond, professor of biology, wrote that in 1907. He blamed the moa for its own demise and suggested we might learn a valuable moral lesson. As if the moa, the naughty thing, got its just deserts. As if it were an ill-behaved child.
FX	*The sound of knocking becomes louder and more insistent.*
Colin	I suppose the cause of that noise must be Mrs Jamison, my secretary. What does she want now? No doubt, I'll soon find out.
Mrs Jamison	Mr Hollings?
Colin	Of that, I am quite certain. Busy, Mrs Jamison!

Mrs Jamison	(Entering) Sorry, what was that you said?
Colin	I said 'I'm busy'. (He begins to type slowly) Flat out in fact.
Mrs Jamison	Never mind me.
FX	*The sound of furniture being moved.*
Colin	Mrs Jamison, what are you doing?
Mrs Jamison	I really don't understand, Mr Hollings, why you insist of sitting in the darkest corner of the room. It would be much better to position yourself closer to the window, to take advantage of the natural light.
Colin	Ah, but I prefer to be next to the bookcase.
Mrs Jamison	Yes. The bookcase. I would if we could move that bookcase . . .
Colin	I find the view from the window can be distracting.
Mrs Jamison	Distracting? Oh, I do apologise! Am I disturbing you? I only came in to say . . . no, it's slipped my mind. I'll remember in a moment.
Colin	Would you mind closing the door? On your way out?
FX	*The door closes. Pause. Knocking again. The door opens.*
Mrs Jamison	I remember. There was a telephone call earlier, while you were busy.
Colin	Which particular moment of the day was this?

Mrs Jamison You were in a meeting.

Colin Oh, proper busyness. Not this other kind.

Mrs Jamison That's right. A Mrs Alice McKenzie telephoned.

Colin What did she want?

Mrs Jamison She didn't wish to leave a message. She would prefer to speak to you directly and will contact you this afternoon.

Colin Alice McKenzie? Who is Alice McKenzie?

Mrs Jamison She can't be local. I'd be sure to recognise the name if she was local.

Colin Thank you, Mrs Jamison.

FX *The door closes. Typing. Pause.*

Colin It took me nearly two years to write the first chapter. It took quite some time to get the hang of it. I'd always wanted to write. History. It's what I was good at when I was at school. I wanted to be an historian. My teacher, Mr Haden, said I was one of the most outstanding pupils he'd ever taught and should I wish to pursue an academic career . . . My father insisted I should be a solicitor, as he was.

Colin's father I've given the matter some thought Colin and I've decided it would be for the best if you made the law your vocation.

Colin It wouldn't do to argue. Even as a grown man I was . . . frightened of my father. He went a bit strange, late in life. Sometimes he used to cry. I hated that, couldn't bear it. He cried liked a small child cries. If he spilt his tea or dropped something on the floor he'd start this blubbering about it.

FX	*Typing. Pause.*
Colin	He used to shout at me when I was a boy.
Father	Colin! Colin!
Colin	I would run away and hide in the woodshed and bawl my eyes out. Then suddenly – it seemed sudden – he was this old man, crying. Somehow it made me what to shout at him.
Father	Colin! (His voice fades) When I get my hands on you boy . . .
FX	*Typing. Pause.*
Colin	I'm not complaining because I ended up a solicitor. It isn't such a bad thing but it wasn't what I really wanted. In the end though, I thought, I should write. I should write something permanent. My wife wanted me to wait until after I retired.
Maureen	Why don't you wait until you have more time Colin?
Colin	Maureen, I told her, I've waited long enough. I try to spend a few hours on my book, every day.
FX	*Typewriter. A page is ripped out.*
Colin	Damn and blast this bloody machine! At one time I thought of asking Mrs Jamison to do the typing

but it would never do. She'd only interfere. She can't, or won't, understand why I'm writing it at all. Why don't you write a local history, Mr Hollings? Heroics and hardships of the pioneers! People would be much more interested in that.

Mrs Jamison	Much more interested.
Colin	Write about Hawera! A history of our community! As if history is no more than local interest, old-fashioned gossip. You need to see the whole thing, Mrs Jamison. You need the whole thing laid out before you. It's like climbing a mountain to see the lay of the land. That's what history is.
FX	*The metallic 'ting-ting' of an old style telephone.*
Mrs Jamison	Mr Hollings? A Mrs Alice McKenzie on the line for you.
Colin	Hello. Hello? You'll have to speak up I'm afraid . . . (Click) How strange.
Mrs Jamison	It sounded long distance.
Colin	I'm sure she'll call back, if it's important.
FX	*The shuffling of paper.*
Colin	Alice McKenzie. It's quite a coincidence but I came across that name just this morning when I was reading about moas. I simply wanted to get the facts straight, the likely date of extinction. I found this book that said the last known sighting of a moa was by a young girl called Alice McKenzie at Martins Bay in the late nineteenth century. It was reported in this book as if it really

happened. As if it was something more than more childish invention. She was seven years old. She wanted to believe it was a moa she saw. It's like when my daughter, Ruth, used to tell me about fairies in the garden.

Ruth   (As a child) You wouldn't believe how many fairies we've got in our garden daddy. You could see them too, if you wanted.

Colin   Are there elves and unicorns as well? Nymphs and dragons?

Ruth   No. Only fairies. They've got ballet slippers like mine.

Colin   She always did have quite an imagination. Ruth was very bright, very good at school. Her report cards were excellent. She got married not long after she left school. I wanted her to go away to university and so did she for a while. She'd known Richard since they were at primary school and he used to tug her plaits or whatever it was that boys did to annoy girls in those days. But by the time she turned seventeen she didn't think he was that bad after all. Three boys they've had. I look at Ruth sometimes . . . it isn't disappointment I feel. I wonder, that's all. I look at Ruth and I wonder if there's any disappointment in her life.

FX   *A telephone rings.*

Ruth   (As an adult) Hello mum, it's me. How are you?

Maureen   Very well, thank you dear.

Ruth   How's dad?

H

A History of Large Birds Disappearing

Maureen He's fine. Wrapped up with his book of course. He still won't let me see it. Not until it's finished, he says. I keep saying – Colin we've been married for thirty-two years, why won't you let me see it?

Ruth I'm a bit worried about him. He seems odd lately.

Maureen That's nothing new . . . I'm a little worried too. Not terribly worried but he can be so distant. We were having a conversation the other day and I swear he'd mistaken me for someone else. He snapped out of it but for a moment I'm not sure he knew who I was.

Ruth What are we going to do?

Maureen To do? Well, there's not much that can be done. A holiday perhaps. Maybe we could go to a beach somewhere.

Ruth The beach sounds good. Dad would like that.

FX *The sound of waves fades into the crackling of an old recording.*

Alice My name is Alice McKenzie. I grew up at Martins Bay. It was a remote area in the South Island. We were a pioneer family. It was not an easy life but as a girl I knew no different. We used to drive the cattle along the beach and my brother and I sometimes saw the prints of a very large bird in the sand. Occasionally, we caught a glimpse of the bird itself. Once, I came across it as it slept on the sand dunes. It had bright blue feathers, brilliant blue plumage. I tied its leg with a flax rope and secured the other end to a sapling. It woke, made a loud, harsh noise, broke loose and ran away into the bush.

Virginia Fenton

FX	*A heavy book is thumped onto a desk.*
Colin	Brilliant blue plumage! What sort of fantastic creature did you Alice see that day? Why would anyone bother to write it down? I might as well put that Miss Ruth Hollings, aged six years, sighted several tribes of fairies living in the garden of her childhood home in Hawera, Taranaki.
Ruth	(As a child) Daddy, I've seen them.
Colin	This will not be the last recorded sighting as no doubt generations of New Zealand children will continue to see fairies in gardens up and down the length of the country.
FX	*Hurried typing fades to background noise.*
Colin	There are no reliable sightings of moas recorded in living memory and all evidence suggests that the great bird died out many centuries ago. The foreign reader must not be misled by the inclusion of such speculation. (His voice fades) Surely the recording of history . . .

Ashes

An extract from a one-act play for the stage

Stephen Phelps

Evening. A darkened set. The burnt-out ruin of a boarded-up suburban house. Mary, smartly dressed, 48 years old, Irish descent, stumbles across the wreckage. She picks up charred items from the blackened rubble – looking to see if she recognises them. Budge, mid-30s, down and out drinker, appears, unseen, to one side.

BUDGE   She's not here.

MARY   (*startled*) Who?

BUDGE   She's fucked off.

MARY   Who?

BUDGE   (BEAT) Jenny.

MARY   Why?

BUDGE   She's not going to hang around waiting for you, is she?

MARY   Who?

BUDGE   You. (BEAT) Police, Probation – whatever you are.

Stephen Phelps

He stumbles into the house, sits in a charred and tattered armchair.

What's she done now?

MARY   You tell me.

BUDGE   She don't need to do anything. Not with you
            bastards. (BEAT) Why don't you just leave us
            alone?

MARY   I don't even know who she is. Never heard of
            Jenny. (BEAT) I'm on a visit. Just looking.

BUDGE   She lives here. (PAUSE) Like me.

He produces the stump of a cigarette from his jacket.

Cigarette?

He lights it himself.

MARY   No thanks.

BUDGE   Looking at what? The dregs. What's interesting
            about us?

MARY   Not you.

BUDGE   What then?

MARY   Nothing. I just . . .

BUDGE   You been here before/

MARY   No, I/

BUDGE   Don't fucking lie. Don't lie to me. I know. I've
            seen you. (PAUSE) How many times you been?

MARY   It doesn't matter. It's not/

Mary is making for the door . . .

BUDGE   Course it fucking matters. To me. It matters to me.

MARY   (PAUSE) I'm sorry, I shouldn't have/

BUDGE   Well you have.

Barring her way.

      So cut all this shit.

Mary runs her hand slowly down the charred door frame.

MARY   The place. This place. I know it. I've been here before.

BUDGE   This dump? We've been here for months. Jenny and me.

MARY   I used to be here. Used to live here. It was a long time ago. A long time. (PAUSE) Look, I'd better go. I shouldn't have come. Not after all this time. I'll go.

BUDGE   Why did you? Come. Why did you come?

MARY   It's not. It doesn't matter. I just wanted to see it. It meant a lot to me. I'll go.

She turns to leave then stops in the doorway.

      I was told there was a girl here. A girl. Who knows something. Is that Jenny?

Stephen Phelps

Budge ponders.

	I can get you some fags. When she's back. (BEAT) Or some drink.
BUDGE	What was it like? (BEAT) Before. Before this. What was it like before this?
MARY	Before the fire? I can't remember, really. (PAUSE) Like a house. Like any other house. I suppose. We were happy here. For a while. (PAUSE) I don't like to see it like this. Sad it should be like this. Still. Sad's nothing though is it? (BEAT) I thought they would have fixed it. Something would have been done. Should have. I thought it would have been a home again. Someone's home.

She looks around touching parts of the wreckage.

	I thought they would have made it nice again. By now.
BUDGE	Nice? What does that mean? Fucking nice?
MARY	Not nice. Just a home. Somewhere someone could live.
BUDGE	I live here. It's my home. My fucking home. Sometimes. And Jenny. This is where we sleep. Sometimes. When we can't get nowhere else. (PAUSE) Or maybe that's not living to you. Not what you call "living". Not the way we live. Not like this.

He is rampaging around the place.

	But this is it. This is where we live. Eat. Drink. Sometimes we even cook. Here.

He kicks some burnt embers around.

> When we can get a fire going. (BEAT) And sleep. This is where we sleep. And fuck. Sometimes. Life goes on. Even when you drink. And you've no job. And you have to steal your clothes. And then someone steals the blankets from under you. Life goes on. That's what you fuckers never recognise. Life goes on.

She has started to cry.

> Oh, shut the fuck up. I don't give a toss about you. Crying's no good. Get used to it. This is how we live. Lots of us.

She is sobbing.

> What's this? A bleeding heart? It's a little bit of Blair's Britain, this – but they don't talk about this bit. (BEAT) Do they? (PAUSE) Don't like shouting? Rather you weren't here. Sorry you came. Changed your mind.

MARY (PAUSE) Someone died. Here. In this room. A long time ago. I slept in this room too. (PAUSE) And made love. Fucked, here. Made love, actually. But then he died. In this room. (PAUSE) And I thought they would have done something about it. By now. It's the last insult, really. They've done nothing. Nothing to put it right. (PAUSE) All that wrong, and nothing to put it right.

Silence while Mary rubs her face dry and Budge shifts uneasily. He starts to ferret around behind the sofa and produces a plastic bag.

BUDGE Beer?

MARY   No. No, I won't. I don't.

BUDGE   Don't what?

MARY   Drink. Any more.

BUDGE   How did he . . . Die. How did he die?

MARY   The fire. In the fire.

BUDGE   But that was years ago.

MARY   Eight years. It was eight years ago. And it's still just the same. (PAUSE) Can't mean much can he? He burnt to death in here. Kenny. And the others. Two others. (PAUSE) He just lay down here, like he always did, and fell asleep, and then it started. But he would have known. At first I thought about the pain. I just couldn't get the pain out of my head. I thought about the burning. His hair. And then his arms. Burning through his shirt, and then his arms. Like meat. Burning like meat. (BEAT) Like cooking. I just kept thinking "like cooking". Did you know that? In the pictures, it's like meat, like cooked meat, burnt meat. Black, like burnt meat. They showed me the pictures.

BUDGE   What is all this shit? Pictures. What pictures?

MARY   They showed me the pictures. The police.

BUDGE   Whose pictures?

MARY   Their pictures. Police pictures. The crime scene.

BUDGE   What crime?

MARY   Arson. The fire. It was arson. Deliberate. Three men (BEAT) burned to death. And they said it was deliberate. (PAUSE) Why would anybody do that?

She wipes away some tears.

But it wasn't painful you know. It wasn't the burning. He wouldn't have known. They said that. He wouldn't have known anything. It's the smoke.

She picks a burnt stick from the remains of Budge's fire.

Apparently. They could tell. Asphyxia. Inhaling the smoke. In a stupor. A drunken stupor. (BEAT) See, it helps. Sometimes.

BUDGE   So why you? The photographs? Why you?

MARY   But I don't believe it. They knew. They knew all right. Else why would they have been by the door? All three of them. Kenny never slept by the door. Even when we were drunk we wouldn't have slept by the door. Kenny and I slept on the sofa, and Mac was always in his chair. (BEAT) Over there.

BUDGE   What about you? Where were you?

MARY   Me? Oh I was there. I was there to start with. But I left. I had a row. With Kenny. And I left.

He offers her a cigarette. She accepts and he lights it for her.

BUDGE   Well you're still here. That's why you're here. Because you left.

MARY   Yes. That's why I'm here.

BUDGE   I mean if you hadn't left, it would have been you too. I mean you would have been burnt too.

MARY   If there had been a fire.

BUDGE   Well there was.

MARY   What if there wasn't? Maybe there wouldn't have been if I was there . . .

BUDGE   But how could you have stopped it? You said it was arson. (BEAT) I mean did they ever find who did it?

MARY   (PAUSE) Me. They said it was me. They said I left, after the row with Kenny, and that I'd set the fires before I left. Three of them. Three different places. I'd say that's pretty determined wouldn't you? That what they said. Three fires. And that's what they took me to court on.

BUDGE   Court?

MARY   They charged me, and I went to court. (PAUSE) And then they convicted me.

BUDGE   What of? (BEAT) What did they convict you of?

MARY   (PAUSE) Murder. What else? What else, if I set fire to a house and three people died?

Budge takes a deep swig from a can of beer.

BUDGE   Well, bugger me. The famous Mary McCarthy – murderess of this parish. You did it, did you? (BEAT) After all these years . . .

MARY   Did I? (BEAT) Do it?

BUDGE   Well they wouldn't convict you if you didn't, would they? I mean, you said you did.

MARY   I said they convicted me . . .

BUDGE   Well that's good enough for me.

MARY   Well what if I didn't? What if they were wrong?

BUDGE   Wrong?

MARY   Yes. What if they were wrong?

BUDGE   Well did you?

MARY   I don't know.

BUDGE   You don't know! You don't know whether you killed three people . . .

MARY   I don't. I don't know. They told me I did and they showed me the photos. And they told me I'd threatened Kenny. In the pub. That evening. Earlier that evening. Said that I'd kill him. Someone said they'd heard me threaten to kill him. Someone phoned the police and said they'd heard me threaten to kill him.

BUDGE   And did you?

MARY   I don't know. You tell me.

BUDGE   You don't know if you threatened to kill him?

MARY   You tell me. I don't know if I killed him. Them.

He takes another swig of beer.

BUDGE   I'm not getting this. You got convicted didn't you?
            I thought you said you'd gone to court and been
            convicted?

MARY   I did. I was.

BUDGE   Well there you are then.

MARY   But now I don't know. Never did really. After I
            got convicted there were people who said I
            shouldn't have been. They said there wasn't
            enough to convict me. And they wanted me to
            fight it. So I did.

BUDGE   Well you would.

MARY   And it worked. It took years, but it worked.
            (BEAT) They got me lawyers, top lawyers.

BUDGE   Oh, excellent. That's fucking priceless, that is.

MARY   They put the papers together, and it was the
            Home Secretary, it went all the way to the Home
            Secretary.

BUDGE   The Home Secretary.

MARY   He said the Appeal Court had to look at it again.
            And they let me off. They said there wasn't
            enough. They said I didn't do it.

BUDGE   Well that's it then. I expect you're happy with
            that.

MARY   I should be.

BUDGE   Well isn't that enough then? Would be for me.

MARY   But that's just it. It isn't. Not for me. (BEAT) You
        see I don't know. I can't (BEAT) can't remember.
        I never have. That night. I just can't remember.

BUDGE   That would be enough for me, I can tell you.

MARY   I remember drinking in the house with Kenny
        and Mac, and the other fella, and I remember we
        were arguing, and then we went out. And that's it.
        Until about two in the morning, when I came
        back, and I walked down the street.

BUDGE   I can never remember two in the fucking
        morning.

MARY   I could smell the burning. Smoking. Still hot, and
        that terrible stench, that awful smell. It sticks in
        your throat. Seven years and I've still got the taste
        of it. And then I realised it was a fire. A fire. And
        it's flesh of a man you love that's burning.

For a moment neither meets the other's gaze.

        I sobered up then.

Remora

An extract from a short animation

Jamie D. Corbman

EXT. CITY. DAY.

It's a bright summer day, and TOBY, a bicycle courier, is hurtling through the streets, dodging cars, jumping the pavement, and scattering pedestrians. He is an adept – if somewhat reckless – rider. Suddenly, the road seems to twist like an amusement park slide. The world spins. TOBY is sitting on the pavement. People gather around him.

> VOICES
> Hey buddy? Are you OK? What happened? He just fell off his bike. Did he hit something? No, he didn't hit nothing, he just fell.

TOBY grips his head and rubs his eyes. He looks up at the people around him. He stands up, and for an instant, he looks down on them as if they are all very much smaller than him. He snaps out of it. He picks up his bike and walks away, unsteadily walking his bike. He seems in a daze, and the crowd grows quiet and parts to let him through.

INT. DR ERWITZ'S OFFICE. DAY.

We are in a gleamingly sterile examination room. The polished white enamel surfaces have a blue-green glint under the cold,

247

artificial lighting. TOBY is sitting behind an X-ray monitor. He sits with a stoop and his arms hang limply at his sides. His whole body seems to have given up on him. We can see his body from his neck down, but his head is behind the monitor, so we can see his skull moving as his head would. On the monitor, there is a small, pulsating red orb within the image of TOBY's skull. DR ERWITZ, an elderly, bent, and balding man is pointing to the red orb with a pointer.

> DR ERWITZ
> Well, this would certainly explain the headaches and the dizzy spells. It's called a Glioblastoma multiforme. A grade IV astrocytoma. It's brain cancer. You have six months.

TOBY seems dazed. He stands up and puts on an oversized jumper. Then he puts on a pair of sunglasses and pulls up the hood of the jumper.

EXT. CITY. DAY.

The city looks much less appealing now. TOBY is walking home. He is buried under his hood and behind his sunglasses. The city is cold, grey, and windy. Wet sleet is falling and forming dirty, partially-frozen puddles. As TOBY walks, the people seem to get smaller. Eventually, he is more than twice as big as many of them. The tiny people scurry past him as if they are train cars running on tracks.

TOBY gets to an old apartment building. He walks inside.

INT. APARTMENT BUILDING LOBBY. DAY.

TOBY takes a key on a chain around his neck from beneath his jumper and fits it to a keyhole next to the elevator doors. He turns the key, and the doors whoosh open. TOBY presses the down button and the elevator reluctantly makes its descent. When he reaches the bottom, the elevator comes to a grinding halt that echoes forever up the shaft. TOBY walks through the doors and into his flat.

INT. TOBY'S FLAT. DAY.

TOBY walks to the mirror and looks at himself. He removes the sunglasses. He takes down the hood. He sighs, and for a moment he recalls the image of his own skull with the glowing orb. The X-ray replaces his reflection in the mirror. He sighs and looks down at the sink. He looks back up at the X-ray. Something about it catches his interest. The red glow is not an orb at all, but it seems to be something like the silhouette of a ballerina. He turns his head to the side to get another vantage point. He seems to notice something about his head. He reaches up and finds that he can open the top of his head like the lid of a box on hinges. A tiny ballerina, REMORA, is pirouetting on his brain. We hear a MUSIC BOX MELODY. He gingerly plucks her from his brain and holds her up to eye level. REMORA twirls and dances on his hand.

TOBY is awestruck. He stares at her.

TOBY

You're . . . beautiful.

REMORA stops spinning. She reaches out a hand to TOBY.

REMORA

Dance with me.

TOBY slowly leans in as if pulled by an irresistible force. He takes her hand. The room spins, and the music box melody switches to a FULL ORCHESTRA playing the same song.

Jamie D. Corbman

INT. BALLET STUDIO. DAY.

We are suddenly in an expansive ballet studio with sunlight streaming through picture windows. The floor is polished wood, and mirrors line one wall. The studio has been in disuse for some time, and white drop cloths hang over some furniture and equipment scattered throughout the room. The air and the mirrors are dusty, but for the most part this is a happy place. It is quiet and away from the rest of the world. TOBY is wearing a white tuxedo with tails, and REMORA is in a pink ballerina costume. They dance and twirl together. This is an odd image, because TOBY is very tall and REMORA is smaller than his hand. At times, she alights on the drop cloth-covered furniture in order to look TOBY in the eye. At other times, TOBY holds out his hand and REMORA twirls on it. As they dance, their shadows grow long at a visible rate. The distorted shadows creeping across the floor appear as elongated ghost images. They finish the ballet and bow to each other. Suddenly, TOBY grabs his head. Something is wrong. He has a severe headache. We hear a ringing noise.

> TOBY
> Something's wrong.

> REMORA
> Dance with me.

He falls to the floor, dropping REMORA in the process. He crashes like a sack of bricks, but her tutu allows her to float gracefully to the ground. She continues dancing and twirling around TOBY's body as he clutches his head and writhes in pain.

> TOBY
> I can't. Something's wrong.

> REMORA
> Dance with me. Dance with me.

TOBY groans in pain.

> REMORA
> (Fading into echoes)
> Dance with me. Dance with me. Dance
> with me. Dance with me. Dance with
> me. Dance with me. Dance with me.

INT. TOBY'S FLAT. DAY.

TOBY is still standing in front of his mirror. He carefully touches his head, but it seems to be a single piece now. His head is throbbing, and the phone is ringing. He answers the phone.

> TOBY
> Hello doctor. Honestly yes, quite a lot of
> pain, in fact. OK, I will then.

He puts his sunglasses back on and raises his hood.

EXT. CITY. DAY.

TOBY is crossing the city again back to DR ERWITZ'S OFFICE. He weaves through other people and avoids everyone. He clearly does not enjoy being out in public. He gets to the building. It is a towering glass and steel affair. People with all sorts of bandages, slings, and casts are filing in and out. TOBY wades through the crowd and disappears into the building.

INT. DR ERWITZ'S OFFICE. DAY.

DR ERWITZ looks in TOBY's ears and eyes. He takes his pulse, looks in his mouth with a tongue depressor, takes measurements with calipers, and makes notes in his pad. He speaks as he does so, and sets down bottles of pills on a tray next to TOBY.

Jamie D. Corbman

DR ERWITZ
Now I can give you these for the pain,
but I'm afraid that they won't be very
effective, so I'm also giving you these.
Now if you take one of these, then you
shouldn't also take one of those until
they wear off. If you're feeling dizzy or
you're experiencing blurred vision, then
you'll also want to take one of these.
Unless you think that the first ones are
causing it, in which case, you should just
switch to the second ones. Now the
second ones are known to cause
digestive problems and nervousness, so
if you experience either of those things,
then you'll want to take this and this. Of
course once you take all of these, you
may begin to feel sluggish, depressed,
and experience loss of appetite. All of
these are normal, but if they interfere
with your daily pattern, or you have an
inability to sleep properly, I can also give
you these.

INT. TOBY'S FLAT. DAY.

TOBY is sitting at the table counting out the pills. He is lining
them up in neat stacks. He gets confused and tries to sort and re-
sort them, but he cannot make sense of which ones he should
take. He seems to be getting very tense, and his head begins
hurting. He rubs his eyes and his temples and mutters to himself
as he counts the pills. His hands begin shaking and he
accidentally knocks over the piles of pills, reducing the order to
chaos.

TOBY
Dammit!

He slams his fist on the table. He begins counting again. As he does so, the top of his head opens and REMORA climbs out. She stares up at him and waits patiently. His eyes meet hers.

INT. BALLET STUDIO. DAY.

TOBY and REMORA start dancing, but almost immediately, TOBY trips over his own feet. He starts again more deliberately, but he still trips. REMORA is unfazed and continues dancing. Her dancing appears lithe and liquid next to TOBY's plodding steps. He starts again, this time staring at his feet and counting out the paces.

> TOBY
> One, two, three. Left, two, three, four.
> Right-no, I mean back, two.

INT. TOBY'S FLAT. DAY.

TOBY is still counting the pills. But now he is doing so intently and feverishly. He seems intent upon completing the task, but the harder he tries, the more complicated it seems.

> TOBY
> Four blue ones, two, three, four. And
> two codeines, those are pink, two, three-
> no wait, orange, two-no not that orange,
> the oval ones.

INT. BALLET STUDIO. DAY.

TOBY is still counting his steps. His rhythm is totally off and he cannot keep up with REMORA. He trips and lands in a heap.

                          TOBY
          Damn. Screw it.

INT. TOBY'S FLAT. DAY.

TOBY knocks over the stacks of pills again and accidentally
spills one of the bottles as well.

                          TOBY
          Damn. Screw it.

He grabs a handful of the pills and chokes them down. He is calm
for a moment. His headache seems to subside, and he relaxes.
Then he grabs the sides of the table and looks around the small
room frantically.

INT. BALLET STUDIO/BALLROOM. DAY.

TOBY is on the floor staring up at the walls. The walls seem to
melt away revealing a decadent VICTORIAN BALLROOM
with a black and white marble checkered floor, flowing red velvet
draperies, and long gilt mirrors on the walls. The place is lit by
flames licking out of tall torches. TOBY looks around clearly
disoriented. He tries to get up but the floor ripples and heaves
like the ocean. He staggers and then sinks back to the ground and
blacks out.

INT. TOBY'S FLAT. DAY.

TOBY struggles to his feet, knocking over his chair in the
process. He fights his way to the telephone. He picks it up and
dials. He leans against the wall as it rings.

                          TOBY
          Yes, may I speak with the Doctor, please?

INT. DR ERWITZ'S OFFICE. DAY.

DR ERWITZ is examining TOBY. He takes his pulse, checks his temperature, then uses his light to peer inside TOBY's mouth, eyes and ears. ERWITZ holds a large hypodermic syringe filled with a thick green substance up to the light. He squirts out a few droplets and then injects the contents into TOBY's neck. TOBY swoons and loses consciousness.

INT. BALLET STUDIO. DAY.

TOBY dressed in his white tuxedo bows to REMORA. He takes her in his hand and they begin an elaborate ballet.

> TOBY
>
> I love you.

INT. DR ERWITZ'S OFFICE. DAY.

ERWITZ turns on the sink. He washes his hands and begins laying out tools. He leaves the water running.

INT. BALLET STUDIO. DAY.

A rainstorm kicks up outside the studio. Rain begins pelting against the picture windows.

> REMORA
>
> You can't love me.

INT. DR ERWITZ'S OFFICE. DAY.

ERWITZ opens each of TOBY's eyes and shines a bright blue light into them.

Jamie D. Corbman

INT. BALLET STUDIO. DAY.

A lightning bolt outside flashes in the studio. TOBY and REMORA miss a step but recover.

INT. DR ERWITZ'S OFFICE. DAY.

ERWTZ takes a long pair of forceps and sticks them in TOBY's ear. He begins prodding around and attempting to pull out any offending bodies.

INT. BALLET STUDIO. DAY.

Something is wrong. The floor begins to buckle and wave like the ocean. The walls sag and then come alive. The whole studio expands and contracts like a lung breathing.

                    REMORA
          You can't love me. Just dance with me.

Two Nice Girls

An extract from the beginning of a screenplay

Verity Peet

EXT. RURAL ROAD, SUFFOLK. NIGHT

A pleasant, moonlit night. Looking down from on top of a long hill, a narrow country lane is stretching away for miles to the horizon. Golden in the dusky twilight, acres and acres of arable stubble stretch across the panorama, broken only by the road and occasional tree.

Caption: Summer, 1985

We notice two tiny specks of white light coming along the road towards us. They become bike lamps and, closer still, the smudgy figures of two teenage girls on their bikes.

Credits sequence over:

ANNA and KATY are excited and breathless from cycling uphill, but mostly from their singing and cider. Faintly at first, and increasingly louder as they get closer, we hear them singing – and they're no angels – a duet from an old American musical, like I'm Just A Girl Who Can't Say No *or something equally upbeat. Katy does a comedy low voice for the male part. They make over-emphasised hand gestures to the song.*

ANNA and KATY get closer to the top of the hill. Singing fades under voice over.

ANNA V/O (AGE 27)
That's when it all started. I'd always had

dreams, but . . . that was the first time I'd ever really told anyone. I mean told anyone and meant it.

Near the very top of the hill the girls have to get off and push their bikes. The singing has stopped; they're too breathless. ANNA has long dark hair, big brown eyes and with her ready smile is naturally beautiful. KATY isn't pretty but is striking with her short spiky hair. ANNA has a blossoming, curvy body. KATY looks like a stick insect.

ANNA V/O
That summer was the beginning. My dreams didn't seem impossible, because they matched someone else's.

At the top they pause for a moment before getting back on. They push off down the other side of the hill. They are heading towards a small town of lights in the distance.

ANNA V/O
It was the summer I met Katy.

The girls gather speed, wave their arms in the air, dancing on their bikes with 'no-hands' and wobbling dangerously and delightedly.

KATY AND ANNA
Wheeeeeeeeeeeeeeeeeeeee!

From back behind the girls, on top of the hill, they become smudgy figures again, disappearing into the distance towards the town. The red back lights of their bikes become specks before vanishing.

ANNA V/O
I'd always thought that I was going to be . . . That I was going to somehow become fantastically beautiful . . . Or discover I had a talent for something . . . That something . . . magical would

happen, could happen . . . That summer
I learned I wasn't the only one.

INT. WINE BAR. NIGHT

A tacky, small-town wine bar. Friday night and it's busy, loud and smoky.

KATY is attempting to look sophisticated in black everything whilst ANNA has dressed to attract male attention in Madonna-esque layered vest tops and bangles. Both girls are making sweeping gestures with their cigarettes and making every attempt to be noticed. They are talking in a language resembling French. Anna is supposedly the French one and Katy the bilingual host. Both sport pronounced French accents and so mostly get away with it (it's a small town) and if they don't, they don't care.

> KATY
> Vous desirez an autre cherie?

> ANNA
> Ah merci, mais je n'aime pas sherry.

> KATY
> Non non non mon petit smart arse. Est-
> que tu voudrais le vodka?

> ANNA
> Ah, mon petit fleur, je pense . . . Je pense
> . . . Er peutetre . . . Nous erm pas de,
> nous n'avons pas de . . . mooch de
> seeeilver?

> KATY
> Que?

> ANNA
> La moneeeee!

Verity Peet

KATY

Ah, l'argent! Alors, pas de probleme.
Regardez a la bar s'il tu plait. Moi pense
il ya les dreeeink complimentaire. Oui?

*Over at the bar IAN and DAVE are watching them. KATY and
ANNA give them the come on and giggle. The lads – who look like
members of Young Farmers – move over to them.*

ANNA

(MUTTERS) Try and get some crisps
too.

The lads arrive. They have pronounced Suffolk accents.

KATY

Well hello.

ANNA

Bonjour!

DAVE

All right if we join you?

KATY

Sure.

ANNA

Qu'est qu'ils peut?

KATY

Jusque a petit grope je pense . . .

ANNA

Please to sit.

The lads sit.

                    IAN
Is that French?

                              ANNA
Ah, oui. You spik French?

                    IAN
No.

Anna looks the question at Dave too.

                    DAVE
Nah. I used to do extra maths instead
. . . Only cause I messed around like.

                    ANNA
Vat is extramass?

Embarrassed pause. ANNA is all innocence.

                    DAVE
You girls want another drink?

                    KATY
Oh, thanks very much. Mine's a pernod,
neat, and Er . . . Desiree's is er . . . what
do you . . . Qu'est-ce vous desiré?

Girls stifle giggles.

                    ANNA
Ah, merci. Le vodka et l'orange si'l vous
plait.

                    DAVE
Vodka and orange, right?

KATY
(*Mock respect*) Right!

ANNA
Alors, Katrina, est-ce que il y a any shance de la grande?

DAVE
What did she say?

KATY
Well she was wondering if . . . Oh no it doesn't matter.

KATY pretends to admonish ANNA with a long nonsense word.

KATY
Ouerdoucherfordilajunegaves!

DAVE
(*But DAVE is smitten*) No, it's all right, really. She was wondering if what?

KATY
Well, she was . . . Well have you been to France?

(DAVE shakes his head)

Well in France the measures are a little more generous you see, and . . .

IAN
I bet she wants a double.

KATY
Do you mind?

IAN and DAVE exchange glances.

ANNA
What you all say?

DAVE
Course not. D'you want one an'all?

KATY
Oh well, all right then, thanks.

DAVE goes to the bar. ANNA and KATY let IAN get uncomfortable.

ANNA
Vat is your name?

IAN
Ian. What's yours?

ANNA
A . . .

KATY
Desiree.

ANNA
Desiree.

KATY
And I'm Katrina.

IAN
That's Dave.

Pause. Gets uncomfortable again.

ANNA
Ave you go France Ian?

                         IAN
          Nah.

                         KATY
          Been anywhere?

                         IAN
          Um . . . Went on the Norfolk Broads last
          year.

                         KATY
          Really? Get as far as Lowestoft?

                         IAN
          No, we only got to . . . *(realises she's taking
          the piss)*

Dave comes back with the drinks.

                         DAVE
          All right?

Ian looks dubious.

                         KATY
          Mais, Katrina! Où la creeeeisps?

The Poetry

Introduction
George Szirtes

About a year ago I was asked to write an article about recent developments in Hungarian poetry, and, not knowing enough, I wrote to a young Hungarian poet to ask her what she thought was happening among her contemporaries. After the enormous changes of 1989 changes were to be expected. The poetry, she said, was denser, more personal, more contemplative. But this was only a tendency, she warned.

There have been no comparable changes in Western society, though changes there have undoubtedly been, the world after 9.11 being some sort of landmark, though the repercussions of that event, as of 1989, may be expected to work their way through the sytem for a while yet.

Besides the ordinary periodic shifts in sensibility that are usually signalled by the arrival of a new defining voice (but how do we know who is decisive, when they are being decisive, and for whom they are deciding), the shifts in English poetry, from Dylan Thomas, to Philip Larkin, Sylvia Plath and Ted Hughes, to Heaney and Mahon and Harrison, to Muldoon, to Armitage, Paterson, Shapcott, there are specific changes in the nature of feeling and thinking that arrive from history's left-field. Shelley famously said that poets were 'the unacknowledged legislators of the world'. It is probably easier, however, to think of poets as parts of the world's nervous system, the nerve endings of language. They register the sensations available to them.

The talents that a course like the MA at UEA brings together are naturally diverse. They come, this year, from Canada, India (via America), Ireland, Germany, Poland and various parts of the

Poetry Introduction

United Kingdom. Their voices, gathered together in this anthology, are as diverse as their backgrounds, and some of the most indigenous writers are among the most European and translatlantic in mode. The New Internationalist movement, if that is what it is, is not a movement: it is simply the passage of a phenomenon. But it is a phenomenon that speak and sings. Are the poems here denser, more personal, more contemplative? I would not say so. They are however in the business of defining shifting transnational territories, various governances of the tongue. The processes of change will be quietly ticking in them. They are, in any case, a pleasure to read.

– George Szirtes

Carol Thornton

Perseid Meteor Shower, 12 August 2002

Nonetheless

Gliding upstream

Ripening

Incarnation

Carol Thornton

Perseid Meteor Shower, 12 August 2002

The earth hurtles through a cloud of ancient dust
with its parvenu companions, SAR-Lupe, Echelon.
Hunched tiny in our place, we flee the city's glow.
Freeland will be dark. I navigate the curves,
hedgerow fingernails scraping the passenger door.

The church's bells toll ten. I spread
the sleeping bag between two leaning monuments.
Pipistrelles in their juddering flight are black
against the sky, the tower their radiant.

The grass resists as I lie back, my feet pointed
at the south horizon. My child right-angled to me,
his head resting warm on my belly.
We find Aldebaran,
Cassiopeia, finally pick out Perseus.

From the Yeoman, *wee-wah* as a car sets its alarm
and a woman's laughing echo.

Stars dance in and out of view at the edge of vision,
each one vanishing the moment it's sought.
The sky darkens and cold seeps in.
'A satellite! I found it myself.' His voice rich.

Vanishing sparks radiate from Perseus.
Then the slow brilliant arc of an earthgrazer
and my son's indrawn breath
reverberating through us.

Nonetheless

Nonetheless, there are parts of the city
where those without shelter
freeze, or huddle over gratings, or
death comes by degree, beginning with this night.

The Technology of Metal, Turning – Kim Maltman

From Carfax tower, Cornmarket seethes in the heat.
Two students pose by St. Michael's tired stones,
their friend balanced on his friend's shoulders, trying out shots.
A bus top-heavy with sightseers sways around the corner
by the Randolph, missing a plaid-skirted woman
who cycles up Banbury Road to the charity
shops. She's there every Tuesday. She opens the windows
wide when the record-collector leaves, treats
the most inglorious shopper with haughty civility.
Nonetheless, there are parts of the city

where the constant, wearing road noises give way
to the gentler traffic of voices, the fizz of bubbles
rising in champagne, as petrous worthies, gowned
and flapping, sip from Lord Crewe's benefaction.
At a signal they form tidy lines like schoolboys
and process out the gate, past the helter
and skelter of tourists vying for a better view.
As the doors of the Sheldonian swallow them up
the onlookers make for the picturesque Covered Market, or
Starbucks, along cobbled lanes, where those without shelter

Carol Thornton

lie in wait. Like her, with her gold front tooth
and her torpid baby. Or him, skin-headed and pierced,
the tracheotomy scar on his throat still pink.
Who will buy his last Big Issue?
A Peruvian band is unloading their kit at Bonn Square,
and outside the Westgate Centre the old troubadour
with the outsized carnival hat shuffles through
a tap-dance parody. There are benefits, aren't there,
and shelters? They won't have to starve, or
freeze, or huddle over gratings, or

all that sort of thing. Elsewhere, Minerva
wheels her trolley up Marston Ferry Road
always watchful for the Satanists who place
coded messages in the News of the World,
got her sacked from lectureships at two colleges,
turned her into a modern anchorite.
Her teeth are brown stubs. She smiles like a duchess
at the merest hint of courtesy or kindness.
Later, as the village lads set her bins alight,
death comes by degree, beginning with this night.

Gliding upstream

A water-snake cuts through the stream leading you
out of the shallows and weeds. Reeds
entangle your legs, the stones scrape your feet.
The sun through the willows marks you with shadows
of green. Your coins are scattered and spent,
but a flash in the darkness draws you on.
There's music in the water, a rhythm in the river
that's turning you on your centre.
Your edges push against air.

> You
> were asleep
> on the riverbank,
> blossoms in your hair,
> seams in your silk stockings.
> In your hand, a pretty villanelle.
> Snake
> skimmed atop the water, before
> the V of subservient ripples.
> You shed your gown
> in narrow ribbons
> that slithered
> from your
> skin.

You are twirling in the morning with catkins in your hair, holes
in your silk stockings, and a book of empty pages
in your hand. Follow the snake up the river,
tripping over roots and secrets the animals know.
They may show you shallow holes
where they stow the bones of tiny creatures,
let you look into caverns where their young
are hidden. If you dance. If you dare.

Carol Thornton

Ripening

In heath and scrub-land, woods or open hillside
ripening berries spend long August days
in hiding from the desiccating rays,
the trenchant peck of a blackbird's yellow bill,
the trumpet call of wild convolvulus.
In shadows underneath the sharp-toothed leaves
the drupels soften, plump and pruinose
but thorny stems rip holes in satin sleeves.

Espaliered on the fence, bramble's loganberry kin
are splay-legged damsels contemplating sin
and mouthing softly 'Ruin us, ruin us.'
Glossy, red, and swollen, toward the sky they thrust.
Pulled from the stem, a *thup* too small for hearing.
A memory of something secret, tearing.

Incarnation

Wait, there is more. I will be the one,
lace hanky in my buttonhole, a red carnation
in my teeth, holes in my socks, and places to go.
Will you stay? Ask me to stay?

Or someday
when the sky is cracked like porcelain
will you beg me to return? I will be ready.
When every dog is silent,
and swallows stitch up wounds in the sky.

I bear no grudges, carry no rucksack –
only stones in my pockets, round and chalky
to smooth away furrows, tuck you in
under blankets of snow, blankets
of snow.

On a windowsill, a green glass bottle,
in its throat a stem of willow.
On the twig a slender spider
writes a message for the morning,
a tiny script I cannot read.
From miles away I see the sun
glinting off the glass.

Andrew McDonnell

Andrew McDonnell

Song of Fugues

Where are you going,
half dressed into the night?

> *I am going where darkness stammers*
> *against the edges of the light.*

Where are you going,
are you going all alone?

> *I am going with the long coats*
> *who are dancing in their bones.*

Where are you going,
how long will be your flight?

> *I will walk the paths in shivers*
> *and return before first light.*

Where are you going,
won't you let me join your song?

> *I cannot take you my darling,*
> *this is as close as you can come.*

Where are you going,
is there nothing I can do?

> *I will walk this way forever*
> *lost from me and lost from you.*

Where you are going
I will come too . . .

> *There is no room for tourists,*
> *passengers or you.*

Where you are going,
I forbid to let you roam . . .

> *I left when I was born,*
> *there is no such place as home.*

Sweet Briar Road

See this site here, said Tömas, poking his finger into the map. It covers about a square mile of land. A whole square mile of pipes and chimney stacks hidden behind conifer and barbed wire. You never see anyone about. You might once or twice spot a security guard, a weird occupation for any person, nothing to speak to but an Alsatian, having to keep a heavy blue jacket on all day, even on humid summer afternoons, where all you need do to break a sweat, is cross and uncross your legs. Anyway, this site produces agricultural chemical, the kind used in crop spraying. Sometimes when the weather is just right, and a north easterly breeze blows across the land, there is a pungent smell in the air, a bit like that of manure, but more gas based, sticks to the fibres of your clothes, hangs in the back of your throat like the taste of cod liver oil. No one in the city seems to mind said Tömas, as if they possess a melancholic resignation to the fact that the smell is here to stay. In the sixties Porton Down floated a giant mustard gas cloud over the city, to see how it would disperse over a built up area, so perhaps the people of this city have been conditioned to sharing their environment with chemicals for so long that they no longer care. This site where they make the chemicals is well hidden. You only pass it by taking a disused railway track that runs from the city centre out into the country, passing beneath old bridges riddled with graffiti, along the edges of great council estates, the tree line reflected in dark windows, the many roads that the path crosses with drivers eyeing you suspiciously from behind glass. There is a constant noise being emitted from the plant, and even though you can't quite define it, it does exist, so low is the pitch of this sound that it rumbles inside the bones makes breathing slightly harder and causing a slight dizziness. For the lack of people, you do see strange things, said Tömas looking vaguely northeast. On one of the tarmac concourses, I noticed a white plastic garden table laid out with four chairs. On the table lay an empty wine bottle that seemed to be attracting wasps. A few days later when I returned, the table and the chairs had all but disappeared, all that remained was one plastic chair lying at the bottom of the bank, right up against the fence, as if it had been thrown into the undergrowth by someone in anger. Another time, said Tömas, I happened to see a man of about forty, holding his hand half a metre above a silver pipe, watching it warp, his fingers elongated, his palm twice the size of his reflected head. But he didn't look amused; his face look slightly pained as if he had seen something else reflected there, something other to his image. I remember a tale from my childhood in Sweden, my grandmother, a beast of a woman who we had to call Mrs Harazbo – Can you imagine such a thing! Children who could not refer to their Father's mother as Grandma, or anything even slightly sentimental for fear of a severe reprimand – I recall the bed time story that she derived from a Scandinavian folk tale, that stated if you saw a green troll-like beast grinning behind your left shoulder, you would be dead within a week. Perhaps the man at the plant had seen something behind him, something hiding in the dark of his history, waiting to pounce. Whatever it was he saw in his reflection, I have no doubt in my mind it was something hideous, as I have never seen a face so grave as on his face that day. Since then I have hardly been back, and I will not go there now, I'll leave you to find it. My wanderings are over. I have no urge to peer into the darkness anymore.

For Your Ovaries

If I were to press my lips
against the flesh below your belly
and sing to your ovaries, to coax one back
from where it hides ill behind your womb,
and knew it would make you sleep easier –
aware of how the curtain material
feels in your fingers, when you pull them apart
to reveal sunlight, that would pour down your body
and could carry you in its arms all the way to Japan

then I would.

But all this distance and confusion over
what once was, of tangled arms
and shy kisses, prevents my singing.
But if you take the phone and lay
the speaker to your belly,
feel the tender cold of the metal
bring goose bumps to your skin,
then I'll start to sing like a bird
something old for you,
and you only.

Andrew McDonnell

Insomnia

I had not fallen asleep for over six months, Julia said. In the first
few months I had been restless and the stress of the insomnia
would often reduce me to tears. But after the third month, I
found a way to stop the stress by slumping against the wall and
fixing my eyes on something on the bedroom floor. Quite often
it would be a hair I would stare at, other times it would be the
light of the moon, creeping through the gap at the bottom of
the curtains. In this state of sleeplessness, I mastered my own
memory. In some ways I like to think that I died that first night
I was struck by the insomnia, and all I had were the nights to
look back across my life. I could remember the development of
my identity, how certain moments made me think in new ways,
said Julia, for example, the man I saw when I was eight years old,
standing in the rain dancing with an imaginary partner, his arms
wrapped around his invisible bride, his suit heavy with water
and his eyes closed up so tight. I had forgotten that man. Now
every time I see people dancing, I think of that man and as an
adult I sense his darkness far more acutely. Another time I
remember seeing a dying pigeon beneath an underpass. I
watched as the city flowed around the tiny shaking body, its
utter helplessness now it was grounded in this place of humans,
so cold and relentless. I can't remember how long I stared at the
pigeon before vanishing back into the crowds. By the fourth
month I decided to leave the house at night and wander. I would
walk the long corridors of the new hospital, and realise that I
was in the company of other ghosts. Drained faces passed me by,
said Julia, never returning my gaze. Some of them would cluster
in one of the two huge glass atriums. The hospital had been

moved out of the city, like the mental hospitals almost two hundred years before, the sick and the ill moved to the peripheries. Now we were drawn like night moths to the lights at the very edge of the city, the easterly wind calling us like the Mistral, to a brownfield site where the cities births and deaths continually happen. As if the huge humming generator at the heart of the building – its tone, forever lurking in the ear like a giant hummingbird, feeding on the sustenance in our heads as if our ears were the entrance to some exotic flower – was responsible for the processing of humans. I cannot remember how long I kept visiting the hospital at nights. Or how many other ghosts I met in those corridors that stretched for more than a quarter of a mile. Towards the end of my insomnia the madness of being unable to sleep finally caught up with me. I was found wandering, shoeless in a white dressing gown on one of the A roads out of the city. I recall the brand of cigarette that the policeman was smoking as he asked me questions. The smell of the burning chemicals in the cigarette, were as vague and distant as his voice. I was then examined by a doctor and this time taken back to the hospital against my will. I remained there for a few weeks before being discharged on medication. I recall sitting in the discharge lounge, the smell of hospital ingrained in the leather chairs, and finding myself being stared at by a former ghost I kept passing on my nocturnal wanderings, said Julia. He was still staring at me as the ambulance men wheeled him out. Now when I go to bed I lay my head on the pillows and breathe the scent of lavender in deeply. I find that I never dream at all.

Agnieszka Studzinska

Lighthouse Hill 1927

A Garden

On The Train

Agnieszka Studzinska

Lighthouse Hill 1927

The lighthouse stands, an albatross
in a backlash of grass –

Between a bowed land the blood of a dead rabbit
surges as if it was a winter cloud.

Now I remember a newborn in your palm
A small black pebble, blind.

You passing this soft stone, unbroken heat;
My childhood in hesitation for hours.

Later I wished they had told me,
your own stone killing you,

the volcano, an eruption of firelight under skin.

I could have sat beside the bed, listened to the pleas
with each sip of water swallowed,

your fists in my palms as if they were two small rabbits.
Tell you how beautiful things have become.

Not even a lighthouse could protect you now.

A Garden

This garden is a handkerchief inside an olive blazer
or the callow swoops of a skirt, lost among leaves.

The gooseberry bush is no longer translucent green,
like a misplaced photograph beside the walnut tree.

Once I hid behind this coppice of fruit and loss,
soft detritus moulds remain.

There is a redolence of left over rain, foreign words
like yeast in my mouth, dough in yours,

rising to a temperature of understanding.
This year I found the handkerchief in a pair of jeans.

Agnieszka Studzinska

On The Train

A woman holds a letter as if it was an orange,
the anonymous smell of childhood saturates skin.

In my hands it is a pale winter, driftwood.

I think about letters buried in the parched mouth
of a riverbank or a frozen cloud

and how the shade of distance is the delicacy of this
season.

I slice it in half.

Lawrence Bradby

Lawrence Bradby

England Is A Soft Touch

though not if you arrive without a map,
stepping straight into its gloomy garden shed
of rusty scythes, rakes, shears, coiled fence wire,
cans of useful poison; not

if you arrive having dead-reckoned the distance gone
by time spent in a sealed, moving truck, jumping out
as instructed onto the dieseled grass that sags beside an A-road
to watch the truck haul away; not unless

you know exactly where to run your hand,
where to press. It is dusk. Headlights soon
will rip their cold incurious regard across you
with your knotted bundle, unless you follow,

follow me, I'll show you where the lay-by holds shadows
scorched by joy-ridden cars that chanced departure in a wild blaze,
but whose bodywork remained –
                              caught beyond their oil and rubber life –
until removed by the authorities.

Now step off the road; I'll show you flat cloud overhead,
                                        a dirty blanket
uplit in smears of lichen orange where the dark is being dealt with.
It's a map of settlement seen from underneath,
a map of population density.

This way, beside a ditch, where blackened sugar beets
steam and stink of sour molasses. They are piled up
inside a straw bale stockade, ready for distribution;
trust keeps them there, or surplus.

Air is moving through the hedge;
                    its particles drag past the tips of thorns
softly, but louder than the road's slow tear that's far behind.
Double-chevroned tracks lead into a huge grey hangar –
the silence of big machines.

I'll take you past a pub that's run aground out in the fields.
In the forecourt, its sign swings from a mast that pokes up
through the muddy gravel. A canned-drink dispenser
glows through frosted glass.

The windows of this village invite one to look in. No curtains,
nothing locked. The main street is a corridor of scented darkness
with warm-lit rooms that open quietly off it; all are empty,
                                    set for someone
to step in and take their place.

Lawrence Bradby

Scent

One night I walked the market, moving
through the cellar smell of spuds, salt
choke of dog-chews and dried pigs' ears, decay
of vinegary fish: each stall's grip
thin and greedy on the air around it.
The shutters were all up; nothing to see
the aisle's length but painted wood and splinters.
I pushed on, turned left or right prompted
by the air's acquired grain and draw,
did the shadow of my shopping rounds,
dropped a coin at every corner taken.
The air bit. I struggled back, picked
each from its chip of bone-white street light,
jammed it in a groove or splintered crack
in the nearest stall, waited for a sigh
or sign or silent out-breath from within.
And if I'd walked an avenue of yew trees
when the berries glowed in their red cups,
the blackbirds would have held themselves as still.

The Familiar Maze

Why would you choose to get lost? How is it possible?
You need simply look for the end of the aisle,
but the view is blocked by women thoroughly
upholstered in conflicting floral patterns.
That one's voice is still strong, though pumiced;
that one's only got a whisper to provide
the dirty punch lines and thumbnail obituaries
which, by moving closer, you hear, just.
A sharp rain pecks at the roofing
like gravel shaken on a metal tea tray,
as just above head-height birds dance
for a slice of toast pitched there somehow;
the diminuendo of the last few crumbs.
Your ear is drawn along the roof valley
to a chimney bringing up the patient hiss
of a geyser, the slosh and dink of mashing tea.
Quieter still, the charm of plastic bags
uncrinkling, light bulbs buzzing: sounds which
shuttle through the pipes between the stalls.
So how can you be lost when you're at home?

Lawrence Bradby

Dewey Decimal

(i) Do He?
The butchers always call him Codex Ed;
when he takes his tea at Ruby's Caf
his mug has 'El Cyclopedia' round the rim,
but if he's there beside you when you shop
noting what you buy and what you look at
with disdain, he'll introduce himself
as Dewey.
           He can talk purr Norfolk
with the ol' boys, or match the neuro-vocab
of the scientists who'd like to scan his brain.
He's a foundling, was discovered crying
in a filing cabinet. He dates his special gift
to that day: *I sprang out like Athena –*
a sense of order fully formed.
              He knows
a wedding ring just fell among the sprouts;
tomorrow, he could list where else it's been.
He heaps his memories in stalls and rows,
pins your face to vegetables you've bought,
so as the traders calmly pack away
his starling thoughts whirl round without a roost.

(ii) He Do
A human loyalty card. A grocery detective.
He reminds shoppers which vegetable they forgot
last time, directs them to their next stall.
(Row E is his meridian or baseline –
he fixes objects by their offset from it.)
He's not employed as such but fills in
as a figurehead.
        Letters arrive headed
Mr Decimal, Market Place, NR2.
The Council has mislaid its bold plans
for a market redevelopment. He hasn't seen them
though that doesn't mean he can't locate them:
his affinities runs to all things with their past
or their future on the market.
                He clears
new paths through what he knows. Each afternoon
he sits by Our Glorious Dead eating toast,
allowing faces, outfits, bruise marks
on deliveries of fruit to settle down
and be recallable. Redevelopment?
It's constant, patterned, and wholly in his grasp.

Sandeep Parmar

Homecoming

Teeth

Elveden Churchyard

Hilltop Mission – Avalon, Catalina Island

Homecoming
After Christa Wolf's 'Cassandra'

Voices spear the darkness. Troy is no more than the glint
Of departing soldiers. We pass in and out of smoke.

Soon, it is morning. It is not morning.
The false night of forensic lamplight is the dawn.

A distant wood reflects, thick with torsos blaring white;
And hands raise, empty on the approaching shore, to deny.

The light accuses every surface. All are mute:
Thorns and swollen lips, stiffen the undergrowth.

I am Cassandra, neé Iphigenia, Cassandra, neé Iphigenia.
I have exited time, prophet and sacrifice, to speak.

Don't you recognize me? This face is the same.
Time bears the burden of my many names.

Through the trees, on a field, sheep appear to kiss the earth
But aren't. They tear it up between their teeth.

The sea is as good as an oracle, she has brought me back
And forth, her waves equivocate with bound wrists.

Sails slip from their poles, and collapse too weak to weep,
Like slave women, who do not tell what they have seen. But I have seen

My city's walls blown through with greed, I have seen its faces sicken,
Black with fear – and fear, I've seen it sicken faster into death, have seen it -

Seen each of my sisters' blood thicken; I have seen its impure color
Sweeten altars, dragged through graves, to be silenced again and again,

Seen the kings and seen the princes, seen the howl of death
And its advances – clattering thousands in helmets and skulls and ears,

And it has not silenced me. I am free. You will undo me
With the stab of revenge – that has wounded only my dreams, till now.

I catch sight of you, and you are watching me, noble and cold as victory.
Father, our weary king, steps from the ship into your marble arms.

Mother it is me – don't you recognize me? I am Cassandra, neé Iphigenia,
Cassandra, neé Iphigenia, neé, neé. Take me to you,

And I am home. Take me to your smooth, perfumed shoulders, to your grieving mask,
And I am you, you – you come back to you.

Sandeep Parmar

Teeth
For Joe Pena

In sleep he leaves her. The radio on the sill too is insomniac,
Blinks through to the glow of hard surfaces, the close walls,
The unshaded, mute bulb. All this is corseted in by fire escape
And brick, by a dither of jazz and the sudden slap of a report,
Talk of war. He sleeps still. Fetches breath too fast to calm her.
But now, she can see him clearly, through the slick sodium drip
From 83rd street. A piano can be heard through the floorboards
On which they lie, as though underwater. She cannot be sure,
But when the playing stops, cards shuffle. It is too late to be gambling
For money, she knows this, and the pianist knows this and so it is not
For profit that the suits, light and dark, foretell the next lone chord.
The reporter's voice again disrupts. It is a hard thing – to know
The whole world is not sleeping. The man wakes momentarily.
He aims an eye at the clock wearily, thinking there'll be time

For this tomorrow, for the gnash of uncertain threats. She listens.
Waits for the music to start again anywhere. What sleep doesn't see
In the dark is still true. The egg crate mat wedged into a corner,
The empty cigarette box lying on its open jaw. The pianist touches
The lower keys somehow more severe. The girl loves coincidences,
Loves the stack of silk shirts his mother bought and that he wears them.
Glares sadly at Modigliani's photograph hung up, brutal as sex,
At the paints there aren't room enough for that are boxed up like good linen.
She herself hardly fits. She turns. A cold wine glass rolls into her back.
And boxes that have nowhere to unpack themselves, casually stare
At the mess of thrown off clothes. There are no shadows, as shadows need
Objects not already pressed up against the dark. On the dresser
There are folded pocket scraps, a single key and the hollow sound of its teeth,
In doors that open and close, but remain locked. He breathes unsteadily now
Into the morning, when he will lean over and ask her how she slept,
Raise up the curtain and show her the tree outside she might have missed,
Bronzing the street. When he will see color. And she will see time.

Sandeep Parmar

Elveden Churchyard

Oh it is black work he does there – and a black propriety
That guides his simple, moral code – the dead prevail –
If you ask him, he'll tell you.

See over there, under that oak, there's the last caretaker.
And do you see that little gap – that'll be his.
He mows it with particular pride and care.

Difficult yes – work worth dying for. His wage is paid
By interest on a sum that is banked and sheared per annum.
This is a matter of loyalty.

A prince owned the estate before, he says, *an ignorant prince.*
He buries his cigarette, muting the flame with his toe
And motions to a gravestone at the far end

Standing silent and shocked. *I'll show you.* He walks over to it,
Claims it like a brother – no –
Like a victor, his arm straight over for the count -

One, nearly two hundred years – finished.
There's his son, dead at thirteen. And his wife, dead too.
Buses of people come. He is surprised every time – by the flowers and the weeping.

I kneel before the stone. The date. Dead, in Paris, where his heart gave out.
I lay down the lilies I have brought. The caretaker's eyes darken and narrow.
Tell me about his house, I say. How much has been changed?

He relishes this – *Ten thousand pounds for a new roof.*
He smiles between the words, or snarls – it is hard to tell –
It was left in such a mess, you see.

Renovations. Lots of them. Such a mess! Peculiar taste –
Statues and tapestries, gold and hideous. Where are they now?
Junked or sold.

Junked? The memory of an empire blotted out. *Empire?*
He draws a transcontinental blank, and looks out over his own plot, itching with fame
Polishes the stone with his hand –

The name of the last Raja under the will of his fingers,
The will of a peasant – they ought to be cut off, truly.
If I put a sword in the hand of the dead – they would be.

Would you like to see the improvements, made by my last Master?
There's a coat of arms with the Guinness harp there on that tower wall.
From the English fog, the stink of beer and piss offends.

Sandeep Parmar

We walk over to it. Cold flint and careless.
He tells me that he has it under good authority
That there is to be another lord, soon.

Splendid. We smile and look up at the pebbles swimming in their cement.
He feels for a cigarette. It is beginning to rain. You'll see more of me, I say.
He is presentably glad, and escorts me off the property.

Hilltop Mission – Avalon, Catalina Island

In a dream, she holds a mirror
between her fingers   pared to white
advances towards my bed and   turns to where I lie

Glass and bone click   the slowing of blood marks the minute
in seconds   an organ abandoned, the mirror rises
I cannot wake   we press our lips to the reflection
La Malinche

A Spaniard, cuckold to time,
fingers his golden watch   to praise this woman
moored at his side   for the red, split tongue
that felled her people

Love is simple   dies fast over four hundred years
of following husbands   to new nations
to be made heroines   and learn the language of confession
that haunts these tubular halls of blood

We followed them to the font   to the baptismal
and there we drowned our children
there we flashed that immortal smile hidden by flesh
which we wear unknowingly   to receive judgement

Father, in all your grace   shave our heads
and leave us on the mission steps   to wail
and hold our rag corpses   those babies we never let be born

We ripped open their soft throats
and there   just under the skin   as you said were the colors
of our disease   silent now7, we repair ourselves to screams.

Nessa O'Mahony

Nessa O'Mahony

Break

Mending has begun.

Stiffness,
cramped flesh,
weight, heat,
pressure
of burning
in a perfect
white L.
Beneath,
calcium flows,
grouting
the wish-bone.
Waiting
to regain
the courage
of two feet.

Five weeks more.

Morning Walk

At this hour
I can still smell
the freshness,
the air carrying
the sweet scent
of weeds, the dew
glistening on
flowered brush.

So I push past
practising the breaths
that will get me
through a day
of returned calls
and meeting protocol.

I ingest
the taste and texture
of this hedgerow,
storing images,
a bush, polythene embraced,
the roadworks sign
a face-down fallen hero,
the portacabin door
ajar to entice,
a crow last-minuting
as he tugs a morsel
from the road,

and a glimpse,
a sleek shape
melting into shade,
long red tail
disappearing
round the corner.

Nessa O'Mahony

Fool's Gold in Norfolk

Because the words won't flow
I drive through flatlands,
speeding under flat skies until land ends
and sea takes up the slack.
I walk along its edge, eyes drawn
to the waves' hiss.
Agate, quartz, obsidian glisten,
tempting my eye to search for amber.
They'll lose their gleam
before I reach the car,
leaving me with pockets full
of sullen geology.

His Master's Voice
In Memory of James Simmons

Charlie hasn't heard it for a while.
The world's gone quiet, his milk-skin eyes
see shadows mostly, nothing to make him rise
in greeting, tail wagging stiffly.

There's been a change, he knows,
the house full suddenly,
people blundering around,
treading on his tail.
Now the room is empty too.
The bed's been made, the box
carried out. They'd stood around it
earlier, lips moving together.
He'd felt the rumble of a lorry
passing by and barked.

In the morning, he lets his nose direct him,
past the sour-sweet smells
on table-tops, the tang of dripping cans
and empty whiskey bottles,
to the patio where a refuse sack lies,
shredded by night-time predators.

The contents strewn,
he quickly finds the scent
among the surgical gloves and swabs,
his master's slippers, his night-gown,
the smell of sweat still clinging.

Not knowing that a stranger
will come soon, tidying,
sweeping up, thieving the lot
as a starving cur grabs a bone
where she finds it.

Nessa O'Mahony

Home Thoughts

Why am I thinking of you tonight
when it's been years?
Why am I feeling it now,
here, in another country,
suddenly distracted by
the way your hand parted me,
slipping in as if
you were just returning home,
the look of remembering,
that dreamy, certain look
as your hand curved me,
split me into segments?
And why am I thinking of it now,
when it's been years,
and I'm whole now,
and in another country
and there's no need of parting,
of wanting to be half?

Slipping Skin

I prefer the snake's routine.
She has enough
of one scene or another
so she gives a shrug
and shimmies out of skin,
discards a dried-out sheath
coiled in the mark of a question
she's not bothered answering.

Henry Cleverly

The Return Journey

Listen, my old mucker, sweetie-pie

Sensational Tapestry

Down on your uppers

Rear-view mirror

Mind field

Henry Cleverly

The Return Journey

So full of reflection
it is hard to say
where one imagination
begins and ends.

Seek the original cut
the first intention

One moment of inspiration
is prone to reinterpretation

A thousand and one nights hardly suffice
to tell what each entails

A generous helping
an open suggestion.

Sell me something else I don't need;
if the whole world depended
on my moods
would I be any happier?

My responsibility. A never ending silence
or more articulate resounding

All affirmation and no denial;
when we come together we fall apart.

Hold on tight, it's not the first time
we have lost everything we wouldn't fight for.

What I put down yesterday
is waiting to be picked up tomorrow,
and as for today, it never comes
as it slips by, last week is long ago

And far away, the years pass.
I can't hold my breath until then.

Henry Cleverly

Listen, my old mucker, sweetie-pie

Wake up and smell the coffee
or go to bed with Ovaltine
and have sweet dreams
all about me.

We are all red with embarrassment
everyone suffers the blues
it is as natural as breathing in water.

I remember you and your voice
like an ache, so deep, reassuringly
downbeat yet undefeated, more sprawl
than drawl. It was the Jack Daniels and coke
that did it, and the 40 Marlboro Light
of a night, writing poems in bars
in the dark and half-dark

You claimed this to be the perfect space
for concentration, this somewhere
you could be and disappear
at the same time, the place you went to
to get away from, to get away from
and survive your arrival

Now, we are all listening
to what appears yet is not the final cadence
so beautiful, we all agree
to forget what we know. All that Art
originates in pain. It started with a scream
this long slow birthday

And you're saying you never trusted poets
or their way of seeing
but still you couldn't help yourself
believing what they said
and before we went to bed
you spelt it out as a prayer for the dead.

Henry Cleverly

Sensational Tapestry

Indelible memory

Dip your fingers in the sunset
and swoon

Rose-hipped innocence
honey tastes golden

The view curves away
from where we are

Over all creation
in contemplation

The senses gather mystic
horses gallop through

Inspiration
while you sit still

And mix colours
to get a fix

On how it feels do draw a breath
but painting bird song never reveals

Eternal auspices spill in time
for the imagination of beauty

Is becoming.

Down on your uppers

Things move on, and we are not ready for them,
we are looking to catch a fading reflection
before it merges into the landscape, to be reabsorbed
beyond the horizon. Back then awhile,
you could measure the distance.

Talk of how many roads there are out of here
but only our favoured routes are tried and tested.
My thoughts are arrested. Outside, it is cold and dark
the stars are shiny and bright, my mind
seems clearer, who knows how deep the trouble goes.

It doesn't matter what you say, but think of something
to take me somewhere I can breathe again.
Talk me through this impending silence
give me something to hold on to, lend me your ears.

The long night is full of accusations
confusing when and where, how and why, for what
have I been doing here, on earth, recollecting my surmises,
recounting the folly? Well, I hope it will all add up to something
more than, who stops here goes further. You know the answer
is no longer to be found in this, rushing between things.
Helter-skelter, scram, begin again with happiness.

Or get lost.

Henry Cleverly

A clear intention, I see no problem, I see no reason
not to let go and start over, as if this were the first appreciation.
What is there to lose, but that which was lost already?
What is there to choose, but that which was, already chosen?
Sympathetic correspondence. God's plan
in the palm of your hand.
Open your fingers gently. These are the ways
of tenderness and compassion.
These are the roads we must travel.
Talk to me, we have until the morning
to dream our lives and remember.

Rear-view mirror

Well, we are all magic
in our better moments
and I can only begin to tell you
how sad I have been since then.

We are better than we think we are

But there is no escaping it
darkness gathers in my veins
the river floods the banks
of memory, so trust in me

A ripple in the water
smoke in a glass, cat's paw
the glint of a needle in a haystack
the twinkle in your eye

Golden rod, silver birch
the ghost of a chance
the shadow of doubt
onus of proof, beast of burden

The sum of everything
that is out of reach
adds up to more
than a hint of splendour

Fancy as ever
will be central
to my folly
when I get carried away.

Henry Cleverly

Mind field

It was flowers put in vases
and the thoughts of our hearts.
A meditation of deeds
and sheep bleating in the meadow
rain falling and time meeting in me
as if I were a cross-roads.
The experience of innocence
and a world made over.

It was always someone missing
and the hunting of the snark
or Alice through the looking-glass
a guest appearance or star turn
not something to be gone-over or done-in.
It is something to be dwelt upon
and lived as reality
is the end of a dream
the beginning of illusion?

The art of possibility
here and now exploding
she and he, me and you
were all messed up already
more both than either
as much neither as one

Being held in mutual fascination
bound by life's finely spinning

All because, this woven web
this stream of consciousness
this veil of tears, this tale of ours.

Fiona Curran

Fiona Curran

On Receipt

M.O.M.A
11 West 53rd Street
New York, NY 10019.

Pollock Coasters	$6.99
Hepworth Paperweight	$35.00
Dali Clock Cuff-links	$17.99
Water lilies Tea Towel	$9.00
Koons Toy Poodle	$14.99
Bacon Triptych Fridge M	$5.50
Warhol-Campbell's Pen	$4.00
Hirst Shark Choc	$8.00
Schiele Sex Manual	$70.00
Subtotal	$171.47
Tax	$3.46
TOTAL	$174.93
CARD NUMBER	***********6941
EXPIRY DATE/0602	
VISA DELTA/ SALE	$174.93

5/14/02 14.16

Please Retain This Receipt

M.O.M.A. NYC.
Thank You
HAVE A NICE DAY

The Rites

We crawl by, photographing you, the bad accident,
something everyone slows to see. We all do.
Still alive your crocus shoot fingers poke through soil,
fit for cattle and crow alone. If I grasped
your green hand, would a tug of war ensue?
You'd have me down there with you
and I momentarily willing – that is respect for you,
there would be none for me, bitch, rival, even whore.

But darling had you seen death before you did it?
The aftermath of the Reaper's work,
skin mottled purple when the blood settles,
in arse, back, elbows. Cold?
Because the fire in the lungs has popped its last crackle.
Those we love die with morphine eyes open,
they glaze before fingers ripple lashes shut
the body vacates, the smell, a final letting go.

Then we wash, wash away, prepare for dust,
absolve the shell in all its paper frailty.
Resting the body sideways, then sideways,
the winding sheet falling into a fold above the heart,
a clean white blossom pressed to the breast:
Then the spirit risen and cloudy as steam
discovers its weightlessness, shouts, 'Result, result!'
Slamming the door on its way out.

Fiona Curran

The Technology of Modern Romance

Wont C U again
then? Charming
way 2 end it I
must say, tk
balls? Bet office
bike lined up nxt,
lucky girl. Ur
shirts R in
Oxfam. Dont txt
me ever. Bastard.

At My Hands

Freckles mutate with dangerous speed into liver spots.
Veins sit proud as speed bumps between knuckles,
joints grind trapping tendons as they flex.
Nails, a short brutality, flaws pronounced, ugly.
Rings rotate, diamonds slip and turn away
their sparkle palmed. Only a fist makes the skin smooth
like a girl's.

When my young lover runs his lips
over the back of my unfaithful hands, the skin ripples.
Follicle geometrics compact into lines, the script of my life.
The epidermis slackens, the outside hanging on the in,
an ill-fitting suit, that needs to be tucked
in all folding places. Surely he must see this?
The Vampire's hands

                    bled white, the undead tissue
a papery pattern. Creation's cowboy blueprints.

Fiona Curran

Home Cooking 2

Bird Blew.
<u>Ba</u>
   da da da da da da da da da
                               dah,
H raised him up, H scaled him
                         <u>do</u>wn
A one man poly   p-h-o-n-y.
        1234
                  Counterpoint's beeeebop soldier,
Square bashing three deuces d<u>ow</u>n,
                    <u>Off</u>
                    Off the parade ground,
                                      Yardbird cooking
                  and MADness brewing,
play my spine from the base do<u>wn</u>
                                        (and all around)
          Alto,
              every spine and make Jazz Jell-o
                   – hey   float
                              this lady's boat
with Crazeology.

                 Then thunder improvised a track
           that rolled Charlie all the way <u>back</u> to Kansas,
                  back
                         a little number finished way too
soon

     he blew and he blew till he blew out
                  Bird Blew.

You Shall Have Your Renown

Coming here to work an escape,
leafing through a stack of old film books,
I found you disguised as David Hemmings
that cruel photographer in *Blow Up*.
Are you happy now my darling?
Knowing my heart has already cast you,
made you into a movie star,
beauteous and untouchable.

Contributor Biographies

Naomi Alderman was born in London in 1974. She has a degree in Philosophy, Politics and Economics from Oxford University. This year, she won the David Higham Award and was one of the winners of the Asham Award. She is currently working on a novel set in the modern-day Orthodox Jewish community. Page 1.

Tash Aw was born in Taipei and brought up in various countries in South East Asia. He was educated in Malaysia and in England, and now lives in London. *When My Father Was Shot* is an extract from his novel-in-progress, *The Harmony Silk Factory*. Page 17.

Carol Baxendale was born in Broughty Ferry, Dundee. She studied Fine Art in Cheltenham, and Printmaking at the Slade School of Art. She has taught Printmaking, held exhibitions and, more recently, published stories in *New Writing 10*, *Birdsuit* and *Spiked*. Now resident in the UK, she has worked extensively in Norway. Page 157.

Lawrence Bradby's poems have appeared in *Rialto*, *Reactions*, *PN Review*, and in a booklet called *The Best Bloody Job in the World* (Sideline Publications, 2002). His first meal on Norwich Market was pie and peas at Reggie's – it appeared he had been sold short but the pie was in fact submerged beneath the peas in the traditional manner. Page 289.

Contains Small Parts

Laura Bridgeman studied at the E.15 Drama School before forming girl/boy, who were funded by The London Arts Board and The Arts Council of Great Britain. She has been commissioned as a writer by Brouhaha, Gay Sweatshop and Radio 4. She is currently working on a novel. Page 11.

Sam Byers was born in 1979 and has a degree in English, Media and Cultural Studies from Birmingham University. He is currently at work on a novel. Page 107.

Aifric Campbell grew up in Ireland. She studied Linguistics at Gothenburg University, Sweden and spent 12 years working in investment banking in the City. She lives in London. *dead cat bounce* is an extract from a novel-in-progress. Page 125.

Colin Carters grew up in Northern Ireland and has lived and worked in Ireland, England, Australia, India and Spain. He studied Fine Art at the National College of Art and Design, Dublin, and has since worked as a teacher of Art, English, and Communications. *July* is his first novel and is set in Barcelona. Page 145.

Henry Cleverly was born in London in 1962. Grew up in Devon. Studied English and Philosophy at UEA in 1981. Now lives in Norfolk and has two collections of poetry: *Walking Willacome Well* (1991) and *Render My Heart* (2001) both published by Laundry Press. Page 315.

Jamie D. Corbman grew up outside of Philadelphia, and earned his BA Cum Laude in English, Creative Writing and the Fine Arts from the George Washington University in Washington, DC where his work won the Astere E. Claeyssens prize for best original writing. He is currently working towards his MA in Scriptwriting at UEA. Page 247.

Philip Craggs was born in Grimsby in 1981. He took a degree in English and Creative Writing in Bolton. He is working on a novel. Page 37.

Contributor Biographies

Nina Cullinane was born in 1975 and grew up in London and on the Isle of Wight. She cocktail waitressed in New York, buttered baguettes on the Island and taught English in Portugal, before receiving an AHRB bursary to study at UEA. She is writing a coming of age novel. Page 171.

Fiona Curran was born in the North of England and currently lives in London. Her poems have appeared in *Staple, Still, Orbis, the reater* and *The Affectionate Punch*. She has performed her work in the UK and the US. And is working towards that elusive first collection.
  Acknowledgements:
  On Receipt was first published by Electric Acorn (issue 13) at <http://acorn.dublinwriters.org>. Page 325.

Diana Evans has worked in journalism as an editor, lecturer and writer and published in *The Independent, Marie Claire, The Evening Standard, The Stage, The Source, Southbank Magazine*, and other titles. Her fiction appears in *IC3: The Penguin Book of New Black Writing in Britain*, and *Kin*, published by Serpent's Tail. She lives in London. Page 131.

Virginia Fenton was born in Auckland and settled in the UK in 2000. She is a graduate of Victoria University of Wellington, with degrees in History and English Literature. She writes poetry, prose and stage plays. Page 227.

Helen Gallacher has written for *The Sunday Times, N.M.E., Cosmopolitan*, and *i-D* magazine. Her work as a director includes *Surrealist Films With David Lynch* and *Heavy Metal* for Arena (BBC2); and *Tuning With The Enemy* (about an American smuggling pianos to Cuba), for Channel Four. She has also performed standup comedy. Page 73.

Michael Gleeson was born in the Republic of Ireland in 1977. Has published stories in the Irish literary magazine *The Stinging Fly*. This is an extract from his novel. Page 161.

Contains Small Parts

W. David Hall teaches writing in the United States. His textbook, *Culture And Context: A Basic Writing Guide with Readings*, was published in June 2003. He is currently writing *Three Cigarettes and a Single Match*, a novel. Page 195.

Tim Hayton was born and brought up in Liverpool, and has worked in a succession of exciting jobs – from road-sweeper to estate agent. He moved to South London thirty years ago and has lived there ever since with his artist wife. This is an extract from a novel. Page 97.

Angharad Hill was born in Swansea in 1980. In 2002, she graduated from the University of East Anglia with a degree in English Literature and Creative Writing. She is currently writing her first novel. Page 177.

Yannick Hill was born in 1980 in Switzerland. He grew up in Devon. He is currently working on a novella called *Book of Bobe*. This extract is two-fifths of a short story called *Look Then*. Page 183.

Margaret Johnson grew up in Hertfordshire and now lives in Norwich. She writes for the stage and radio as well as fiction. Her novellas for people learning to speak English are published by Cambridge University Press, and her stage play *Goddess* was premiered at Cambridge Drama Centre in 2000. Page 215.

Jennifer Kabat has lived in New York, London, San Francisco and Washington, DC. She has written for *The Financial Times*, *Wired*, *The Guardian*, *The New York Times* and *Condé Nast Traveller*. She has served as an editor at *The Face* and *Arena*. She is working on a novel, *McGovern's Campaign*. Page 79.

Rob Kinsman worked in professional theatre for six years as Administrator, Stage Manager and Press Officer before coming to study the Scriptwriting MA. He has written three full-length plays, one of which, *Perfect Love*, is currently being produced in London by the Breezeblock Theatre Company. Page 219.

Tom Lewis was born in Cambridge in 1980. He lived for several years in Australia before reading English at the University of East Anglia. He writes fiction for young adults and children. Page 61.

Andrew Mackenzie has degrees in Philosophy from Bristol University and the LSE and in French Literature from the Sorbonne. He has worked as a management consultant throughout Europe and as a director of a London AIDS charity. *Apples on Fire* is an extract from his first novel. Page 119.

Dawn Marrow was born in London in 1980. She studied English and Drama at Brunel University and is currently writing a novel. Page 31.

Andrea Mason studied German and Russian at King's College, University of London. She was an artist in London, the former half of collaborative duo Andrea + Philippe. They had solo shows at The Independent Art Space, London and The Showroom, London. She has written for *frieze*, *The Art Newspaper* and *zing*. She currently lives in Norwich and is writing her first novel. Page 101.

Andrew McDonnell was born in Shoreham, Kent in 1977. He has a degree in Cultural Studies from the Norwich School of Art and Design and his work has appeared in *Poetry Life*, *Reactions* and other publications. He lives and works in Norwich. Page 277.

Michael Miller was born in California in 1979 and received a Bachelor's Degree in English at UC Irvine. He wrote for the *Los Angeles Times* for four years and published a book of poems, *Thief After Dark*, from FarStarFire Press. His poems have also appeared in *Faultline*, *Poetry Now* and *Iota*. He is currently working on his first novel. Page 45.

Contains Small Parts

Nessa O'Mahony was born in Dublin in 1964. Her poetry has appeared in Irish, UK and US periodicals, including *Poetry Ireland Review*, *The Shop*, *Fortnight Asylum*, *The Sunday Tribune*, *The Stinging Fly*, *Agenda*, *Iota* and *Atlanta Review*. Her first poetry collection, *Bar Talk*, was published by iTaLiCs Press in 1999. She edits the literary ezine, Electric Acorn at <http://acorn.dublinwriters.org>. Page 307.

Sandeep Parmar received her BA in English and Creative Writing at the University of California, Los Angeles and is currently completing the MA in Creative Writing at UEA. Page 297.

Verity Peet has sold a drama series, *La Noche Buena*, to Granada International, had two short films produced and is engaged in various radio and television development deals. Her screenplay *Two Nice Girls* was showcased at TAPS and BAFTA. Verity is currently dramatising London's history for a new media project involving Stephen Fry. Page 257.

Stephen Phelps has spent ten years running his own TV production company, specialising in miscarriages of justice. Before that he was Producer of BBC's *Rough Justice*, and Deputy Editor of *Watchdog*. Educated at Oxford University, he began his broadcasting career with BBC Radio following five years as a car dealer. Page 235.

Sarah Raymont was born in Mexico City in 1976 and educated at Brown University. *Nearly Sealed* is an extract from a novel-in-progress. Page 167.

Marcus Robinson studied at the University of Wales, Cardiff and Indiana University, where he held a Fulbright Scholarship. His first script, *Underground*, is currently being made into a short animated film. Page 205.

Iain Ross was born in London in 1975. He has a degree in English from Lady Margaret Hall, Oxford. He worked as an editor for an art publisher until 2001. He was awarded the Curtis Brown scholarship in 2002. Page 7.

Tom Rowson was born in 1975. He is currently writing a novel called *The Little White Town*. He has lived in Cheltenham, Southampton, Bideford, Eastbourne, Canterbury and Pulham Market, but he considers Bideford as home. Page 51.

Alyssa Russo is originally from New York and was born in 1979. She earned a degree in Art History and English from New York University, and is in the midst of writing her first novel. Page 85.

Anna Sayn-Wittgenstein was born in 1978. She is German/Swedish, and has a Bachelor degree in History and Politics from Stanford University. Before coming to UEA, she worked in Communications Consulting in Paris, France. Her work has been published in *The Mind's Eye, Pharos* and *Tank*. Page 151.

Chantal Schaul was born in Luxembourg and has studied Media Arts and English Literature in the UK. Her writing celebrates non-realism, using elements of the fairy tale and the grotesque. Her novels are hybrid scrapbooks in which she explores human faults and weaknesses through humour and defamiliarization. Page 23.

Claire Sharland has lived in Nigeria, Istanbul and Paris, where she studied mime with Jacques le Coq. She has worked as an aromatherapist, nanny, artist's model, cast member of a 'murder mystery dinner' company and bookseller. This is an extract from her first novel, *The Butcher's Daughter*. Page 57.

Agnieszka Studzinska was born in Poland in 1975 and has lived in England since 1983. A postgraduate in a Cultural Studies Degree, she has worked in PR and Broadcasting and is currently completing her MA in Creative Writing at UEA. Page 285.

Contains Small Parts

Jasmine Swaney Hewitt was born in 1978. She divides her time between Michigan and England with her husband, Seamus. Page 91.

Carol Thornton was born in Canada. Her poetry and fiction have been broadcast, and published in magazines and anthologies in England, Canada and the US. Her radio drama, *Corps Samples*, was broadcast by the Canadian Broadcasting Corporation, and a poem was short listed for the ARC's Poem of the Year competition.
   Acknowledgements:
   The four line epigraph featured in *Nonetheless* is taken from 'The Technology of Metal Turning', in *Technologies/Installations*, by Kim Maltman (Brick Books, Canada, 1990) and is given by permission of the author. Page 269.

Charlie Thurlow was born in London in 1978 and grew up near the Peak District. He is writing a novel. Page 113.

Jo Wroe taught in the UK and the USA before working in educational publishing for over ten years. Now a freelance writer and editor, she is a published author of fiction and non-fiction for children. *Skating in the Cremator Room* is an extract from her novel-in-progress. Page 139.

Alex Watson was born near Manchester in 1980 and has since lived in many different places. He went to the University of York and has written computer games reviews and careers advice for various publications. *Logical Value* is a piece of a longer story which is in turn part of a novel. Page 67.

Tegan Zimmerman was born in Cape Breton, Nova Scotia, Canada in 1980. This short story was written while completing her English degree at Acadia University. Page 189.